What people are saying about

Confessions of a Teenage Hermaphrodite

"The writing is strong, the characters are likeable, and with a love story to carry the reader through, everything comes together nicely in the end."

—*Rainbow Book Reviews*

"Read this book!! It's awesomely unique, you have never read anything like it before and it's just wonderful."

—*Lost in a Y.A. Wonderland*

". . .effortless prose and authentic characters. . ."

—*A Battalion of Words*

"Simon takes great care with her writing and the result is a gentle novel about a strong girl. . ."

—*Christi the Teen Librarian*

"So emotional and well written."

—*I'd So Rather Be Reading*

"It leaves the reader with a lot to think about…"

—*Christian Book Reviews*

"You'll enjoy this book and, at the same time, you'll learn a great deal about these marginalized members of our society. . ."

—*Shelly's LGBT Book Review Blog*

"I've never read such a deep emotional book. . ."

—*The Paige-Turner*

". . .an enlightening, eye-opening experience. . ."

—*Young Adult Book Reviews by Liz Winn*

"This book is really ground-breaking, especially in the YA industry, and I'm proud to be a part of its delivery."

—*The Book Babe*

Confessions of a Teenage Hermaphrodite

a novel by

Lianne Simon

Faie Miss Press
Lawrenceville, GA

Confessions of a Teenage Hermaphrodite
Lianne Simon
ISBN 978-0-9851482-0-1

Published by Faie Miss Press
1032 Old Peachtree Rd NW Suite 401 PMB 115
Lawrenceville, GA 30043
www.faiemiss.com

PUBLISHER'S NOTES

This is a work of fiction. Names, characters, places and incidents either are the product of the author's imagination or are used fictitiously, and any resemblance to actual persons, living or dead, business establishments, events, or locales is entirely coincidental.

The publisher does not have any control over and does not assume any responsibility for author or third-party websites or their content.

Unless otherwise noted, all Scripture quotations are from the King James Version of the Bible.

Individuals depicted in the images are models and used for illustrative purposes only.

This book is available in electronic format from www.museituppublishing.com.

Set in Garamond

Printed in the United States of America

For Mom,

who stood by me when it mattered most.

Foreword

Lianne Simon's novel *Confessions of a Teenage Hermaphrodite* offers an intimate view of the struggles and celebrations of a young person affected by a disorder of sex development (DSD).

This is the story of a person who is faie coming to terms with their own—and society's—expectations of gender. As a researcher and educator whose focus has been on DSD for the past fifteen years, I found that the narrator of this work provides an authentic and accurate description of a person living with DSD.

The obstacles faced by Jamie, the protagonist of the novel, reflect the real-world experiences of children and young adults with DSD. Ms. Simon beautifully describes the importance of connecting with others who are also affected by DSD, and obtaining access to caring and knowledgeable medical staff, in order to bring answers and peace to a person who is quite literally torn between living in two worlds—male and female.

Upon opening this book I was hooked. Ms. Simon develops characters who are dealing with friendships, romance, school, and family dynamics while trying to understand DSD. Any reader, whether affected by DSD or not, will benefit from reading this enchanting story of a young person coming of age who must determine which path to choose.

—Amy B. Wisniewski, PhD
Associate Professor and Director of Clinical Research
The SUCCEED Clinic
The University of Oklahoma Health Sciences Center
Oklahoma City, OK

Acknowledgments

I woke one morning, suffering from a peculiar form of insanity, one that demanded I tell a story. My loving husband encouraged me in it, even when it became clear that my obsession meant giving up my financially rewarding career to spend my days writing about some intersex kid with gender issues.

Mixed Gonadal Dysgenesis was well known to me; I'd spent a decade answering inquiries about it. But I could never have written accurately about an intersex teen without assistance. A number of adults who have intersex conditions made helpful suggestions, but special thanks are due to Peggy, a friend with Partial Androgen Insensitivity Syndrome, who changed her legal status to female as a young adult.

My friends on the Atlanta Writers' Club online critique group helped me learn the basics and remained patient through endless rewrites.

My critique partners—what can I say?—Mary Hall, Vivian Hubbs, and Carrie Lewis—you're the best.

Several authors, and especially the cracker queen herself, Lauretta Hannon, encouraged me.

Sean Kennedy was instrumental in getting me to share from the heart—the heart of a troubled teen.

My editors at MuseItUp Publishing—Judy Roth, and my dear zija, Tanja Cilia, held my hand and watched over me through the process of making my manuscript ready for publication.

Above all else, the hand of my Lord directed my steps and provided everything I needed.

Whatever good qualities this book has, are largely due to others. The faults are entirely my own.

ଓଃ 1 ଚଃ

Coral Gables, Florida — December, 1970

Pain, sharp and insistent, dragged me back toward consciousness. I kicked the covers away and struggled to raise my head. One hand swept my lower abdomen, searching for blood, or perhaps the handle of a stiletto. Instead, a gauze bandage meant the healers had already treated my wound.

"How are you feeling?" An angel hovered beside my bed. Western eyes dominated her beautiful Asian face. Black hair cascaded over tanned shoulders. A sleeveless silk blouse clung to her perfect figure. As I stared, the mild concern in her eyes brightened into amusement. "Jamie, I'm Lisa. Remember?"

Lisa—my one true friend in college. The mists departed, leaving me groggy and sore in a hospital bed. "Thanks for coming. How'd you find out I was having an appendectomy?"

Shadows drifted across her brow, darkening her face. "Your Neanderthal roommate left a message saying you were in labor."

Ooh! A chuckle died in abdominal pain as my muscles contracted. I reached a hand down and applied gentle pressure against my recent incision, hoping that would help. Frank majored in teasing his little roommate, but he also protected me from more serious abuse by the other boys in the dorm.

"Frank's okay," I said.

Doubt blossomed across her face. "What's that med student see in him?"

Yeah. Her. Sharon considered my small frame and unusual face evidence of a rare disorder begging to be diagnosed. "I think they were high school sweethearts." Frank had worked at his dad's car dealership for a couple of years before starting college. With his new Trans Am and his masculine good looks, he was pursued by a number of girls. I searched Lisa's eyes, wondering what *she* found of interest in a boy like me.

Lisa sat on the bed, her hip brushing against my bare knee. She grinned, teasing again. "You should show a little leg more often."

"Hmpf." Exposing my smooth skin would only provide one more reason for boys to ridicule me. My golden-red mane grew thick and straight, but the rest of my body was free from hair.

Footsteps sounded in the hallway outside my room. Lisa pulled the covers back up, kissed me on the forehead, and tousled my hair. "Rest. I'll drop by tomorrow."

I closed my eyes, glad to have a friend like her.

When I woke again, I saw someone standing beside my bed. *Ooh!* My mother must have taken the red-eye to get to Miami from Illinois so soon. "Mom, you didn't need to come all this way. I'm okay."

"Jameson, if you had—" She paused and brushed the hair away from my face. "—a daughter in the hospital, wouldn't you visit her?"

Come on! Okay, so you haven't seen me with long hair since I was nine, but I'm not effeminate, and I don't wear girl's clothes. So why make such a big deal out of it? At least Mom only hinted at her displeasure over my looks. Dad would probably go ballistic.

Rather than argue, I changed the subject. "I'll miss my finals."

She smiled and patted my arm. "That's all right, sweetie. They'll understand. No one expects you to take exams while you're in the hospital."

Alicia sat on the other side of the bed. The thirteen-year-old was six inches taller than me, but she was still my little sister. "Hey, Ali. Enjoy the trip?"

She nodded. "Yeah. Flying's neat." Alicia took my hand and returned a grin.

Only four months had passed, but I missed her like it had been years. I didn't want to upset her by admitting it, though. "Does this count as a home school project?"

"I'm supposed to write an essay when I get back."

My sister held a paperback in one hand, so I asked her what she was reading.

"Mom's making me read the books on your favorites list. I finished *Pollyanna* and *Anne of Green Gables* last week. I brought *Jane Eyre* with me on the plane."

Mom brushed her hand against my arm, capturing my attention again. "It took too long for the hospital to reach me in Springfield. I gave Kaylah a medical power of attorney. She lives in Coconut Grove now, so in an emergency, she can authorize your treatment. I want you to carry her phone number in your wallet."

What's with that? Mom and Dad hadn't been on speaking terms with my cousin since I was nine. "Okay." Had they forgiven her? Talking to Kaylah again would be awesome.

"The doctors should release you on Thursday or Friday. We'll drop you at the Piersons' before we leave. You can stay with Sharon and her brother over Christmas break."

Sharon? I was doomed! My eyes popped open and I sat up, or rather tried to. Pain brought tears to my eyes as I sank back down. "No, Mom. I'll be okay in the dorm."

"Frank won't be there, and I don't want you alone in your room so soon after surgery."

"But Christmas break is three weeks long!" Way more time than I wanted anybody examining me under a microscope. Who knew what Sharon might come up with? "I'll be back to normal in a couple of days."

"This is not open for debate, Jameson. We can't afford a hotel for that long."

"Yes, ma'am."

Mom pulled her chair close to the bed and put a hand on my arm. "When I arrived, a young woman in a white coat was in your room. I know how you are about doctors, so I asked her to make certain the examinations were kept to a minimum. She apologized and introduced herself as Sharon Pierson, saying she was only a medical student visiting you. We had a long talk. Her parents are spending the winter up north, so she'd appreciate some company. You're blessed to have someone like her as a friend."

A friend? I shut my eyes and groaned. Frankenstein chased creatures from *The Island of Doctor Moreau* through the fields of my imagination.

* * * *

I checked out of the hospital on the fourth day, hoping never to get near the place again. Bad enough that I had surgery, but did everybody on the planet have to examine me?

Alicia and I waited in the lobby while Mom walked out to get the rental car. My sister grinned at me and brushed the hair out of my eyes. "I'm surprised Mom didn't say anything. Your hair's gotten kinda long."

Long and shaggy. Dad had cut my hair the previous spring and I hadn't so much as trimmed it since. "Please don't bring it up, okay? I don't need to be hassled about anything right now."

"Okay. I won't. You're pretty with long hair, though."

Alicia was my best bud ever, but she wouldn't let some things alone. "Come on, Ali. I just got out of the hospital. Besides, lots of guys wear their hair long."

"Yeah, but Dad says they're all pot-smoking hippies and draft dodgers."

"Who cares? I don't do drugs, but I'll burn my draft card when I get one."

"Jamie! Don't say that. Dad's already ashamed of you. Scott died a hero in Vietnam, but you're half girl. Even if you got drafted, you know they wouldn't take you, so what's the point?"

"Last year they shot students at Kent State. Not violent criminals, Ali. Just unarmed kids. Ideas are important, even if your actions are only symbolic."

Mom pulled up in the car, so I slid into the passenger seat. On the way to Sharon's we stopped by the dorm to pick up my clothes and some other stuff. Unbelievable that my mother would make me stay with Sharon. I scowled at her when she wasn't looking. The medical student already ran Frank's life. Why did she have to run mine too?

I opened the car door and got out as soon as we stopped. Sharon was unloading grocery bags from her car. When she eyed me, her smile reminded me of some mad scientist plotting an evil experiment.

After Alicia helped Sharon carry her groceries in, everybody hugged and said their goodbyes. Then my mom and my sister got into the rental car and left for the airport.

I offered to help put stuff away, but Sharon reminded me not to lift anything heavy yet. So I eased down into a chair at the kitchen table and watched her. "When's your brother supposed to get here?"

Sharon sat down opposite me, holding a sheet of paper with both hands. "Actually, Tyler left a note…His unit's on high alert…He'll call as soon as he hears anything…So we're alone for the next few days. Is that all right? If not, I can drive you back to Eaton Hall."

My mother wouldn't be happy if her son was alone with Sharon or disobeyed and went back to the dorm. On the other hand, Dad might actually like the idea of my being alone with a girl. "No. Mom wanted me to stay with someone." I chuckled nervously. "Please don't tell her we were alone, though. She'll have a hissy fit."

"You're sure this is all right?"

No, actually. The situation was horrible, but what other options did I have? "Yeah. Well, better than being alone in the dorm." I shrugged. "And better than going home."

"Why? Is your family so bad?"

"No. I love my family, but Dad would want me to get a buzz cut. He thinks I look like a girl when my hair's long."

Sharon tilted her head, studying me. Then she stood up and got a couple of containers out of the refrigerator. "Are chicken salad sandwiches all right? I was going to reheat the pot roast, but I'm not very hungry."

"Yeah. I'm not exactly starving, either."

The two of us sat down for a dinner of sandwiches and potato chips. Sharon's laser eyes burned into me. She was examining her specimen already, so I put on my innocent-little-kid smile and leaned closer. "What's up?"

"I was thinking how pretty you are when you smile," she said.

Like I need three weeks of this! "Thanks, Sharon. I love you, too."

"No. I'm serious. Perhaps that's why your father thinks you look like a girl."

I put my sandwich down and shook my head. "That's not how things work. I frown and he still makes me cut my hair."

"Why do it then?"

Why was obeying my father so hard to understand? "He's my dad." I poked at my sandwich, no longer hungry. "If short hair is what will make him happy, I'll get it cut."

Sharon frowned at her empty glass and got another soda out of the refrigerator. "Why's your father so sensitive about your appearance anyway?"

Like I should tell you? I scowled at my plate, pleading the Fifth by my silence.

"You can trust me. I wouldn't tell anyone."

Yeah. Right. "Hmpf." She would probably blackmail me. One more person under her control. One step closer to world domination.

Sharon set her fork down and breathed deep. Her face softened and her body relaxed. Sadness touched her eyes. Was Dr. Jekyll becoming Miss Hyde? Wow. Like maybe she was a real person with feelings and all. When Sharon next spoke, her voice was gentler than I'd ever heard it. "Jamie, Doctors Hospital is a teaching hospital. Earlier this week I watched them examine someone with a rare disorder. The patient was sixteen, less than five feet tall, and had strawberry blonde hair. He was still unconscious after having his appendix removed. I didn't recognize his face until the end, or I wouldn't have stayed." She shrugged, looking apologetic. "I'm sorry."

My stomach muscles seized, almost making me hurl my lunch. I grimaced, nervous that my heart might not start beating again. For a few seconds the only sound was the ticking of the kitchen clock. Then my pulse came crashing back, pounding in both ears. What more could anybody take from me? I drew in a long breath, closed both eyes, and exhaled. "You stole his secret," I whispered. "What will happen if every-body knows?"

"No," Sharon whispered, with a gentle shake of her head. "I'm the only one who recognized you, and I won't tell anyone. You can trust me to keep your secret."

Fear and uncertainty raced across my mind. Did I have any choice? I stared at her without blinking, eyes unfocused. How much did she know? "What did the doctor say about him?"

Sharon put on her medical student face. She would have looked perfect in a white coat. "You have a genetic condition resulting in short stature, a pixie face, and a sexually ambiguous body. The doctor pointed out parts of your anatomy. And," she added, in a conspiratorial whisper, "he said you should have been raised female."

I stared at the table, wondering who would ever want some nosy medical student as a friend. But since she already knew everything, I longed for her acceptance. I closed my eyes again, trying to calm shattered nerves. "What if he was?"

"What do you mean? I don't understand."

How could anybody explain a childhood like mine? I put my plate into the dishwasher and retreated to the living room. Outside the picture window white clouds drifted across a pale blue sky. A small child's laughter echoed across the years. I'd been happy once, blissfully unaware of what awaited me. Out of my field of vision I sensed Sharon's silent approach. In a hushed voice, I said, "Maybe when he was little he thought he was a girl, but when he got older his mom and dad didn't like that."

"So you're a boy because that's what your mother and father want?"

Rejected, the little girl had run away from the pain in her father's eyes. She'd hidden in the one place no one could ever find her. *Should I tell you the truth about Jameson? Would you help if you understood?* In a small voice, I said, "She might have built a pretend boy to fool them all."

A wing-back chair sat in one corner of the living room, a lamp stand next to it. I sat down, pulled my feet up under me, and opened a magazine. What good was dwelling on old wounds? The girl had died long ago.

Sharon stopped in front of me, concern written across her face. "Someone should tell her I'd like to be her friend." She reached out a hand, hesitated, and then touched my arm.

Still withdrawing, I got up and walked toward the guest room. At the door I gazed back at her with a growing heaviness in my chest. "She hasn't talked to anybody since she was nine."

ℭ 2 ℬ

I collapsed on the bed in the guest room. Long ago I'd realized that someone would eventually find out Jameson wasn't a regular boy between his legs. But I'd never expected anybody to discover he wasn't much of a boy between his ears either.

Sharon wanted to be my friend, and yet she was too much like a doctor. They'd already done something evil to her brain. Why had I admitted anything to her? Packing and returning to the dorm seemed the safest thing to do, but she had me trapped in her specimen jar. What choice did I have? If she wasn't my friend, she might tell Mom I really did have gender issues. Then I'd be history.

Jameson existed as a thousand boys-don't and boys-do rules. Deep inside, I brushed the dust off the end of one. Was shutting off a part of him even possible? I pulled, gently at first, and then more firmly. With a quiet popping sound, the rule slid out. I waited, probing for any adverse reaction, ready to replace it. A slight easing of inhibition was all I noticed. Down the corridor each way, as far as the eye could see, stretched more of Jameson. This would take time.

One of his rules stood off alone, like a shepherd watching over the others, guarding and caring for them. When I brushed my fingers over it, an electric thrill ran through my vision. Images flashed rapid-fire, jumbled sounds crashing softly in my ears. Kids at a party. I didn't remember anything from my early birthdays. Was this a memory block? Why forget about a stupid party? Ignoring the sights and sounds flooding me, I yanked on the end—and got swept into the past.

* * * *

I didn't have any clothes fit for an elfin princess, so my cousin Kaylah let me borrow some hand-me-downs one of the Fair Folk had given her. She shook her head as she held a white velvet skirt up in front of me. "I don't care if that old book says the Kirkpatricks are faie. Your face is *bean shìdh*, but the rest of you is *brùnaidh*."

At five I was only a little taller than my two-year-old sister Alicia, so the clothes were way too big for me. "Please, Kaylah. The brownies are elves too. They're just not as tall."

"All right, then." Kaylah safety-pinned the white velvet skirt to my slip, so the waist stayed up under my arms and the hem brushed the floor. The satin sleeves of the woodland green blouse hung down past my fingertips. She wrapped a silver lace belt around my waist twice and made a bow in the back. A spider-silk flower went on my shoulder. I sat down so she could tie the ribbons of starlight ballet slippers around my ankles. "There you are!" She clapped her hands together. "Princess Grace herself doesn't dress any finer than that."

Fancy clothes weren't all an elfin princess needed to be dressed for a party, so I sat facing my reflection and waited for my maidservant to finish. She stood behind me in the wall mirror, intense concentration twisting her face. I grinned as she pulled the soft foam rollers out of my locks and fluffed, brushed, teased, and sprayed until my hair was perfect. It wasn't very long, but the color was pretty, somewhere between ripe pumpkin and the gold of the earrings she clipped on my ears.

Face full of wonder, Kaylah held a glass vial before my eyes. "There's a river so high in the Mountains of the Moon that the water turns silvery-blue." She pulled the stopper out of the shiny bottle and dipped a small brush into it. "I'm going to paint your nails with moonlight. Sit still until it dries."

In the mirror sat a beautiful elfin princess—golden hair aglow, large emerald eyes, small red mouth, and rosy cheeks sprinkled with freckles. She was the happiest elf-maiden of the realm. I stood, grabbed a handful of white velvet on each side, curtseyed to the lady in the mirror, and spun around so my skirt would fly.

"Pretty!" shouted Alicia, one finger in her mouth.

"Both my girls are beautiful." Kaylah bent down and kissed my little sister on the cheek.

"Are you ready, birthday girl?" She grabbed my hand and held it high. "Your court awaits you, my lady." I spun around on tiptoes, a lovely ballerina, my shoes sparkling like stardust in the night sky.

Jimmy the Pirate swaggered into the kitchen, wooden saber at his side and a black patch over one eye. Alicia danced in her little pink tutu and a pair of angel wings made from coat hanger wire and crinoline.

Gladys was dressed like Dorothy from *The Wizard of Oz*, red shoes and all. She had even brought Toto, a stuffed toy animal that might once have resembled a dog. Kaylah wore a tattered pair of bib overalls, a gingham blouse, and an old straw hat.

They had all chipped in and bought me a present. Kaylah must have wrapped the package because the edges and folds were all straight. I pulled the tape off, careful not to rip the paper. Inside was a new Raggedy Ann. A squeal of delight burst from my lips, and I hugged the doll to my breast. "Sofie! I'll name her Princess Sofie!" I scooted over on my throne, set her on the seat beside me, and straightened her dress.

Kaylah winked at me, set my birthday cake on the kitchen table, and lit the candles. I blew out all five with one breath and grinned at Jimmy. They say you shouldn't tell anybody your wish, but he already knew I wanted to be his wife.

The pirate grinned at me, eyes flashing, and waved a saber over his head. "Yar! Cut the cake!"

Kaylah was the one who baked my birthday cake. I think she got the recipe off a Hershey's Cocoa tin. Anyway, she made the yummiest chocolate cakes. I cut Jimmy a ragged chunk and passed him his plate.

"Princess, you're making a mess." My cousin, gentle as always, cleaned the frosting off my sleeve and cut slices for the rest of us.

I was halfway through eating mine when I heard the front door open. *Ooh!* Dad was home early. Seeing the little princess would make him sad. My fork hit my lap, chocolate cake and all, and bounced to the floor. Arms trembling, I sprang up, thinking to run away.

"No, Jamie. It's okay. Today's your birthday." Kaylah grabbed my arm and gently pushed me back down into my seat. "He should see how pretty you look."

Kaylah was only twelve, but she'd pretended to be my mom ever since she was seven. My real mom home schooled Kaylah, and me, and my brother Scott every morning. In the afternoon, while our moms worked, my cousin, and Alicia, and I played together. Scott didn't hang around with girls, so he went to his pal Joey's or played kick-the-can outside the old schoolhouse on Polk Street.

I didn't have a magic ring to make me invisible, so Dad found me as soon as he strode into the kitchen. His eyes—those deep wells of disappointment—locked on the elfin princess and sucked the life out of her. "What's going on?"

Kaylah stepped between me and Dad, saving me from certain doom. "It's Jamie's birthday, remember? The kids are all wearing costumes for his party. We were reading *Old Scottish Fairy Tales* and he wanted to dress like an elfin princess."

I peeked around Kaylah's waist, hiding Sofie behind my back. The air around my father seemed to crackle with lightning, but he only nodded and smiled at me. "I got you a new softball. After your party, let's play catch. Okay, sport?"

So my dad played catch with the elfin princess, tossing her the ball underhand from a few feet away. I missed the first one; it went right between my outstretched arms. The second rolled off my fingertips. The third bounced off my hands and hit me in the face. Boys seemed to learn right away, but I didn't think I'd ever be able to catch a ball. I shut my eyes to hide my frustration, but the tears were too many.

"I'm sorry, Jameson. Are you okay?" Dad knelt down and hugged his little princess tight, but the disappointment in his eyes hurt her worse than the ball had. Scott said I threw like a girl, but all the ones I knew played catch better than me. I got hurt when I played boy games. Every time. That's one reason I preferred playing with Kaylah and Alicia.

Dad led me back inside. While he searched for the ice pack, I sympathized with the princess in the mirror. Her face resembled a raccoon's now, with a dark half-moon under one eye. *Poor girl. Another black eye. Won't you ever learn?*

* * * *

A knock on the door meant it was almost bedtime. I put Barbie into her case and picked up my little china tea sets. Alicia began gathering the Lincoln Logs that were scattered across the floor. "Mom knows," she said as she slid a box on the shelf.

"What?" I collected the dolls, and stuffed animals, and all and put them into the closet.

"That you don't play with your cars."

Every morning before Dad left for work, I got my Matchbox cars out of their carrying case. After breakfast Mom home schooled us. In the afternoon I played with Alicia and Kaylah. When Dad got home, I packed the cars back into their case. Seeing me put them all into their little slots made my dad smile. Like he thought I'd been playing with them the whole day. After supper Alicia and I read or played with dolls in our room.

My sister touched my shirtsleeve. "If you're an elfin princess, how come you always wear boy clothes?"

I glanced into the mirror. The elfin princess wondered why, too. "I don't have any dresses, you know. Kaylah's old clothes are only for dress-up, and they're too big anyway."

Alicia hugged me like I was *her* little sister. "You can wear mine."

I glanced at her and shook my head. "I don't want to wear somebody else's clothes."

"Mom says we're supposed to share, and besides, we're twins."

Alicia was my best bud ever, but sometimes she said goofy stuff. "We can't be twins. I'm seven and you're only four." I picked up Sofie and put her on my bed so she could sleep with me.

Alicia held her hand above my head and slid it toward hers, like she was measuring us. "We're the same size and we're sisters." She bobbed her head as if that settled everything.

We stood next to each other in the mirror. Alicia really was as tall as the elfin princess. Our hair and eyes were the same color. She was human and me part elf, but we were both girls. Not twins, though. When I shook my head again, she pouted. "Jamie, please. I want to wear jeans."

She had some cute corduroy overalls with a flower sewn on the front, but no blue jeans. What could I do? I hugged her and said okay.

She squealed and ran to my dresser, where she picked out a pair of jeans. Then she ran to the closet and found a blouse like the one she was wearing. A minute later we were giggling and jumping on my bed, dressed like we were identical twins or something. We scrambled to get ready for bed when someone knocked on the door again.

Mom stared at me for several heartbeats before she tucked me in, but she didn't say anything about Alicia and me wearing matching night-gowns.

* * * *

The doorbell rang a third time. I glanced at the bathroom door, wishing Kaylah would hurry. Alicia peeked around the corner as I took

another step across the living room. "You'll get us in trouble," she whispered.

"What if it's Aunt Elizabeth?" She'd be mad if I didn't let her in.

"Kaylah said never, ever answer the door by yourself." She shook her
head in emphasis. "Never."

A fist pounded on the door, insistent. What could I do? I turned the
handle and pulled.

The tall lady on the porch smiled and leaned close. "You must be
Alicia. Is your mother home?"

Never, ever talk to strangers. That's what my mom always said. "No,
ma'am. My name's Jamie. Mom's not home."

Alicia poked her head around the corner, and then ran to stand next
to me. "We're twins." She tugged on the sleeve of my dress, beaming.
"See. We have the same clothes."

I stared at my sister. She always insisted we dress alike. Our hair was
even cut the same. In her mind, that was enough. That was okay, I guess.
We liked each other better than any real twins I knew.

The lady studied her notebook for a moment, frowning. Then she
shook her head. "Our records indicate a nine-year-old boy named
Jameson and a six-year-old girl named Alicia reside at this address."

Always helpful, Alicia said, "Jamie used to wear boy clothes."

"Who's there?" I turned to see Kaylah approaching, her face pale.
Was she sick?

The lady held out a hand. "I'm Stephanie Pollock, from the school
board."

* * * *

The sights and sounds dispersed, finding their old homes in my
memory. A curious child's imagination drew me into the bathroom.
Golden hair surrounded her face. Large green eyes, small nose, cute little
mouth, freckles spread over her cheeks—the ethereal face in the mirror
belonged on an elfin princess. Before I'd made Jameson, I'd seen her
every day. All of the stupid behavior rules would have to be put back
before returning to the dorm, but I swore I'd never again hide away her
memories.

I unpacked Jameson's clothes and other things, and dressed in his PJs. I could disable the rest of his rules while lying on the bed. Sharon would think me asleep.

A flash, a crack of thunder, and an old wizard appeared in the doorway, inviting me on a quest. I slammed the door in his face. Jameson lent stability to my life. Other kids teased me, but I could live with that. People got killed on adventures, especially ones involving old wizards. Safety lay behind my mask, living my life in my books. No one would ever suspect —or so I had thought.

He shattered the door with his staff. "You're too late," he intoned. "Jameson's doom is sealed. The young mage has seen and won't rest until she frees the elfin princess from his grasp. You must learn to live without him."

My arms and legs trembled at the thought of losing Jameson. How could I face the world alone? He was the one who remembered all those rules about how to be a boy. No. I would only remove my mask long enough to make friends with Sharon, so she would leave me alone and not go blabbing to Mom. Just for one day. Then I'd put Jameson's rules all back and make my world safe again. I stared at the imaginary old wizard and sighed, wondering if Sharon had any idea what she'd unleashed.

❧ 3 ☙

Lying on a feather bed underneath a pile of quilts, breathing the cold night air—could even a princess have asked for a more pleasant sleep? Stretching and yawning, I rubbed my eyes with balled fists. Muted noises somewhere in the house meant Mom was up. Soon she'd be telling me and Alicia to get ready for home school. I rolled over, bunched the soft pillow around my head, and pushed the hair away from my face. The last little bit of sleep was always the best.

An errant ray caught my eye. Bright light peeked around the drapes, too intense for an Oswego winter morning. This could only mean one thing. *Snow!* The little princess bounced up out of bed, clapped her hands together, and squealed at the thought of a white Christmas. I poked my head between the drapes, expecting a winter wonderland.

Bright sunshine dazzled my eyes. Tears formed as I blinked away the blinding colors. Behind the neighbor's house a majestic rainfall stretched skyward to heavy cumulus clouds. God's rainbow soared off into the distance. Memories of the previous day awakened me from my half-sleep and brought me back to the present. *Ooh!* The world was so much more alive without Jameson.

In the yard a magnolia tree spread limbs heavenward, dozens of lilac and cream blossoms declaring the beauty of creation. Great drops rolled off their petals and fell to the earth. Nearby, mist rose from puddles already returning to the clouds. Butterflies played tag among the hibiscus blooms. A hummingbird dallied within arm's reach outside my window, winked, and zipped away. An enchanted land, it seemed, that fair place the humans named Coral Gables. Fully awake now, I pulled the drapes open, spun around on tiptoes, and waltzed to the bathroom.

A shaggy-haired girl frowned at me from the bathroom mirror. She wasn't a real princess, you know, but even a waif expected to have her hair trimmed once in a while. She narrowed her eyes at me, but I spread my hands apart. "You shouldn't expect Jameson to keep his hair all pretty. At least he didn't cut it short." The girl glared at me from under her brows until I turned away.

"It's not my fault his hair's a mess," I whispered as I brushed out the snarls. "And look," I said, holding up a golden lock. "Isn't the color pretty? There's more sun in my hair now. You can't tell whether I'm a blonde or a redhead anymore." She stared back at me, unimpressed. "Okay," I whispered, "So maybe Sharon will trim the ends for us."

The princess in the mirror scowled at me when I took off Jameson's pajama bottoms. She didn't like seeing what was down there because it proved she wasn't a girl like she thought. She only had a pretty face and small size. "Don't be sad, princess," I tried to reassure her. "Sharon said you were supposed to be a girl. Maybe you will be when you grow up."

I took a quick shower. Boy clothes were all I had—I couldn't expect Jameson to keep girl clothes, now could I? He had no fashion sense anyway; all he wore were T-shirts and blue jeans. I dressed in the cleanest ones I found and went in search of my new friend.

Sharon was making coffee when I walked into the kitchen. "Good morning, Miss Sharon. Would you please trim my hair?"

She flinched and turned pale before nodding. "Trim…Sure…Go shampoo. I'll find some scissors."

In the guest bath again I glanced at the princess. "Should we use the sink to wash our hair?" I grinned at her, feeling a little mischievous. Jameson had to use the shower. That was one of those stupid boys-don't rules. Back when being a girl was okay, Mom used to wash mine in the sink.

The little princess strolled out of the bathroom about ten minutes later, a towel wrapped around her head. I grinned when I realized that was breaking another of Jameson's rules.

Sharon studied me from under her brows. "Would you like your hair cut short?"

Memories of my first buzz cut almost knocked me down. Even as a teenager, I fought against tears whenever Dad got out the clippers. My hands rose instinctively to shield my head. "No, ma'am. I only want my hair trimmed."

Sharon smiled the way Mom used to whenever I got scared. She pulled up a kitchen chair and asked the little princess to sit. Then she wrapped a towel around my shoulders. "Your hair's beautiful. You should take better care of it."

My hair had gotten so tangled up with the whole boy-girl thing, letting Jameson do anything at all with it was hard. I craned my neck to gaze up at Sharon. "I'm sorry. Jameson isn't any good at that."

Sharon stared at me. I counted heartbeats until she pulled up another chair and sat down facing me. With one hand she brushed the hair out of my eyes. "Where's Jameson now?" she whispered.

Deep inside, stacks of rules were all there was of him. I touched one to make sure everything was still okay. Then I smiled and tilted my head. "I took him apart. He's not a real person, you know."

A wisp of cloud crossed Sharon's face, leaving a faint trail of distress. "Are you?"

"I hope so." I chuckled, a soft melody at first, like wind chimes in the breeze. How long had it been since the little princess made a sound like that? When I realized that giggling was against another one of Jameson's ridiculous gender rules, the insanity of it all bubbled up out of me as musical laughter.

The sound appeared to banish Sharon's concern. Her smile turned carefree. "So…what's your name?"

"I'm Jamie. You said you wanted to be my friend."

"I do. I'm sorry. I was confused, that's all."

"You said you'd trim my hair."

"I will."

Sharon stood in front of me, a hand on either side of my head. Her face knotted up in concentration as she studied the little princess. "I think you'd be pretty with your hair cut just below your chin. Is that all right?"

Ooh! "That sounds neat."

When Sharon finished, she asked me to go look in the mirror. The pretty little princess reflected there squealed with delight. She started crying, though. The princess hadn't had a girl's haircut in forever. I brushed my hand across the glass to wipe away her tears. "It'll be okay now," I whispered. *You shouldn't lie to her. You know Jameson can't go back to the dorm like that.* I dropped my hand and turned away, whispering, "Let her be happy for a while. Okay?"

I went back to the kitchen and thanked Sharon for the pretty hairstyle. Mom didn't want hair in Jameson's eyes, so I asked my friend for a barrette.

"There's one on the dresser you can use. I'd like to speak with you after you get it."

"Okay," I piped and headed for the guest room again. The girl in the mirror grinned at me this time, her green eyes flashing as I pinned her hair back. It was only for a day, but neither of us cared. I winked at her and bounced back down the hall to the kitchen.

Sharon motioned for me to sit at the kitchen table, and then sat across from me. I imagined her with her white coat and stethoscope, hair tied back and face all intense. For some reason I found her medical student seriousness amusing. It only broadened my grin when she leaned toward me and asked, "Last night, you said you were a girl when you were young. Would you explain that?"

It seemed a strange question to ask first, but perhaps this was a medical student's way of making friends. "I was small. When I played with boys, I got hurt, so my parents let me play with other girls. When I asked, Mom taught me cooking, and sewing, and all. My parents bought me dolls. I thought being a girl was okay."

"What did you play?"

"Kaylah, and Alicia, and I played house and dress-up—" An old memory derailed my train of thought, leaving behind an image of Dad's sad eyes when his happy little princess explained why she had a pillow tucked under her shirt. My sad eyes glanced at Sharon. "Sometimes I was a mommy."

Sharon's eyes lingered on mine. "Kaylah's your cousin who was at the hospital?"

Had Sharon met her? "Yeah. We used to be neighbors."

"You're living as a boy now. What happened?"

Images from my childhood tumbled across my vision, like leaves on a windy fall day. My hands clenched on the wooden edge of the kitchen table as my world spun. I lay on cold steel, crying and alone. Doctors surrounded me, talking to each other. One poked my belly. Another examined me between my legs. "When I was nine, we went to a doctor in Chicago because my parents thought I was too small."

I took several deep breaths, trying to slow my racing heart. My body trembled on the examining table. *Why isn't Mom stopping them?* "I told the doctor I liked being a small girl. He said I had to be a boy." I tore my eyes away from Sharon, trying to hold back the surging ocean of depression. "We moved. In Springfield they didn't let me do girl things, and I couldn't play with Kaylah anymore."

Waves crashed over me, sweeping me off my feet. I had been hysterical when they pulled me away from my cousin. Alicia and I had clung to each other as our family left Oswego for the last time.

A barricade snapped into place, shutting out the images, protecting me, leaving only the indistinct shadow of childhood memories. The pain receded, but I struggled to catch my breath. "Mom took away my dolls. My parents kept my hair short."

Tense muscles eased somewhat. I glanced at Sharon. A single tear spoiled her medical student detachment. I smiled, sure she was my friend. "Last year, my mom took me to one of the doctors she works with. He gave me shots. After a while, my voice started to change. I hated that, so I figured out how to get early admission to college, and here I am." I stared down at the table and grimaced. "Or at least here Jameson is."

"What do you mean?" Her voice was soft and gentle. Not the usual Sharon.

"I'm not allowed to be a girl, so I built a pretend boy. I started making him when we moved to Springfield. He's not a real boy, you know, but he's good enough for most people."

"Why don't you be a girl?"

"I'm not allowed. You saw me without clothes. I'm not a girl between my legs. So—"

"You're not a boy either," insisted Sharon.

Because I was part elfin princess? Because I had to sit down to pee? Because I wasn't good at boy things? At times I wanted to be a boy more than anything. "It would be neat to be tall, and strong, and fast, and play sports." I shrugged, still wondering what Sharon was thinking. "I'm not good at being a boy, but I'm not allowed to be a girl either."

Sharon stared at the little princess, wheels turning. She appeared to be planning my future. I wondered whether she would ask me what I wanted or be like all the doctors who did whatever they liked. After a while longer, Sharon nodded. "Why not be a girl until you graduate? You wouldn't need to tell your parents."

"They aren't stupid, Sharon. I can't stay here until I graduate. Mom and Dad want me home for the summer." They wouldn't like the elfin princess. They'd cut her hair.

Sharon sighed, and then stood up. "Well, I promised Tyler I would do some baking for Christmas."

The princess had her own little red apron. White streaks of flour ran across the front. The small dark spots were probably either butter or lard. How many times had I helped my mom cook? I jumped up out of the chair. "May I help? Mom and I used to bake cakes and cookies for Christmas."

"Sure. Why not? Why don't you find out how much flour and sugar are in the pantry? Look, don't lift. I'll find some recipes."

"I remember our recipes for shortbread and for sugar cookies, and the Hershey's Cocoa tin has a recipe for chocolate cake."

Sharon made a yummy face. "Mmm! Shortbread sounds good. Why don't we begin with that?"

"Okay. You start with two cups of flour, two-thirds of a cup of sugar, and a half teaspoon of salt in a large mixing bowl."

Sharon measured the ingredients with care and mixed them.

"We need to cream in the butter. This way." I smiled, picked up a stick in each hand, and squeezed them both through my fingers.

Sharon blinked at me. "Wouldn't it be easier to melt them first?"

I shook my head, serious. "You don't want the butter to melt the sugar." I stuck both hands into the mixing bowl and began blending the mixture with my fingers. "You want the butter to break up into tiny pieces." The little princess held a handful up in front of Sharon's face to show her. "See?" Small bits fell to the floor.

"Jamie, you're making a mess." Sharon bent down to pick up the pieces. I reached for the washrag and accidentally bumped the bag of flour. A handful of the soft white powder spilled over the front of the cabinets. When Sharon stood again, she had flour in her hair and down one cheek. "Jamie!"

I grinned and covered my mouth with one hand, getting dough on my chin. With the other buttery hand, I tried to wipe the flour off

Sharon's face. "I'm sorry." Giggling, the little princess began licking the batter off her hands.

Sharon scowled at me for a second before her lips trembled, and she started laughing. Seeing the always serious medical student crack up sent me into a fit that ended in tears.

♋ 4 ♌

Later in the day I settled into one of the wing-back chairs with a book, a glass of milk, and some artistically decorated cookies. Sharon sat on the rug next to me. "I'm going to dress up a bit. Why don't you?"

What would I wear? A different T-shirt? "I don't own anything fancy."

"I'll let you borrow something of mine. I'm quite a bit taller than you, but I have some things that might fit. I can do your makeup as well."

You want me to be your Barbie Doll? "No. I don't want to wear somebody else's clothes."

"All right, then. Why don't we open presents? We have a tradition— We can each open one before Christmas."

You didn't need to be a little princess to love watching people open their gifts, and I had brought something I thought Sharon would appreciate, so I picked up her present and handed it to her. "This is from me."

Sharon pulled off the bow and unwrapped the package. Inside was a book, an old leather-bound edition of *The Comedies of William Shakespeare*. She beamed at me with a big grin. "Frank must have told you about the plays."

"Plays? No. He only talked about how much you like Shakespeare."

"I love The Bard, but I also produce a play each year at the country club. We do a dinner theatre for charity. The club donates a lavish buffet. The cast waits tables. Everyone has a wonderful time. We're always looking for people."

"That sounds like fun."

She handed me a present. The folds and edges were all straight. Who would have expected any less from someone as meticulous as Sharon? Whatever the package contained was soft. Clothes, no doubt. I grinned at Sharon and peeled back the paper to reveal a set of baby doll pajamas and an embroidered peasant blouse.

The little princess squealed, hugged Sharon, and ran off to the bedroom to try on her new blouse. The girl in the mirror bounced up and down, holding up the top, impatient to rid herself of the old T-shirt.

I bobbed my head at her and grinned. "Yes. You're right. This is the nicest present I've ever gotten." It was the only blouse anybody had ever given me—a perfect fit.

The girl's eyes went wide and she pointed at the blouse again.

"Huh? Ooh! How did Sharon know what to get us for Christmas?" *How would I know?* I shrugged at her. "Maybe she was going to give these to Frank's little sister. We're the same size."

She seemed to accept that, so I washed my face and rushed back out to thank Sharon.

"You said you'd do my makeup." I grinned at her, trying not to burst.

"Sure." Sharon smiled, took my hand, and led me back to the guest bath. She applied a little bit of mascara and lipstick. The girl in the mirror kept grinning at me and at Sharon. She was the happiest princess in the whole world.

We walked back into the living room. Sharon seemed as happy as I felt. I sat in the wing-back and tucked my feet up under me. When I reached for my book again, Sharon asked me what I was reading.

"I found a copy of *A Little Princess* on your shelf. I read it when I was four, but it's one of my favorites."

"Yes. Mine as well."

She looked a little misty-eyed, so I hopped up out of the chair and hugged her. "Thank you, Sharon. This has been the best day ever."

* * * *

Sharon closed the door to her room. Even over Christmas break my friend studied. I frowned and went to change into my new PJs. A chenille bathrobe hung from a hook on the guest room door. The elfin princess wrapped the softness around herself and went to sit in the wing-back again.

The clock said eleven, but I'd already spent so much time in bed the past week I didn't think sleep would follow me there. *A Little Princess*, though pleasant to read, I set on my lap. With some stories, I would read for a while and wander off into my own little world. Dreaming was important when real life sucked.

Sadness drifted over my head. *Why delay the inevitable any longer? Time to put Jameson's rules back into place. Get it over with. Change back into his PJs and go to bed.* I brushed my fingers across the end of one rule, hesitated, and picked up the book again. Just one more chapter before the elfin princess had to go. What could it hurt?

A mad dash for the guest room was my first thought when I heard the front door open. I was sitting cross-legged on the chair and my feet got all caught up in the robe, so the princess nearly ended up face down on the floor. That would not have done at all. By the time I recovered, he stood in front of me, grinning. "I'm sorry if I startled you."

"No. That's okay," I said, my voice wandering up the scale like some kid's slide whistle. I hid my face behind my book, my eyes peeking over the top.

He eased the volume out of my hand and examined the cover. His grin shone white in the dim light. "Tyler Andrew Pierson, my little princess," he said, bending one knee before the throne.

I took his hand, intending to shake it, but he raised mine to his lips and kissed my fingers, like a storybook hero would. "I'm Jamie," the little princess whispered, out of breath.

"Good to meet you, Miss Jamie."

Tyler Andrew Pierson grinned like the Cheshire Cat and seemed able to appear and disappear at will. His brown eyes sparkled with mirth and his smile confessed that he had his hand in the cookie jar. Perhaps he would teach Alice the rules of Wonderland.

Tyler wasn't as tall as his older sister, but it seemed a spirit of adventure gave him an energy I'd never seen in Sharon. He wore what looked like a one-piece, casual uniform. "Are you a pilot?" I asked, eyebrows raised.

"Yes, miss, I am."

"What do you fly?" I bit my lip. Warmth spread across my cheeks. The little princess didn't believe in love at first sight, but she was having trouble keeping her smile under control.

Sharon pulled the door to her room open. "Hi, Tyler. Jamie, you should be in bed. You two can talk in the morning."

Yes, I should, I thought, studying Tyler. But first the princess must grant him a boon for his kindness. I leaned close to him and whispered, "Don't tell anybody, but there's homemade cookies in the kitchen."

* * * *

The elfin princess opened the drapes as the dawn painted red and purple streaks across the clouds, and early morning mists rose from the ground. I preferred to pray when the world was quiet, and my day not yet begun. As always, I finished by asking God if he would make me a boy and, if not, then make it okay for me to be a girl.

Mom and Dad were proud of Jameson's intelligence, his reading comprehension, and his stellar ACT and SAT scores. But if he was so smart, how come he couldn't figure out something simple, like how to be a boy? I was pretty sure most people didn't have to think about what sex they were.

Someone knocked on the door as I finished dressing. When I let Sharon in, she nodded, her face apologetic. "I'm sorry about last night. Tyler was supposed to call first."

"Okay, but what do we do now? Mom said Kaylah was coming here for Christmas. I have to be a boy with her around. What about Tyler?"

"Your cousin's all right with you being a girl."

So much for keeping my secret! "You talked to her about me?"

"Jamie, if your whole family were like her, the war would be over, now wouldn't it?"

"Sharon, I don't need you starting World War Three. People will get hurt."

"What's the problem? Kaylah accepts you the way you are. Tyler's interested in my cute little redheaded friend."

One day, and already I was in trouble. The more Tyler liked me, the madder he'd be when he found out I wasn't a girl. "Is that what he said?"

"Yes."

Better get it over with. "I have to tell him."

"Jamie, wait." Sharon blocked the doorway. "My brother won't be back until tonight. We'll tell him, but give him some time to get to know you first. He thinks a twelve-year-old girl recovering from surgery could use a little cheering up."

My jaw dropped at the boldness of her lie. "You're kidding. Right?"

She gestured toward the mirror. "Look at yourself. Am I really so far off?"

I studied my image. A prepubescent girl smiled and waved at me. *Yeah. Close enough.* "We tell him right after Kaylah leaves?"

"Right before you go back to the dorm."

That was almost three weeks. I chewed on my lip, wondering if he'd kill me. "Okay."

Sharon left, pulling the door closed.

Or maybe he'd be my friend by then.

03 5 80

I studied the kid in the mirror with a critical eye. Kaylah was due to arrive any moment. What would she say? With my new hairstyle and top, I thought I looked like a girl, but a whole swarm of butterflies gathered in my stomach. I waited in the entryway, tense.

Five minutes seemed like hours. I pulled the door open when Kaylah arrived. She hesitated while I stood inside, a frightened little girl. Then my cousin grinned and hugged her little princess. She remembered me! My heart leaped like a gazelle.

Kaylah handed me a bag. "I stopped by the Salvation Army. These should do for now."

Tyler would be home soon, so I hugged my cousin, and rushed to the bedroom. It was okay that the clothes were hand-me-downs, I thought, examining an old Mod-style dress. All that mattered was Kaylah still loved the elfin princess.

As I got dressed, I stared at the girl in the mirror, wondering how she might pass for a sixteen-year-old. A moment later I walked down the hall wearing one of the dresses Kaylah had brought. Sharon grinned and said, "You're pretty. A twelve-year-old, but you look good."

* * * *

Kaylah and I joined Sharon and Tyler in the living room for snacks, conversation, and celebration. After we had opened presents, Kaylah handed me a bundle, saying, "She belongs to you, but I thought I'd wrap her anyway."

I removed the covering, careful not to rip the paper. "Sofie!" I held up my old Raggedy Ann and hugged her tight. "My little Princess Sofie," I whispered.

Kaylah's eyes overflowed with a tender sadness. "You left her at our house when your family moved."

Several drops ran down my face when I tried to blink them away. I wondered how many additional tears Santa would bring me.

Sharon touched my arm. "You said you sang in a choir. Do you remember any of the songs?"

I thought over the music I'd learned. After taking a deep breath, I started singing, "Angels we have heard on high, sweetly singing o'er the plains."

Kaylah grinned and took up her part. "And the mountains in reply, echoing their joyous strain."

We sang the chorus in harmony. "Gloria, In Excelsis, Deo!"

"Wait!" Sharon ran to the piano and started playing as she sang alto.

Tyler laughed, picked up a songbook, and sang bass.

When we finished all the verses, Tyler turned toward Sharon. "How long has it been?"

"Too long." Sharon stretched and yawned.

Kaylah winked at her little princess. I grinned at her and mouthed, "Thank you."

* * * *

Daily walks through the neighborhood helped me build up my strength. Tyler accompanied me whenever he was home. I'd never been treated so nice by a boy, but a girl sure could get used to the attention. I wasn't actually a princess, you know, but he seemed like Prince Charming to me.

On one walk I asked him what he wanted to do with his life.

He paused, put a hand to his chin, and flashed that grin of his. "When I get back from Vietnam, I'd like to start my own crop-dusting business or fly for one of the emergency transport companies."

"Vietnam?"

"Yes. I'm supposed to go sometime this spring or summer."

I turned my head away and sighed. "Do you have to go?"

"Let's talk about something else." He took both of my hands in his. "What are you going to do when you grow up?"

Heat flowed into me through his hands. My heart crept up my throat. Most of the time Tyler treated me like I was his little sister, but part of me wished I was sixteen to him. "I'm not sure," I whispered, hoarse. "My parents want me to go to college. I'd rather get married and have children."

"Did you get what you wanted for Christmas?"

Yes, I had. Time with a boy named Tyler. A gentle older brother. Someone safe for the little princess to have a crush on. I grinned. "Yes, sir, I did."

"You're not going to tell me what you got, are you?"

"No. I'm not."

"Sharon said you go to church. Are you a Christian?"

"Yes, sir."

Tyler's eyes grew large. "Would you please stop doing that?"

"Sir?"

"Yes, that."

"Okay, Mister Tyler."

He laughed and shook his head. "I'm only nineteen. You don't need to be so formal."

"Okay."

"Do you read the Bible every day?"

"No. I don't read it much."

"Would you like to read the Bible together? Perhaps pray together?"

"I'd love to. Can we sing a couple of hymns?"

"We'll do that," he promised. He took my hand and we continued walking. "Jamie, does your life glorify God?"

"Jesus died on the cross for me. I try to obey him, but—" I lost myself in his eyes.

"But what?" he asked, his smile encouraging.

I stared at the ground. His eyes had grown so intense. "Knowing what's right isn't always easy."

"That's why he gave us his Word and his Spirit." Tyler was silent for a moment, his eyes studying mine. "Is the little princess well enough for a Bible study this evening?"

Warmth filled me when Tyler stood next to me. He would make someone a wonderful husband. His way of leading was so gentle. "Sure."

* * * *

Sharon, and Tyler, and I sat around the kitchen table, the remains of dinner growing cold in front of us. My nervousness exploded into terror. Sharon had told Tyler I had something to tell him before I left, so we sat around the table in silence.

When was it okay to share your secrets? Too soon, they could push a person away. Too late, and they might think you'd deceived them. If you didn't share, they might find out anyway and think you didn't trust them.

Sharon knew mine and she was my friend; maybe Tyler would be, too. He'd been so sweet. I looked up to find Sharon staring at me. My heart caught in my throat. Words failed me.

We sat for several minutes longer before Sharon said, "Tyler, I asked Jamie not to tell you about herself until you'd spent some time with her." Tyler's dark brown eyes turned my way, expectant. "She has a rare disorder that results in short stature. She's sixteen."

Tyler shook his head. "She's, um…not very well, um…endowed."

"Flat-chested," I said, nodding my head. "I haven't had my puberty yet."

Sharon glanced my way. "Her condition also affected her reproductive system. She'll have to take estrogen once the situation with her parents is straightened out."

Tyler's eyes sought mine again. "Sixteen?"

I bobbed my head. "I'm a student at the University of Miami."

His eyes withdrew. At least a part of Tyler was no longer in the room. "What's going on with your parents?"

Why couldn't I be like everybody else? *I'm a circus freak, okay?* Words got all caught in my throat, so I stared at Sharon, pleading for help.

She coughed and said, "Jamie's parents don't understand she's a girl."

Dark clouds formed over Tyler's brow. I sighed and bit my lip. The battle was lost. "I room with Frank in Eaton Hall. He doesn't know." There. I'd said it. I studied my lap, bracing for the explosion.

"You're a boy?" Tyler's voice rasped, almost a whisper.

"No, Tyler." Sharon slid right back into her big-sister-lecture voice. "She was born with one testis and one ovary, but what does it matter? I'm her friend. I was hoping you would be as well."

One reason I didn't argue with my mom and dad about being a girl was that letting Jameson live life for me hurt less than facing reality myself. The Pollyanna in me wanted to believe Tyler would ignore the freak show and befriend the princess instead.

I waited, avoiding eye contact with him. "How do you relate to someone like that? Can I hang out with a guy who's half girl or date a girl who's half boy?" Hurt, disbelief, and a touch of anger carried in his voice.

"You related fine yesterday, Tyler." He didn't move, but his eyes turned away. The day before, I'd been a twelve-year-old little sister to him.

Tyler was short for a guy, but he had broad shoulders and muscles and facial hair. My older brother had been tall and strong. He'd even played football before he went into the Army. Why not me?

Alicia was six inches taller than me. She was only thirteen, but she already had her curves and her period. Was that too much to expect?

Okay, so I had to take hormones to have a puberty. Boy hormones would make my situation worse. At least female hormones would make me look like a short girl. That would be okay, except I'd still have to tell anybody I cared about that I was a freak. And be sent away.

Tote in hand, I rushed out the door. Gray clouds followed me back to the dorm.

ℭℬ **6** ℰ℞

As soon as Christmas break ended, I made up my final exams. I was anxious to get back on track. After registration I bought my textbooks and dropped them off at the dorm. The weather was cool and sunny, pleasant winter weather for Miami. My favorite bench by the lake was unoccupied, so I sat there. Most always I brought a book along, but that day I wanted to relax in the sunshine and enjoy the flowers. I leaned back, closed my eyes, and drifted.

"Hey, lookit what we have here—Sleeping Beauty." I turned my head to discover my nemesis leaning over the back of the bench.

"Hey Ron, leave me alone. Okay?"

"Or what, you little fairy?" Ron grabbed me by the hair and yanked my head back. "You still owe me the cash I gave Frank for your little nightie." He pushed my head forward and stomped off toward the dorm.

Lisa walked toward me from under a nearby magnolia tree. "What is his problem?" she exclaimed, her face twisted in anger.

"He took a nightgown from Frank's little sister—from their house, I guess—and left it on my bed as a prank. Since I wouldn't return it, he had to buy her a new one."

Lisa's eyebrows crept up her forehead. "You kept it?"

"Sure. Mom always said I should try to make a bully's actions cost him something."

Lisa covered her mouth with one hand as she giggled. Then she glanced toward Ron and frowned. "Does he bother you often?"

"Yeah. Most every day."

"Why don't you report him?"

"That would only make the problem worse."

"Too bad no one protects you."

We both sat and watched some baby ducks play in the shallows. Finally, Lisa asked, "So, what did you sign up for this semester?"

"French Lit, Honors Lit, Creative Writing, and a couple of history classes… There's another anti-war protest today. Are you taking photos?"

"No. Just enjoying the scenery."

I breathed deep as the breeze brought the scent of flowers. "Don't you love the honeysuckle?"

"Yes, and I think there's some jasmine around the other side of the lake."

I bounced up off the bench. "Ooh! Would you show me where?"

Lisa grinned. "Sure. Up this way."

I smiled and fell in beside Lisa, hurrying to keep up with her longer stride.

She glanced at me and slowed her pace. "Do you remember the photo I took of you under the magnolia tree?"

"The day school started? Sure."

"Would you mind if I took some more?"

"No. That would be okay."

"Is Monday good? Around ten? At the bench?"

"Yeah." It was neat to have a friend like her. She was always cheerful and didn't make fun of my new hairstyle. "Why did you want a picture of me, anyway?"

Lisa stopped, her eyes sparkling. "I collect interesting faces." She scanned mine again. "Yours is—What's the word?—Like your mother was an elfin princess in some fairy tale."

A long-forgotten memory struggled to the surface, a page from an old book Kaylah had shown me. "Faie," I whispered. "The Kirkpatricks are thought to be faie. That's an old Middle English word meaning enchanted."

A grin exploded across Lisa's face. "Oh! Yes. Exactly. That's why I wanted to take your picture." Her eyes teased me as she tousled my hair. "Are you a changeling then, left in place of some human babe?"

I studied her face, wondering what she'd do if she met the elfin princess.

* * * *

Back in the dorm, I thumbed through my new French books to see how difficult they'd be. *Vol de Nuit* had won some literary prize. *Madame Bovary* was supposed to be Flaubert's masterpiece. *Les Misérables* seemed interesting. Reading had been a passion of mine since I was four. My French Lit class provided a welcome challenge.

The phone rang. I groaned and reached for it, not wanting to talk to anybody. When I heard Tyler's voice, I almost hung up. "Hi, Tyler."

"Can we get together? I'd like to talk."

"I can't."

"Sharon says you haven't been at church since Christmas break."

"I haven't been feeling well."

"You can't run from God, Jamie."

"I need some time alone. Okay?"

"This won't take long. Should I come over?"

"No! I'll drop by the house."

On my walk over to the Piersons', memories of my time with Tyler twinkled like lights on a Christmas tree. My stay with Sharon had been a little girl's dream, but not something I'd asked for, nor expected to ever repeat. Jameson's rules were back in place, and I wanted no more risky fairy tales. Let Sharon go study somebody else. And Tyler—was he expecting to befriend the girl he'd met?

Tyler waited at the end of the driveway. Why had I thought him the Cheshire Cat? His grin was nowhere in sight. He held out a hand when I got close. "Let's take a walk."

Did he expect me to be his little sister again? I kept my hand at my side. "I'll go with you, but I have to be a boy."

He stood for a moment longer, arm still extended, frown growing darker. Finally, he nodded and stuck his hands in his pockets. "All right."

As we walked north on Granada, Tyler seemed to struggle to find the words. "I'm sorry I hurt you."

Mom always said you had to forgive whenever somebody asked. I didn't much feel like it. "Okay."

He stopped and scanned me with his dark eyes. "I had fun. Didn't you?"

I breathed deep of the tropical breeze, remembering our walks together. "Yeah. I did, but I should have told you about myself right away."

His grin returned in force. "'Hello. I'm Frank's sixteen-year-old hermaphrodite roommate?'"

"I should at least have told you how old I was."

"Would you be offended if I thought of you as a sixteen-year-old girl with a few medical issues?"

"Not as long as you understand I have to be a boy right now."

Still grinning, Tyler shook his head. "You'd make a stunning young woman. Delicate and pretty's a good combination for a girl."

He just didn't get it. I turned around and started walking back to the dorm.

Tyler caught up and put a hand on my shoulder. "No, wait. I'm sorry. I won't pressure you any more. All right?"

I studied his face, thinking he'd probably be praying about my situation. Well, that was okay. My dad wasn't likely to listen to God. "I have a doctorate to finish before I can even think about gender issues."

"A PhD? I thought you weren't interested in school."

"My father was always limited because he didn't have a degree. He wanted his sons to graduate from college. My brother died in Vietnam. I'm all that's left."

Emotions warred across Tyler's face. Anger. Pain. Sadness. "You're not the only one who could use a friend."

You need me? The ace helicopter pilot? Do you hurt, too? "What do you mean?"

Tyler's eyes grew serious. "I take a lot of flak for being the shortest guy in my unit. I work twice as hard as anyone else." The muscles in his face grew taut as if he were fighting back tears. "I volunteered because I want to show my parents I can do something. I was supposed to be the doctor, but…"

Sharon had done what Tyler's parents expected him to do. "I'll be your friend."

Tyler extended his arm again. I raised an eyebrow, but risked shaking his hand anyway. He held it longer than necessary, but at least he didn't kiss me.

He nodded toward Ponce de Leon Boulevard. "I thought maybe we could walk over to Little Caesar's and grab some pizza. Then come back and resume our Bible study."

Little red lights flashed, warning me that spending time with Tyler wouldn't be good for Jameson. I tried to come up with a reason to avoid it, but only nodded instead. Sometimes you had to take risks. I bit my lip hard to keep from smiling.

* * * *

On Monday morning I brushed my hair, grinning at my image in the mirror, not caring if I looked like a girl. Tyler wanted to be my friend.

I bounded down the stairs and out the door. The gardenias were in bloom, so I stopped to inhale their sweet perfume before heading to the bench. Lisa arrived ten minutes later, carrying a shoulder bag. Her grin was nearly as broad as mine. "I know where there's an awesome crepe myrtle with pink flowers. The tree's off campus, but only three blocks from here. You mind?"

"No. Sounds neat."

A short walk brought us to our destination. I gawked at the tree, wondering why it had bloomed so early in the spring. The blossoms overwhelmed me with their beauty.

Lisa unpacked, set up for the shoot, and waved me over. "Would you mind looking at something?" She handed me a photo. The image captured the joy of summer in South Florida. One could almost smell the magnolia blossoms surrounding the girl's pretty face. My face. The photo she'd taken my first day of school, six months earlier. *If my appearance was that feminine then, what must I look like now?*

I studied Lisa's face. What was her point in showing me the picture? My stomach groaned. "I remember the shot." I smiled, hoping I sounded nonchalant.

It was the first time Lisa had been timid around me. She reminded me of a lost kitten. "The photo's good, but there's one thing that would improve the image dramatically. I was wondering if you might be willing to wear a little, ah..." She averted her eyes, apparently expecting me to say no to something she hadn't even asked.

I studied the picture again. My stomach started doing somersaults. The photo would be better if the girl wore a bit of makeup. Lipstick and perhaps a bit of mascara. No wonder Lisa couldn't ask her question. You didn't ask a boy to wear lipstick. I chuckled to myself. Except one like me, maybe. Why couldn't I just be normal? I sighed, wondering if she'd tease me. "Okay."

"Huh?" Lisa looked confused.

"Didn't you say you were a makeup artist before you became a photographer?"

"Yes. I still am. Some of my models—" Light dawned on her face.

"I'll wear whatever you think is right for the shot, but I'd like to learn to apply it myself, and I want the makeup cleaned off when we're finished."

The smile on her face told me she and the elfin princess would be good friends someday.

❀ 7 ❀

A month into the semester I had settled into my routine. I was studying when the phone rang. After a brief conversation Frank handed me the receiver. "Sharon," he said.

"Hi. What's up?"

"Last Christmas I told you about the plays I produce. This year we're putting on *Twelfth Night* over spring break. Are you familiar with it?"

"No. I've read quite a few of Shakespeare's plays, but not that one. A comedy, right?"

"Yes. One of his mistaken identity comedies. I'd like for you to play Cesario. I think you'd be perfect for the part. There aren't many lines and the production is for charity. What do you say?"

"Over spring break?"

"Yes."

Better than going home. "Sounds like fun."

"Wonderful. I'll give Frank a copy of the script next time I see him. You can stay at my place over spring break."

That afternoon, after my last class, I walked over to the Piersons'. Tyler and I had been meeting three or four times a week to have supper together, and talk, and read the Bible. We weren't dating or anything, you know. Two boys didn't do that.

Tyler stood, waiting next to Sharon's car. "One of the guys in my unit gave me a coupon for dinner for two at the Jamaica Inn. I figured…"

So far he hadn't paid for any of my meals. Not that he hadn't offered. Every time. He was old school—the guy picked up the tab. So I couldn't let him. I shook my head. "I—" Well, it was only a coupon. It wasn't like he was paying money. "Okay, but I leave the tip."

Tyler grinned all the way to Key Biscayne. Maybe I'd made a mistake.

Our booth had walls on three sides—nice, and cozy, and quiet. The only problem was the air conditioning vent blew frigid air down my back.

When my teeth started chattering, Tyler took off his jacket and handed it to me. I hesitated until his grin went lopsided. "It's a boy's jacket."

Boy's or not, I was freezing. I wrapped it around my shoulders, grateful for the warmth. A not-unpleasant musky scent brought back memories of Christmas break. He'd been wearing the jacket when he set up an evergreen tree in the living room. Guilt softened my mood. "Did I ever thank you for how you treated me over the holidays?"

Tyler's eyes sparkled in the dim light. "No, but you're welcome."

A waitress drifted up to our booth. Still lost in Christmas memories, I missed what she said.

"I'd like an iced tea," Tyler said, smiling eyes intent on me.

The young woman leaned a little closer. "And you, miss?"

"An orange juice, please." I nodded my pretty little head. A waitress mistaking me for a girl wouldn't kill me. When she left, I smiled at Tyler and said, "Sharon talked me into playing Cesario in her production of *Twelfth Night*. What can you tell me about her plays?"

His grin lit up the entire booth. "Cesario, huh? Do you know anything about the part?"

"Nah. Only that he doesn't have many lines."

Tyler rested his chin on his hands and stared at me. "Perhaps I should ask my sister to let me play Orsino. We could practice our lines together."

"You'd help me learn my part? That would be neat."

* * * *

A couple of days later Frank brought me a copy of the script. When I read through the play, I was only mildly surprised to discover Cesario was Viola, a girl. That's what I got for making a promise without knowing what I was getting into. The reaction to my hairstyle had been bad enough. When people found out I had played a girl, I'd never hear the end of it. But even if Sharon had tricked me, I still wouldn't break my word.

I went and sat on the bench by the lake to read through *Twelfth Night*. My concentration was so focused I barely noticed when a young man sat next to me. I said my lines under my breath, trying to get the feel for the part.

"Are you practicing for a play?"

Startled, I glanced up. The man had dark brown hair, the scruffy start of a beard, and steel-blue eyes. His smile glowed, warm and friendly. He looked kinda cute, actually. "Sorry, I didn't mean to interrupt. My name's Sean. You appeared to be practicing a part."

"I'm Jamie. Yeah. I volunteered to be in a play."

"Here at the school?"

"No. Up at a country club in North Miami. My roommate's girlfriend produces plays. For charity."

"Indeed? Good of you to help out then."

"Thanks… What's your major?"

"Oh, I'm not a student here. I'm waiting for a young lady who works for my boss."

"What do you do?"

"I provide security for a club on Miami Beach."

So Lisa thought I needed someone to protect me, and poof, this guy appeared on my bench. I grinned, wondering if Lisa had arranged a bodyguard for me.

* * * *

I had no cause to be mad at Tyler. He was only taking advantage of the situation, using it as an excuse to spend more time together. Well, no harm done; I was learning my lines.

Tyler worried me, you know. His eyes said he was becoming more attached to me than I was allowed to be to him or any other boy. Well, okay, so I was growing fond of him as well.

"Look, just trust me," he'd said, refusing to tell me what was up. It had been a long day, and I was already worn out, but he insisted. So I threw on my denim jacket and walked over to his house as the sun settled below the western horizon. Red and purple striations pierced the clouds.

He grabbed my hand and started walking back across campus. I would have argued, but I was having trouble keeping up with him. Tyler led me to the intramural field. When I saw the carnival spread out before us, I forgot boys weren't supposed to hold hands.

We walked hand-in-hand among the rides and games, talking, laughing, eating popcorn, and watching the people. Stars awoke and the moon rose, seeming to hang above the crowd. A cool breeze brought the smell of approaching rain. The chatter of a hundred conversations and the music of the carousel organ nearly drowned out the distant sounds of traffic on South Dixie Highway.

One young couple standing near us seemed lost in a passionate embrace. Energy drained from my spirit as I watched. I pulled my hand away from Tyler's. "I should go." Romance could never blossom in my life.

Tyler sighed, exhaling slowly. "One more ride and we'll leave." He took my hand again and led me to the Ferris wheel. We climbed into a seat and waited while the other passengers got on. My mood dampened, I faded fast. When Tyler put his arm around me and pulled me close, I hardly minded.

* * * *

A month before spring break I dropped by Sharon's house. She waved me in as soon as I walked up the drive. "Thanks for coming."

I forced a smile and followed her inside. "Sharon, I know you meant well, but you tricked me into being a girl for this play. I was tempted to back out."

Sharon frowned at me, but nodded. "I'm sorry. Would you have agreed if I'd told you up front?"

"Probably not. I don't mean to be rude, but why did you ask me over?"

"I need to measure you for your costumes."

"Are you sure you want me to play Viola? What happens when the audience figures out Cesario's being played by a boy?"

Sharon shook her head. "A boy? That won't be any problem." She shrugged. "Besides, we've done authentic Shakespeare before. A friend of Tyler's played Celia in *As You Like It*. He was horrible as a girl, but the audience loved him anyway. Most of the lines are for Cesario. Besides, practice starts next week. We can't replace you now."

"I'm not an experienced actor."

"The character's a girl pretending to be a boy. You should be able to handle that." She wasn't frowning, but her eyes said not to argue with her.

I sighed and turned away.

In a gentler voice, Sharon said, "One other thing. Tradition dictates that the happy couples kiss at the curtain call. Including Orsino and Viola."

My heart caught in my throat. "Tyler?"

She nodded, smiling. "Yes. Tyler."

He knows and he wants to kiss me? In front of everyone? Terror ran up and down my spine. I shook my head and opened my mouth to tell her no. "Okay," I whispered. Maybe Frank wouldn't be around.

After dinner I followed Sharon over to the kitchen counter. I was dying to learn more about my condition, and this seemed the ideal time. "Will you explain my medical stuff? The doctors talked about me with each other but didn't tell me anything."

Sharon leaned against the counter. "I can try…Ordinarily a boy has one X and one Y chromosome in each of his cells, and a girl has two X chromosomes in each cell."

Yeah. Basic human genetics.

"Turner Syndrome's a condition where a girl has only one X in each cell. Turner girls are short-statured."

"Shorter than me?"

"Yes. I think that the average adult height in Turner Syndrome's around four foot eight."

"Wow."

"They don't develop sexually and sometimes the heart or kidneys are malformed." Sharon continued in a softer voice. "You have Mixed Gonadal Dysgenesis. People with MGD have an X and a Y chromosome in some cells and only one X in others."

"Some of my cells are girl?"

Sharon chuckled and shook her head. "Well, individual cells aren't actually male or female, but yes, you're a mosaic of Turner Syndrome female and normal male. Some babies with MGD are born with one testis and one ovary. Like you."

"An ovary?" I bit my lip at the thought.

"Well, Turner Syndrome ovaries are only streaks of tissue. They don't produce eggs or estrogen, and you'd still need a uterus to have a baby."

I chewed on my lip, eyes down. "At conception I was only one cell."

"Yes…with one X and one Y chromosome. During one of the first few cell divisions a Y chromosome was lost. The cell without a Y continued to grow and divide like all the rest."

"But I started as a normal male conception?"

"Yes. I guess you could say that."

"So God means for me to be a boy."

Sharon looked thoughtful, but then shook her head. "How tall's your father?"

"Six-one. Why?"

"You have a brother?"

"He was six-two."

"You're less than five feet tall because you were missing Y chromosomes in some cells. Does God mean for you to be six feet tall?"

"Don't be absurd. I can't change my height."

"Exactly."

ℭ 8 ℬ

After my last class I walked to the Piersons'. Spring break had arrived at last. Sharon answered on my first knock. "Jamie? Hi. Come in."

"Hi. Is everything ready for the play?"

Sharon nodded. "We're getting close." She pointed down the hall. "I left some things on the bed for you. Go ahead and change. You can't be flat-chested for the play, so you might as well start wearing a bra. Tell me when you're ready. I'll do your hair and makeup."

"Okay."

Curious to see what Sharon had selected, the little princess examined the items laid out on the bed—PJs, peasant top, a new hairbrush, a purse, a bra that had some kind of padding, some inexpensive jewelry, and the clothes Kaylah had brought at Christmas.

When I returned to the kitchen, Sharon motioned me to a chair. "Sit down. I'll fix your hair." She handed me a mirror when she was finished. "That's a French braid," she explained. "When there's time, I'll teach you how to braid my hair. Frank can't seem to get the hang of it." She smiled and checked the time. "Let's do your makeup. Then you can help me fix dinner."

The little princess in the mirror looked cute with her hair all fancy. The French braid drew more attention to her face without taking anything away from her hair. What a neat style! I would have known more about such things had I allowed Jameson to read any of Mom's or Alicia's magazines. Would Mom and Dad have cared so much?

* * * *

The next morning a light breeze ruffled the drapes, sending waves of light across the ceiling and walls. Soft noises elsewhere in the house indicated someone up and about. The little princess stretched and yawned. She didn't need a mirror to tell she was glowing. *Lord,* I prayed, hands clenched, *I should be the same person on the outside as on the inside. Please help my inside be like the boy on the outside, the boy my parents want me to be. Lord, please make me a boy, but if not, please make it okay for me to be a girl.*

I showered and washed my hair, dressed, and applied my makeup, starting over several times before I was satisfied. I winked at the princess in the mirror and headed for the kitchen.

Sharon and Tyler were already in the dining room, drinking coffee. "Good morning, Miss Sharon, Master Tyler." I found a soda in the refrigerator, got out a glass, and joined them at the table.

"We were just talking about you." Tyler grinned. "Sharon says you know your lines well enough for us to take the day off. I thought the two of us could go to Coconut Grove, and then down to Matheson Hammock Park."

Sharon smiled at me. "Go ahead. I need to run some errands. The two of you have fun. Eat something before you go. A cola isn't breakfast."

Come on, Sharon. I'm almost seventeen. "Yes, Mom."

"I'll get the bike out."

"Bike?" I asked, my eyes growing wide.

"Yeah. We'll take my Kawasaki. A motorcycle's much more exciting than a car. You ever been on a bike?"

"Yeah. A couple of times."

"You'd better put on some jeans. I don't think you can ride in a dress. By the time you change, I should be ready."

The little princess returned to her room and changed into a pair of jeans and a fuzzy sweater. I sat on the bed, trembling as I remembered my last motorcycle ride with Dave, one of the neighbor boys. The longer we had ridden, the more aroused I'd become and the worse my feelings of guilt. Those things had never happened before taking testosterone, and they still frightened me. I considered telling Tyler I'd changed my mind, but then I decided the shots must have been the reason.

When I stepped out the front door, Tyler was sitting on a motorcycle. I climbed on the back and put both arms around his waist. As a girl I was free to relax and just hold him tight. I pulled myself close. Tyler eased the bike out on Granada Boulevard and took off. The front wheel came up off the ground. A burst of adrenaline hit me when I slid back on the seat and almost lost my grip. The Kawasaki was louder and higher-pitched than Dave's bike, the acceleration much quicker. Tyler was older, taller, and stronger than Dave. He wouldn't let me get hurt, but I held him like my life depended on it.

After crossing Ponce and South Dixie, Tyler turned on Hardee Road. The pavement beneath us became a dark blur. Tree limbs overhanging the street rushed by inches away. We rocketed down a long tunnel of black and green. He eased off on the throttle as we turned on Main Highway. When we were close to Grand Avenue, he pulled to the side of the road and stopped. Tyler pulled off his helmet and grinned over his shoulder. "You can let go now. We're stopped."

The princess leaned her head against his back and held on for a few more seconds, trembling. My heart was still trying to catch up with the rest of my body. The vibration had left me numb. Adrenaline coursed through my veins. There hadn't been time to think about anything else. I pulled off my helmet and shook my hair loose. "That was fun! How often can you go that fast without losing your license?" I got off the bike, pulled a brush out of my purse, and went to work on my hair.

Tyler dismounted and set both helmets on the seat. "We weren't speeding. It only seemed like it because Hardee is two lanes with no shoulders." He pointed to the side street. "You ever been to Commodore Plaza?"

"I haven't even been to Coconut Grove before. What's at Commodore Plaza?"

"Shops and restaurants mostly." He turned and pointed across the intersection. "The Barnacle is one of the oldest houses in the county. The place was here before Miami was even a city."

On the other side of the street were lush greenery and a drive blocked by iron gates. "What would you like to do?"

He grinned his brightest, eyes twinkling. "I'm going to Vietnam in two weeks. A pretty girl's standing in front of me. What do you think I'd like to do?"

I looked away, my whole face warm. Tyler was a nice boy. Why should I read anything into his question? And why did I always think about marriage and babies anyway? I bit my lip and stared at the ground. *Why should I be so scared? He knows what I am.*

I stepped close, put my arms around him, and smiled. "No one ever kissed me on the lips before." The princess dreamed of a fairy tale come true.

He ran a hand through my hair, around the back of my head, and pulled me close. As his lips touched mine, something wonderful stirred deep within me.

ᘓ 9 ᘔ

The final dress rehearsal started early the morning of the play. Tyler and I were putting away our costumes when Sharon approached me. "I've got a few errands to run. Why don't you tag along? We'll go shopping, and I know a fabulous little place to eat."

Sharon had been pushing me, one gentle nudge at a time, into being a girl full-time. When she'd first told me she wanted to be my friend, I'd only intended to be a girl for a single day. Tyler's unexpected arrival had turned one day into an entire Christmas break. The play meant people other than Tyler and Sharon seeing me as a girl. If I ran errands with her, I'd be out in public, doing everyday sorts of things as a girl. The time to stop was before my parents found out. Way before. "I better not. You go ahead. I'll wait here."

Sharon glanced at Tyler, who shrugged. She pulled me by the hand saying, "Come on. We need to talk."

After we walked around the corner, she asked me what was wrong.

"The play's one thing. It's not real. My parents wouldn't like me being out in public as a girl. My ride with Tyler yesterday was bad enough."

"Would they be any happier if you sat here, in a dress, clinging to Tyler all day?"

Sharon was probably right. Either one would get me grounded forever. Maybe I was wrong, but I also heard a hint of blackmail in her voice. "No ma'am. You have a point." Where would it all end?

Sharon gave me a few tips on my acting as we walked out to the car. "Don't worry about overdoing the boy thing. Presumably, this is Viola's first time pretending to be a boy. I would expect her to mess up. My advice is to relax and enjoy yourself."

Sharon started the car and glanced at me. "I need to drop by the school bookstore. I'd like you to pick up some books I ordered. I'll drop some others off at the library while you're doing that. We can meet back at the car."

I stared out the window, butterflies growing in my stomach. Being a girl around Sharon and Tyler had been safe. The play wasn't real. Would people at the bookstore think I was a girl? Almost everybody ridiculed Jameson. Would they tease Jamie as well?

Sharon managed to find a parking spot on Miller Drive, between the library and the bookstore. Outside, a couple of Campus Security officers stood, talking to each other. I waited while a young man walked out the door. He nodded to the younger-looking of the two officers. "Semper fi, man." The officer nodded and grinned.

I pushed the door open, did a quick scan, and walked in. My stomach dropped into my shoes. Ron stood in the magazine area, holding a copy of *Road and Track*. He'd glanced my way when I came in, but I wasn't certain he'd recognized me. Was it too late to run? Head turned away from him, I made a beeline for the special orders desk. "Ma'am, I'm supposed to pick up some books for Sharon Pierson."

A few minutes later the woman returned with several books. She checked the titles against the order and double-checked with her copy. "Right here," she said, handing me a paper and indicating where to sign.

I picked up the books and turned to go. Ron stood near the door, leaning against the wall. He was looking my way with a smirk on his face. Pretending to ignore him, the little princess meandered toward the door, stopping at various displays along the way. I prayed that he'd leave me alone.

Ron blocked my way when I tried to leave. "Excuse me, please." I tried to push past, but he was a foot taller, twice my weight, and strong. "Please let me go."

Ron shook his head, scowling. "Or what, you little faggot?" He gestured to the nearest clerk. "Hey! Call security. Pervert alert!" He pointed at me. "This is a boy. He lives down the hall from me in the dorm."

I tried to shake loose from his grip. "Let go. You're hurting me." I didn't yell, but my voice did get louder and higher in pitch. Tears started to cloud my vision. A gathering crowd of people stared at us. Ron had one hand around my wrist; with the other he grabbed my arm. I dropped my shoulder and spun, hissing, "Leave me alone!" Although I didn't break free from his grip, I did hear my sleeve rip. *Excellent.* A hand still free, I wiped the tears from one eye down across my cheek. A bit of mascara came away on my hand. *Good.*

The books slipped from my hands when he grabbed one of them. "Lookit. *Sex Errors of the Body.* A pervert book."

I didn't need to fake my tears; they started streaming down my face on their own. When I managed to get close enough, I kicked the door. The glass didn't break, but the noise was loud enough to attract attention. One of the Campus Security officers walked into the bookstore. The other stood in the doorway. When Ron shoved me toward them, I stumbled into one, stooped to pick up my books, and turned away from the officers. With my head down, I pulled out one of my barrettes and let my hair fall down across my face.

The officer scowled. "What's going on here?"

Ron pointed at me. "He's a boy. His name's Jameson. Lives in our dorm."

The older officer glanced at me and walked over to the nearest clerk. "What's going on?"

"She came in, picked up some special order books, and was headed out the door when he refused to let her leave."

The officer turned back to Ron. "I'd like to see some identification, please."

Ron frowned, pulled out his wallet, and showed the officer his student ID. "What about him?" He pointed at me again.

The officer sighed, shook his head, and turned to me. "I need yours as well, miss."

The little princess was still crying. "My name's—*hic*—Jamie. I don't have a driver's—*hic*—license. Can't I go? My boyfriend's—*hic*—sister's waiting for me."

The younger officer put his hand on my elbow. "Someone is outside who can verify who you are?"

I nodded. "Sharon."

When the officer walked me out of the store, Sharon got out of her car and rushed to meet us. "What happened? Are you all right?"

The officer glanced at me and smiled at her. "You're Sharon?"

"Yes. Why? Is there a problem?"

"No, ma'am, but I need to verify her identity."

"Jamie Kirkpatrick. She's staying with us until my brother leaves for Vietnam. Her brother rooms with my boyfriend in the dorm."

"Her brother's name?"

"Jameson. Why?"

"Your brother's deploying?"

"Yes. Tyler leaves Thursday after next."

"He's a Marine," I whispered as I examined the rip in my sleeve.

"You're his girl?" The officer examined my innocent elfin-girl face and ground his teeth.

I sighed and whispered, "Yes, sir."

"Semper fi." He turned on his heel and strode back toward the bookstore.

I watched the officer walk away. Everybody believed me a girl, even with Ron insisting I was a boy. Without me acting or anything. I could have a life as a girl! But would my parents ever allow it?

* * * *

So many people! In awe I contemplated the audience. The tables had been nearly empty during dress rehearsal. Sharon had assured me she'd keep Frank busy with errands, away from the play. Well, no time to be nervous; I had drinks to fetch.

Each table had a placard with a number and cast member name. Sharon had organized everything so that nothing could go wrong. I still found ways to mess things up. The elfin princess would never be a waitress. Fortunately, people appeared to be more interested in chatting with Viola than in complaining about my mistakes. I was surprised how much fun I was having.

The cue came. The cast walked up on the platform and filed offstage. Tyler grabbed my hand and led me, stage left, to an old couch. The director ran around making sure everything was ready while Tyler idly played with my hair. All day he'd seemed nervous, always starting to say something and never quite finishing. I hoped he would remember his lines. The time came for him to go on stage, and he leaned over and planted a kiss on my lips. Like that, he was gone, grin and all. I wondered if I would remember my lines.

The first scene was short, so I stood offstage and watched. Scene II opened and I walked on stage with the captain and the sailors. Everything went well until I saw Lisa sitting at a table, front and center, grinning at me. At that moment I realized someone other than cast and crew might recognize me. "What country?" someone whispered from offstage.

Look at the Captain. Project! I slid into character. "What country, friends, is this?"

Captain frowned at me before getting into character himself. "This is Illyria, lady."

At the end of Scene II, I walked off stage, grabbed my skirts, and ran to change costumes. Scene III was almost over by the time I returned as Cesario.

Scene IV, I walked onstage with Valentine, but my primary interaction was with Orsino. When he asked me to woo Olivia for him, a pang struck my heart. I had memorized my lines and was having a blast playing Viola-as-Cesario. My parents had often told me I had an overactive imagination, but the pain confused me. Was I experiencing what Viola would or did the thought of someone else marrying Tyler hurt that much? A subtle undercurrent ran through our interactions on stage. I imagined more in Tyler's grin than simply Orsino's fondness for Cesario. The scene progressed, and the tension within me grew, becoming a tightness in my throat. Cesario's final line was an aside, directed to the audience, but I couldn't tear my eyes away from Tyler's. "Who'er I woo, myself would be his wife." Did his grin burn a little brighter? *What peculiar insanity!* Through the rest of the play, I wondered at my heart, that I could hope to marry Tyler one day.

∾ 10 ∾

The little princess woke up late and yawned. Another beautiful morning. I was packing my things when Sharon walked into the guest room. "You don't need to leave yet, do you? Tyler would like you to stay and have lunch with us."

"I suppose I can, but I need to leave right after we eat."

When I walked to the kitchen and offered to help, I found Sharon holding a cake with seventeen candles on it. I had hoped nobody would remember my birthday.

She set the cake on the dining room table. Tyler smiled and held out a small case. "Sharon and I got you these."

"Thanks." I opened the cover and pulled out a pair of gold hoop earrings. "Ooh! These are beautiful." Long-forgotten memories played before my eyes, like an old newsreel, all scratches and spots. I had begged my mother to pierce my ears the day she did Alicia's. The back of my legs still remembered the switching I'd gotten for trying to do it myself. "I love them, but I don't have pierced ears."

Sharon fingered her own hoops with a smile. "I can pierce them for you if you'd like. I did mine a couple years ago."

Black clouds roiled around my head. Sharon should have known better. Piercing my ears would do more damage to Jameson than every-thing else I'd done. "This was sweet of you, but I'm not allowed." Not allowed to be a girl. I held out the box to Tyler, biting my trembling lip.

"You're not allowed? Ha! You really are twelve, aren't you?" He reached over and pulled five candles out of my cake.

"Tyler!" I studied my love's face and reconsidered. Yes, I would wear them for him. "Okay, I'll keep them." *You're sending Jameson back with pierced ears? You're insane, aren't you?* I pointed to the candles. "Put those back." Then I turned to Sharon. "Will this hurt?"

"Not much, but you'll need to keep posts in the holes until they heal. People are going to notice. You think you can handle that?"

"I can always take them back out."

"True, but they may close up."

Not merely insane; suicidal. "So I'll leave them in."

Ten minutes later Sharon and the little princess returned from the guest room. I ran up to Tyler and hugged him. "Thanks. I always wanted ones exactly like these."

He brushed my hair back and kissed me on the forehead. "Don't ever grow up." He took me by the hand, his eyes smiling. "I can get a pass to spend the day next Thursday here with you. Will you do that for me? One more day before I leave?" He put his arms around me and pulled me close. "I don't want to sit around all day. Stay here Wednesday night, and we'll do something exciting together on Thursday."

"I have classes…You're sure you want me to stay?"

Tyler nodded, his Cheshire Cat grin bright.

The little princess stood on tiptoes and kissed him on the cheek. "Okay."

* * * *

Thursday morning, I rolled over and yawned. The days had flashed by, while I tried in vain to study. Wednesday evening I'd walked over to the Piersons', only to find a note from Sharon saying she'd be out late. I stretched one last time, and then got dressed.

Tyler took us up Interstate 95 and across the MacArthur Causeway to Ocean Drive. He parked the bike, set the helmets on the seat, and escorted his little princess to the beach. Shoes in hand and pant legs rolled up, we walked hand-in-hand along the water's edge.

After walking some distance, I gazed up into Tyler's face. "Why am I here?"

"A handsome young prince brought you on his white stallion?"

No doubt my smile revealed my sadness. Who would be interested in a girl who couldn't bear children? "Why would a handsome young prince care anything about me?"

Tyler stopped walking. He motioned toward the street, away from the water. "Let's go sit where the sand's dry." He squeezed my hand and led me up the beach. "Here. Sit with your back to me. I'm pretty good at back rubs." Tyler began kneading my shoulders. "What's so hard to understand about my wanting to spend time with you?"

"You're going to Vietnam. You're spending your last day here with me. Why? I don't have anything a boy would want."

"Oh, but you do." He sat next to me then, face-to-face. "The society bimbos Mother tries to set me up with don't have your sense of humor or your brains. You're pretty, and your body will develop. I'd be surprised if Sharon doesn't straighten out the situation with your family before I return from 'Nam."

My brother Scott and I had never gotten along, but he was still family. He had died in Vietnam. Why should Tyler have to risk his life? "If they're gonna send our brothers and boyfriends to war, they should at least let them win. Why do you want to go, anyway?"

"Jamie, my draft number's three. I don't have many choices. I don't like the war any more than you do."

"You'll be killing people in an ungodly war. That's not right."

"No. I'm a pilot. I'll be flying Medevac, trying to keep people alive."

"I don't want you to go. You might die."

Tyler got all serious. "Yes. Medevac's dangerous. If I die, I go home to be with the Lord, but I'm hoping you'll be praying for my safe return."

"I'll do that." A thick mist had hung over Oswego the day Dad told me Scott had died. My brother had volunteered for the infantry. Why did boys always want to be heroes, anyway? The war seemed so pointless. "When I turn eighteen, I'm gonna burn my draft card."

Tyler stood beside me and laughed. "You try to register, and they'll throw you out of the building."

The little princess leaned toward him and stuck out her tongue. Tyler laughed again, put his arms around my waist, and pulled me close. "You know, the one thing you messed up on in the play was the kiss at the curtain call. We should work on that. One other thing—stop calling me sir."

"Yes, sir." I grinned.

Tyler brushed the hair from my face and kissed me.

Lord, please, somehow, let me be his wife.

* * * *

Wolfie's corned beef tasted yummy. I looked up from my lunch and studied Tyler. I hated to be a party-pooper, but I'd learned from painful experience how much sun I could endure before burning.

Tyler glanced up from his *latkes* and pastrami. "Why the sad eyes?"

I sighed, staring at my plate. "I need to stay inside the rest of the day or I'll burn."

"Why didn't you say something?"

"I think I just did."

So after lunch we headed home. I was grateful for the cool wind after a morning of sun and salt air. With my arms around Tyler, my world was secure. I leaned my head against his back and enjoyed the ride.

Sharon met us at the door, smiling. "Good. I was hoping you wouldn't be all day."

I put the helmets away and headed for the guest room. "I think I'll shower. Shouldn't be too long."

"Why don't you wear that dark green belted smock? I'd like to take some snapshots of you and Tyler."

"Okay."

After showering and getting dressed, I joined Sharon in the Florida room. All the photographer contraptions she had set up brought a smile to my face. "Is all this necessary?"

Sharon bobbed her head. "Yes. You want the lighting perfect—and your makeup as well." She grabbed my elbow and dragged me to the master bathroom.

By the time she was happy with my hair and makeup, Tyler was standing in the living room in his dress uniform, looking striking. My heart stuttered, sending crazy chills through me. The beautiful princess grinned and planted herself next to her handsome prince, one arm slinking around his waist. I imagined us standing together in front of a pastor to take our vows. The heat wave surging through my body wasn't all from too much sun. What would I do when he was gone? Sharon tripped the first shot before we were ready. After an hour she ran out of film. I offered up a prayer of thanksgiving, wondering if I could be blackmailed for any of our poses.

Tyler spent what seemed like several hours on the phone, talking to his parents. They still didn't approve of his flying Medevac, but at least they'd called to bid him farewell. My heart twisted within me with sympathy for him. I prayed that someday his family would be proud of their son.

Later in the afternoon Tyler, and Sharon, and I rode to the bus station. Tyler kissed me a good long while. Hand still on my cheek, with a tender caress, he smiled. "I'll write and let you know my address." He stepped back, gazing at me a moment longer.

I fought to keep from crying. "I'll miss you." A single errant tear ran down my face.

Tyler wiped away my sorrow and kissed me on the cheek. "The Bible says men shouldn't marry and run off to war."

Then don't go! My chest heaved. Tyler grinned his Cheshire Cat grin and pulled me close "We couldn't marry anyway until we convinced your parents you're a girl. When I return, we'll work on that. Be patient until then, okay?" He kissed me again.

Another tear rolled off my lashes. My arm reached for him, zombie-like, and then dropped.

Tyler studied me, chewing on his lip. He mumbled to himself and shook his head. Then he pulled something shiny out of his pocket and walked up to me.

A necklace with…a locket? He clasped it around my neck. Curious, I pulled it up until I could see that the necklace held a gold ring with a large diamond. My vision went dark and I grabbed his arm for support.

Tyler's grin burned bright, and his eyes laughed. "My great-grand-mother's wedding ring. Will you hold it for me?"

All I managed to say was "Unh."

He chuckled. "We can work through this when I get back. If you can't wait, leave it with Sharon. I'll understand." He turned and left me staring at his grin.

Tyler kissed his sister on the cheek, boarded his bus, and was gone.

Outside, Sharon gazed across the car at me. "He told me he was serious about you, but I had no idea. What do you think?"

I looked down and rolled the ring between my fingers. "I love him, Sharon. Something deep inside me comes alive when he's around." But what chance was there the elfin princess would ever be set free? I sighed, hope failing me. My fairy tale wouldn't have a happy ending. "I'll hold his ring, but I'm not allowed to love him the way I do."

"You should consider seeing Dr. Parker. I think he could explain your medical condition to your parents. If they understood, I'm sure they'd let you be a girl."

Doctors would only make my situation worse. "Explain what? That I need to sit down to pee? Don't you think they know that? Sharon, nothing good comes from going to a doctor."

Sharon's lips thinned. "Do you mind if we stop by a little shop on the way back?"

The little shop turned out to be one of the more expensive clothing stores on Miracle Mile. Sharon led me in by the hand. "There's a dress over here that would be perfect for you. Stand in front of this mirror while I get it." A moment later she held up a green satin gown. "Imagine yourself wearing this. You've been on hormones for a couple of years, so you've developed a more feminine shape. You and Tyler are dancing. He's holding you close."

I gazed at the girl in the mirror, imagining his ring on my finger and three little children standing next to me. Yes. Marriage would be nice, but could only ever exist in my dreams. I shook myself. "I can't live in a fantasy world. My parents will never change, so I need to." I left the store and started back toward the car.

Sharon caught up and grabbed my hand. "Jamie, your trying to be a boy is irrational. You can't waste your entire life for parents who haven't a clue who you are."

I frowned and tried to pull away. "Leave me alone. Okay? They're my family, and I love them." I pulled free, stumbled out into the crosswalk, and nearly got hit by a bus. Shaken, I continued across the street.

On the drive home, I sat in silence, trying to concentrate on the trees passing by, instead of my impossible situation. Sharon offered to give me a ride back to the dorm, but I declined, saying I needed some time alone. We hugged and I walked down the drive. I laughed, a little crazy, thinking back on the day Sharon had told me I should have been raised a girl. Friendship with her had cost me my sanity. My heart longed for Tyler. To be with him. To be his wife. I held his ring up so it caught the first rays of sunset. I had never wanted anything so badly as to wear it for him. So close. And yet impossible. My fists clenched as tears pushed their way past my defenses.

Hoping to avoid running into anybody who'd recognize me, I followed Granada all the way to Ponce. The sun's evening warmth consoled me. *Lord, this is madness! I lost a brother I hardly knew. Now Tyler's gone and taken my heart with him. How can I ever live without him here?*

How had I let myself fall in love with a boy? I had to be Jameson. *Lord, I know you want me to be the same person on the inside as on the outside. How can I be Jameson on the inside if I can't even keep the one on the outside working right?*

∽ 11 ∼

Little Queen. Back at the dorm someone had scratched a message on the door, welcoming me back to reality. I ignored the graffiti, unlocked the door, and went in.

Frank's stereo was gone, the bed bare. My bag hit the floor. A note on my desk read, *Jameson, you're a good friend, but I can't stay with you in the dorm. Frank.*

I collapsed on the bed and pulled off my shoes. What was the point of pretending to be Jameson anymore? I turned away from the windows and closed my eyes. Sharon might have meant well, but was the time with Tyler worth all the heartache it had caused?

Without Frank the room seemed empty. Without Tyler…

* * * *

Steppenwolf fell to the ground. What a horrible story. Who needed to read depressing fiction when they were already down? I rested on the bench near the lake and soaked up the late April sunshine. The empty dorm room only underscored my loneliness. At least out by the lake I enjoyed the sun's warmth.

"Do you mind if I join you?"

I looked up. Sean stood in front of me. "No. Go right ahead." My protector, huh? Well, at least Ron didn't bother me with Sean around.

"You don't appear to be much interested in your book."

"No. I had to read it for Honors Lit. The book's junk."

"Is that what's bothering you?"

"Hmm?"

"You seem down."

"This semester's bad, and everything I do makes things worse."

"You did right well in that play."

I grimaced and studied my hands. "What play?"

"*Twelfth Night.* That was a brave thing to do."

"Or just stupid."

"It's all right to make a fool of yourself for a good cause. The play was for charity, no?"

"Yeah...You told a girl named Lisa Alexander about the play?"

"Of course. My sister asked me to look after you. She's rather fond of you. We didn't realize what part you'd play, but no matter."

"You don't..."

"No. Lisa's my half-sister. My mother died soon after I was born. My father remarried about a year later."

I closed my eyes, wishing I could start the year over.

* * * *

Every day I waited at the boxes for the mailman to arrive. I longed to hear anything at all from Tyler. Nearly a month had passed and I hadn't received a letter yet. I'd written notes to him, but I didn't have his address, so they were all stacked in my dresser drawer. Had my love forgotten me already? Changed his mind? Should I return his ring?

Thunder rumbled in the distance. Dark clouds hung low in an overcast sky, a steady drizzle falling on me. A trickle of water ran off my hair and down my back. My soaking wet T-shirt clung to my skin. Water squished between my toes in my sneakers. None of it mattered—the gloom suited my mood well. Depression had grown thick and dark, like molasses, and a constant companion. The bottom of the downward spiral rushed up to greet me. Even my health was fading. My lungs congested, I labored to draw each additional breath. So many things going wrong. Jameson broken. Frank gone. Tyler away for a year. *Lord, if you don't help me, I'm not gonna survive this.*

A car pulled close to the curb and slowed. Water surged across the sidewalk. I glanced that way and saw Sharon in her Toyota. She pulled up ahead of me and stopped.

Why can't she leave me alone? I squinted up into the rain, pushing the wet hair away from my eyes. I stepped through the mud, waded around to the driver's side, and fidgeted while Sharon cranked down the window. I braced myself for another lecture, but when I leaned down, her eyes were all red and puffy.

Tyler. Please God, not Tyler! My stomach muscles seized. Bile rose in my throat. Losing Tyler was more than I could ever bear. The rain became a downpour, drowning me in sorrow, washing away all my hopes and dreams. "Don't tell me out here in the rain." I stumbled back around to the passenger side and climbed in.

The drive to the Piersons' home was quiet. I followed Sharon into the house and stood, dripping on her living room carpet. She sat down on the sofa, head down. "Mother called me this morning. Tyler's helicopter went down near Hue." She stared at me, eyes hollow. I sat down next to Sharon, and we held each other. "They can't get to the wreckage. A flyover reported seeing no survivors." She leaned against me and wept.

'He just got there!' my heart protested. I didn't even have his address yet. Too stunned to make a sound, I prayed, *Lord, please let Tyler be alive. Please protect him and bring him safely back to us. Please comfort Sharon and her family.* After a while, I asked aloud, "Is there anything I can do?"

Between sobs, Sharon said, "Can you stay with me until Frank gets back? I don't want to be alone right now."

"Okay." Leaving seemed pointless anyway. I'd only lock myself away somewhere.

"I had thought you and Tyler would get married one day."

"Some dreams can never come true. Tyler will come back—I'm sure of it—but he'll marry somebody else."

Sharon shook her head. "Tyler's dead."

My stomach muscles tightened again. "No." I refused to believe him dead. "He can't be."

"I'm sorry, Jamie, but you have to accept it."

He had to come back. "No, Sharon. If you stop hoping, you'll stop praying for him, and if you don't ask, how can you expect God to send him back to us?"

* * * *

I was sitting at my desk, studying for finals, when the phone rang.

"Hi, Jameson. Frank. How're you doin'? Only a week before finals."

My smile was weak and one-sided. "I'm okay, but it's too quiet here without you. How've you been?"

"Great! I've been stayin' at my folks' place up in North Miami. My birthday's the week after finals. My parents are up north, so I'm throwin' a party. Wanna come? You can stay in my sister's room. Wear her clothes if you wanna."

"Not funny, Frank…Did you invite Ron?"

"Nobody told you? He got himself booted out of school for harassin' some chick in the bookstore."

That got my attention. "Really?"

"Yeah. So, you wanna come or not?"

I gazed out the window. What were my plans? "Yeah. Can you give me a ride to your place?"

"I guess so. Meet me at Sharon's?"

"Yeah."

An idea had been rolling around the back of my mind, just out of my field of vision. There might be a way to make Jameson's rules permanent, like they were a natural part of me. If so, I was pretty sure I could use the same process to fix my gender issues and forget about the elfin princess. I'd still be tiny and have a feminine face, but—well, anyway, I needed time alone to work it all out. I finished studying, put my books away, and dialed home. My sister answered.

"Hi, Ali."

"Are you all right? You sound sad."

"I'll be okay." I never was any good at lying to her.

"What's the matter?"

"I'm sick of my entire life revolving around my gender. I'm tired of being in-between. I want to be normal."

"What are you gonna do?"

"I don't know. Life's such a struggle. I think about giving up sometimes."

"Don't say that!" My sister's voice trembled with pain. "You should come home. Talk to Mom and Dad."

"No, Ali. I can't until I get this all straightened out."

"You have to. We're moving to North Carolina."

"I'll think about it, okay?"

"Jamie, I miss you. Please come home."

"Pray for me." It was the only thing that might help.

* * * *

Finals were over. I'd survived my first year of college. Now I had to figure out how to live life. I was packing my things when the phone rang.

"Mom. Hi. How are you?"

"I'm looking at a photo of a young man in uniform holding his sweetheart. It arrived special delivery today." My mother's voice sounded as cold as the February winds blowing off Lake Michigan.

"Mom?" I asked in a hushed voice.

"They both look so happy."

Of the pictures Sharon had taken, my favorite showed a dead-serious Tyler being kissed on the cheek by a moon-eyed elfin princess. As my mother described the photo, I stared at the copy on my desk. Sharon had betrayed me. I was dead. "Mom, I…" I rested my forehead on my hand. A drop of sweat rolled down my nose.

Gray clouds rolled in off Lake Michigan, an inland nor'easter from the Great Lakes promising heavy snows and gale force winds. "Jameson?" she asked in a quiet voice.

"Yes, ma'am."

"Did you tell Sharon you're only pretending to be a boy?"

I shuddered, unprepared for the blizzard approaching. "Mom, I—"

"Jameson?" she asked in a voice so quiet it echoed through my soul.

"Yes, ma'am."

"Is that true? Are you pretending?"

A muscle in my arm twitched. I forced myself to take deep breaths. "Yes, ma'am." Green lightning flashed across the sky.

"You could talk to Sharon about this, but not your own mother and father?"

A cold wind stung my eyes. "I'm sorry, Mom. I was afraid. I'm a girl. Okay?"

"You're a girl? Fine." The wind hissed, icy breath turning to crystals.

I stared at the handset in terror. "Mom, I can—"

"Listen to me. I spoke with your Aunt Elizabeth. You're her daughter for the summer."

The little princess closed her eyes. My throat began constricting. "Mom. I only—"

"Alicia says you weren't planning to come home."

Snow melted and flowed down from my eyes. "I only need to—"

"No! I've had enough of this. Come home right now and go back on testosterone or go stay with—"

Poison or banishment. "Mom, please!" The plea echoed in my ears.

"Jameson!"

I remained silent for a ten count, shocked at the intensity of my mother's voice. No quarter. No terms. Only unconditional surrender. "Yes, ma'am," I whispered.

"Enough, Jameson. Do whatever you need to do at your aunt's this summer, but get this out of your system."

"Yes, ma'am." The storm abated, leaving utter devastation in its path.

"Call your cousin Kaylah. She'll tell you how to get to her parents' house."

"Yes, ma'am. I love you, Mom."

"I love you, too."

I slipped the phone back into its cradle. An eternity passed, but my heart refused to slow down. Thoughts clashed through my brain. Sharon had set me up. What would a summer living as a girl solve? I was sure I couldn't face testosterone.

ଓଃ 12 ଞ୍ଚ

I picked up Tyler's photo and gripped it tight. He provided the one stable point in my chaotic universe. Sharon insisted he had died. A tear ran down my cheek. If they left me alone long enough, I could fix Jameson. Make everything stable again. Safe.

I finished packing, set my bag on the bed, and called Kaylah.

"Hi, Jamie. You're quiet. Your mom must have called."

"Yeah. I never heard her so mad before."

"My mom isn't happy either. She thought this was all settled long ago. So, will you be spending the summer with us on Saint Andrew's?"

"You're going? I thought only Aunt Elizabeth, and Uncle Stephan, and I would be there."

"No. I'm going back to my parents' for the summer."

That might make my situation bearable. "Wow! Does my dad know?"

"No."

"What do your parents think about this?"

"I'm not certain. Perhaps they think this will bring our families closer again. All they told me was your mother asked them to treat you like their own daughter."

"Oh, joy. I remember how strict they were with you."

"You can still go home and take your shots."

I grimaced, recalling the effect of the testosterone on me. "No, thanks. I'd rather wear a dress all summer."

Kaylah laughed. "Well, there you are! I guess you get your wish. Is testosterone so bad?"

"Yeah. I get nervous thinking about it."

"Anyway, didn't you want to be a girl?"

"Yeah, but this is only for the summer, and it's make-believe."

"How do you know you'd like it anyway?"

"What does liking have to do with anything? Do you always like being a girl?"

Kaylah laughed again. "No. There are times when I think being a guy would be better. But, I'm not. So there you are. Is everything packed?"

"Yeah—well—everything I had in the dorm is packed."

"You'll have to repack for Saint Andrew's before we go. No sense taking things you won't need."

I sighed, feeling worn out. "I guess so. *If* I go to Saint Andrew's."

"Whatever. I'll meet you at Sharon's in an hour. She's expecting us for supper."

"Okay."

Sharon had said she wanted to be my friend. She'd encouraged me to be a girl in public, but then sent a picture to my mom. What kind of person entrapped someone that way? What right did she have to ruin my life?

After I'd finished cleaning my room, I sat down to rest for a few minutes. I checked everything one last time, locked the door, and went to the lobby to return my keys.

I kicked a palm frond lying on the sidewalk. All Sharon and I would do was argue. Why go right away? When I walked along the path by the lake, I noticed Sean standing by the shore, so I dropped my bag next to the bench and sat down. "Hi, Sean."

"Jamie!" He grinned. "How've you been?"

"Okay."

We both sat in silence for a while before Sean turned to me. "How'd your finals go?"

"Pretty well."

"Well, that's good then. So what now? Home?"

My attention wandered out across the lake. What was I gonna do? "I don't know. Mom wants me to stay with my aunt for the summer."

"You don't sound like you're too fond of that idea."

"I need some time alone."

"You in trouble with your mother then?"

I sighed. "Yeah."

Sean remained silent while a bird hopped around near the bench. "Because you were a girl in that play?"

Concern shone in Sean's eyes. He had never belittled me. I shrugged. What did I have to lose? "Because I was a girl when I wasn't in the play."

"Were you now? How did your mother find out then?"

"Somebody sent her a picture."

"You posed for someone? Now that was stupid."

I dug the photo out of my bag and handed it to my friend. Sean studied the picture. "Ah. I see." He smiled, eyes intense. "You both look happy there."

"My mom said the same thing, only I'm sure she wasn't smiling."

"Is the gent your boyfriend then?"

I considered the photo. "Yeah. He went to Vietnam. They say he's dead."

Sean squeezed my hand. "Wow. I'm sorry. I hope he comes back."

"Thanks." I chewed on my lip, eyes closed, thinking about Tyler.

"Do you sing?"

"Yeah—well, I used to sing in a choir anyway. Why?"

Sean smiled, looking mischievous. "Sing something first."

His good humor proved contagious. The thought of singing something brought a smile to my face. "Okay." I took a deep breath and started singing *Puff, The Magic Dragon*. Midway through the third verse I stopped, tears in my eyes. I shook my head. "Sorry. Bad choice."

"No. You did right well. You've a fine voice. If you'd like a job for the summer, I think—"

"Jamie!" Kaylah's voice sounded behind me. "I've been looking all over for you. I said an hour. Come on."

I smiled at Sean. "Sorry. Gotta go."

* * * *

The aroma of lamb made my mouth water. The sun broke through the overcast and melted away my troubles. I sat across from Sharon, waited while Kaylah said grace, and then dipped my spoon into my bowl. "This stew is as good as my mom's."

Sharon smiled and nodded. "Thank you. I thought I remembered you saying you liked lamb."

"It's my favorite. Did you make much?"

"Yes. Why?"

"Maybe I should stay for a couple of days and finish it."

Kaylah narrowed her eyes at me. "No. Your mother wants you to leave tomorrow."

Why had she turned against me? "Aw, come on, Kaylah. You can't blame me for trying. I want a few days alone first. That's all."

Kaylah frowned and shook her head. "I have some last-minute errands. I should be back here at eight tomorrow morning. Be ready to leave at ten."

Sharon frowned at me after Kaylah left. "You're right to be upset with me, but we should talk this through."

"Why should I be mad?" I glanced up at her. "You sent my mother the photo, didn't you? Did you plan to wreck my life when you asked to be my friend or was this a spur-of-the-moment thing?"

"Jamie, your mother called me last week. She seemed frantic. She wanted to understand why you were running away. I couldn't explain it all to her, so I sent her the photo to show her who you are and how happy you could be. I'm sorry. I should have told you."

"I wasn't running away. I only needed to straighten some things out."

"You told your sister you weren't going home."

"I was going to stay at Frank's for a couple of days."

"And then go home?"

"Yes…no." What had I planned to do? "I don't know. I need a little time alone. That's all."

"To do what?"

Sharon wasn't going to like hearing the truth. "I think I found a way to make Jameson permanent, but I need to be alone for a couple of days."

Sharon's face paled. "Permanent? What about Jamie?"

I studied my bowl, pushing a couple of peas around with my spoon. "I don't think Jameson would even be aware of her."

"Jameson would be a real person?"

I shrugged, pretending not to care. "Yeah. At least I think so."

"You're going to kill Jamie? I thought you wanted to be a girl."

My words might hurt her, but how else could I explain? I wasn't the person she thought I was. "I *am* a girl, Sharon." I pointed to my heart. "Here, but not between my legs where it matters."

Sharon pushed back from the table, dark clouds troubling her eyes. "What are you talking about?"

Life had been okay before I met Sharon. Well, at least my world had been stable, and hiding behind Jameson safe. "Haven't you screwed things up enough for me?"

"Me? You don't even know what's between your legs."

My throat tightened. Sweat trickled down my back even though the room was cool. I didn't want to argue with her. "I'm a boy, Sharon. A dress doesn't change that."

"You aren't male, Jamie." Sharon's lower lip twitched.

"Get real. You're a med student. You saw what I've got. All I need's a minor repair."

"Have you ever seen what's between a normal boy's legs?"

"Give me a break, okay? I've changed diapers. Stop trying to make me something I'm not. Give up and go find some other rare disorder to torment."

Sharon stood up, glaring at me. Lightning crackled around her head. When I picked up my empty bowl, the storm broke and she rained down hard on me. "Sit down! We're not finished."

I carried my dishes to the sink, took my time scrubbing the food off, rinsed them, and put them into the dishwasher. When I tried to brush past her, Sharon grabbed me by the arms and hissed, "Sit down." She blocked my way, glaring at me.

Too weary to push any further, I sat down again.

Sharon stomped out of the room and returned a moment later with a large book. She shoved the remaining dishes aside and slammed the hardback down in front of me. Then she sat next to me and started going through the pages. "Here. This one's your age. That's what you'd be like if you were male."

The guy in the photo might have been my age. Hard to say with the black box across his face. Hair covered the pubic area, extending onto his thighs and up past his belly button. The genital skin was darker than the surrounding area. The boy's penis was—well—I frowned at Sharon from beneath my brows and shook my head in denial.

Sharon nodded and pointed to the caption. "Tanner Stage Five. Age sixteen to eighteen. That's normal development."

My eyes refused to focus and my brain fled, but the image made it past my defenses and struck home. Sharon snapped the book shut and walked away.

In the guest room I sat on the bed and pulled off my shoes, wondering how long I could avoid thinking about what I'd seen. No amount of testosterone would give me a penis like the boy in the picture. Not even close. No behavior rules would make me a boy. No surgery. Nothing. I wasn't a boy. Or a girl.

We were leaving for Saint Andrew's in the morning, so I took Jameson apart again. Every rule, each bit of Jameson now represented one more lie I'd been told. Without concern even for my own sanity, I tore the rules out, screaming at my parents and the doctors, releasing all the emotions I'd pent up for nearly a decade.

Tattered images from my childhood swirled like large snowflakes in a blizzard. Mom taking away my dolls and the miniature china tea sets. My hair falling to the floor as clippers buzzed across my skull. Dad making me sit on my hands so I wouldn't use them when I talked.

Bits of Jameson's rules rained down on my head. My feet slid out from under me—and I was back in Oswego, running through the driving rain, scrambling for a place to hide before my father overtook me. When I found one, I curled up inside, shivering in the darkness. All the while I'd been pretending to be a boy, they'd been pretending I was male. I peeled away the wasted years, washing them out of my life with my tears.

* * * *

The next morning Kaylah found my sanctuary, just like when I was little. Her eyes got all wet when she opened the closet door and found me sitting in the corner with my chin on my knees. She sat down, cross-legged on the floor and made a sad smile at me. "Did you eat breakfast?"

I'd spent the night in my hiding spot, so I pursed my lips and shook my head no.

"Sharon might have some rolled oats. You still like oatmeal, don't you?"

Yummy with brown sugar. I glanced up at her and nodded.

"You're coming to stay with me for the summer, remember?"

Last time they had taken my dolls, so I pulled Sofie close and held her tight.

Kaylah brushed the hair out of my eyes. "It's all right, Jamie. You can bring Sofie. Now go take your bath. Okay?"

They lied to me. I wasn't a boy. The little princess crawled out of the closet and walked to the bathroom. At the door I turned back. My mouth opened and closed, but nothing came out. A single tear slid down my cheek.

Kaylah stared at me and nodded. "Yes, princess, I know."

When I was dressed and all, I walked into the kitchen, Sofie tucked under one arm. My cotton dress had a cloth belt, so I went to Kaylah and turned around for her to tie my bow. After my cousin finished, she turned me around and kissed my forehead. "Run and get your brush and a couple of hair clips."

Everything would be okay. I rushed back to my room and grabbed my things. Kaylah brushed my hair and clipped it back on both sides.

Sharon crouched down next to my chair. "Your breakfast is ready."

After a while, she leaned close. "I'm sorry. We're still friends, aren't we?"

My world was a smoking ruin, but I didn't blame Sharon for the hurt. I glanced at her and nodded my head.

"Good. Promise me you won't ever make Jameson permanent. All right?"

Jameson? Did Sharon have any clue what she'd done? I ate another spoonful of my oatmeal and nodded my head again. Jameson was gone. I wasn't a boy, you know.

os 13 so

Out the window, through the gaps in the low cumulus clouds, the elfin princess thought she spied an island that might be Saint Andrew's. We'd been airborne for quite a while. I glanced at Kaylah, who appeared to be asleep, her head swaying with the motion of the aircraft as it sailed above the sea.

When the pilot announced our approach and the thrumming of the engines eased, Kaylah stretched her arms and turned her head. She ran the back of a finger down my cheek. "We'll be landing soon."

My cousin brushed the hair from my eyes. "Sharon thought my little princess needed treatment for mental health issues," she whispered, almost too soft for me to hear. "Something called schizothymia. But I remember her before the doctors interfered with her life. She got quiet when she was in pain. She'll be all right now."

Kaylah had always been a second mom to me. Someone else might have told a seventeen-year-old girl to leave her Raggedy Ann behind, but Kaylah understood why I clung to a scrap of my shattered childhood. She also knew why I needed the photo of Tyler in my hand and not in my tote. To her, I didn't have to be a grownup yet.

The seaplane banked, turning on its final approach to the port at Saint Andrew's, an area of protected water reserved for landings. I shut my eyes and tried to relax, wondering what the summer would bring.

* * * *

The little bus hit a pothole that bounced me up off the seat. I grabbed Sofie to keep her from falling to the floor. Kaylah sat next to me, eyes closed, a smile of perfect contentment on her face. How did she sleep with so much going on?

The bus had only a thin canvas top to give a little shade to its passengers. The scents of flowers and food, dust and diesel fumes swirled through the air. Crowds of tourists and local vendors milled about on the sidewalks, some crossing the street between the slow-moving vehicles.

Tropical birds, tree frogs, and insects called to one another. Our seats squeaked for every little bump in the road.

Sofie leaned against my shoulder so she could see too. She was only a doll, but sometimes I liked to pretend she was my daughter, my own little princess.

A hand on my arm drew my attention back inside. Kaylah smiled at me. "We'll be getting off soon. Let's put the picture in your tote so we don't lose it. All right?"

The little princess kissed Tyler and stuck the photo into her tote. She asked her Lord to bring her prince safely home.

The bus pulled to a stop next to a street sign that said Ireton Close. Kaylah took her little princess by the hand and led her out to the sidewalk. Townhouses, stores with apartments over them, and small parks lined the street. Back along Fairfax Avenue, in the direction we'd come, the street descended past an old stone church.

"Here, Jamie. Hold my hand. You carry Sofie. I have your tote."

Old stone and wood townhouses lined each side of the narrow lane. Half a block away children kicked a ball around. The street didn't even seem wide enough for two cars to pass.

Kaylah led me past a walk-down with a sign that said Counselor Levinson and up a short flight of steps to a door. I tilted my head back, looking up at my aunt and uncle's townhouse. There was one more level above where we stood, and a roof with a dormer above that.

"I'm sure the door's not locked, but I'd like to surprise Mother. Okay, Jamie?"

I glanced at Kaylah and nodded, so she rang the bell.

Aunt Elizabeth did a double-take, eyebrows shooting up. Didn't she know it was the little princess visiting instead of Jameson? I put on my best happy smile for her.

"Hello, Mother." Kaylah grinned.

My aunt hugged us both.

Inside, Kaylah brushed my hair. "The bathroom's at the top of the stairs. Why don't you wash? Then we'll have something to eat. All right?"

I nodded and started up the stairs. With a dry washrag, I cleaned the dust off Sofie. After I had washed the stickiness off my own face and hands, I smoothed down the skirt of my dress and walked back down.

Uncle Stephan joined us for a lunch of soup and sandwiches. After he had asked the Lord to bless our meal, he frowned at me. "Did you wear a dress on your trip?" His voice sounded pleasant enough, but frost formed in the corners of his eyes.

I frowned at my skirt, wondering what might be wrong with it. My clothes weren't as nice as what a real princess would wear, but they were the best I had, and I'd been careful to keep them clean. I glanced up at him and nodded.

After a moment he dipped his head. "Well, no harm done, I suppose."

I released my breath and grinned at Kaylah.

When Uncle Stephan finished his soup, he pushed his bowl away. I glanced at him again, nervous, but his expression remained neutral. "You'll need a name. Jameson won't do."

Didn't he remember my name? I sat up straight, eyes darting around the table.

"She likes to be called Jamie," offered Kaylah.

"Very well." My uncle nodded. "Jamie." He stared at me and nodded again. "When we all lived in Oswego—I think you were nine—you said you were a girl." He glanced at Kaylah and sighed. "We all thought you got over that. Since you've never lived as a girl, your mother thought doing so might help you get this out of your system. Are you with me so far?"

I glanced up at my uncle again and bobbed my head.

"She'll welcome you back like the prodigal son as soon as you're willing to take testosterone. When you're ready to go home, all you have to do is ask. All right?"

"It is decreed!" announced the old wizard, holding up a scroll. "The elfin princess is hereby banished until she agrees to let the mages transmogrify her into a hirsute little beast of a dwarf."

My lips quivered. Mom and Dad hated the elfin princess and had ordered her death by testosterone poisoning. Things would have been so much easier if I could have been Jameson for them.

I didn't realize I was crying until Uncle Stephan pulled me up out of the chair and hugged me. "They're only doing this because they love you," he assured me.

Aunt Elizabeth brought a box of tissues. After I blew my nose, Kaylah nodded toward the stairs. "Come on. I'll show you our bedroom."

* * * *

Sunday shone bright and warm. I held my chin up while Kaylah adjusted my hat. Then I followed my cousin out the back door of the townhouse and down a short flight of stairs to a small patio area where Uncle Stephan and Aunt Elizabeth waited. On the other side of a walkway was the churchyard, a large grassy area with ancient trees, and to the right, the old church I'd seen from the main road.

When Aunt Elizabeth turned our way, she rolled her eyes.

I grimaced, wondering why dressing up for church should be such an issue.

Kaylah shook her head. "Mom, this is her first Sunday here. She's going to be meeting people. I thought the hat would be cute."

The little princess was wearing her new drop-waist dress. Kaylah had loaned me a neat hat with a wide satin ribbon around it and had tied my long hair back into a ponytail. Aunt Elizabeth frowned at both of us and shook her head. "She looks like Pollyanna."

That was good, wasn't it? The princess put on her best Pollyanna grin and curtseyed for her aunt. Kaylah chuckled, grabbed my hand, and started toward the church.

I sat still through the sermon, trying to absorb everything, trying to worship a holy God and wondering what He thought about His little princess. *Lord, please help me be the person you want me to be, and please bring Tyler safely home.*

* * * *

Late the next morning Kaylah led me out the back door and across the old churchyard to a street called Martin Lane. My cousin pointed out an old three-story structure of stone and wood—the manse. Wisteria crept up the stone sides and over the tiles on the slate roof, even covering a few of the windows. The building sat at the front of a large field of grass and ancient trees. Vines all but overran the old stone fence enclosing the property.

Four girls in light yellow dresses ran across the field, screaming and laughing. Kaylah smiled and gestured toward them. "The two youngest are Stephanie and Melissa, the Ainsworth twins. They're four."

Kaylah had said I would meet our pastor, his wife, and the foster girls who were staying with them. "They're orphans?"

My cousin grinned when I spoke to her, but turned more serious. "Yes. The tall girl with long black hair is Maria Honasan. She's fourteen. Her father's a Filipino sailor. She's waiting for her aunt to come take her home."

"It's sad they don't have moms."

Kaylah nodded. "The other girl is Heather Campbell. She's seventeen."

"She's an orphan too?"

"Her parents threw her out. She's pregnant."

Baby juices flowed through the elfin princess. *Ooh! I want one of those!*

"Don't envy her. The life of a single mother's hard. Even here."

The pastor met us at the door. "Kaylah. How are you?" He hugged my cousin, and then smiled at me. "And you must be Jamie. Welcome to Saint Andrew's." He bent down and hugged me as well. "Come on in." Inside, he motioned toward a couple of chairs. "Have a seat. I'll fetch tea. Abi made scones this morning. I believe there are a few left."

Kaylah grinned and whispered, "Abigail Gillespie makes the finest scones you'll ever taste."

Abigail was a frail-looking woman with white hair in a long braid. She joined us for tea and scones. Tea wasn't my favorite back then, but the scones were truly yummy. Like her husband, Mrs. Gillespie exuded gentleness. When she set the tray down, Kaylah hugged her tight, kissing her cheeks, and then stepped back, frowning. "Mother says you were ill. You're still pale. Are you taking care of yourself?"

Abigail smiled and nodded. "I'm getting more rest now. You've lightened my load enough for me to catch up, I think."

Kaylah introduced her little princess, and then poured milk into her tea.

The pastor was holding a sleeping toddler when he returned. "I thought you might like to meet our newest addition. Rachael's ten months old."

Ooh! A baby! I stood up to take a closer look. Her eyes were shut, so I couldn't tell what color they were, but her curly hair, what little she had, was golden.

"Robert, do be careful not to wake Rachael. She's pretty cranky, with her mother no longer around."

Right on cue, the little girl woke and started crying. Abigail took the child from the pastor and started rocking back and forth. The toddler gurgled but kept crying. "Hush now, honey. Everything's all right." Abigail rolled her eyes and frowned at her husband.

"Here. Let me try." Kaylah took her from Abigail and rocked her in her arms. She patted her back, but Rachael kept crying. Kaylah tried for several minutes to comfort the child before she sighed and walked over to me. "Would you like to try?"

The poor baby had lost her mommy. I touched the side of Rachael's face with my fingertips and stroked her hair. I picked her up, held her against one shoulder and started whispering to her. "It's okay, pumpkin." After a few seconds of loud protest Rachael quieted down. I sat in a chair and started rocking.

Kaylah arched an eyebrow. "I don't recall your being around little ones much."

The baby started playing with my bracelet, so I shifted her to my lap. Then I smiled at Kaylah. "A couple of years after we moved to Springfield, I started babysitting for one of our neighbors."

"Would you like to sit for her?"

Baby juices surged through me once again. How could the little princess not want to babysit a toddler? I grinned at Kaylah. "May I?"

Abigail poured herself a bit more tea. "You'd have to change her diapers."

"That's okay. I don't mind." My best puppy eyes begged my cousin. "Please, Kaylah."

"Don't ask me. That's up to Mrs. Gillespie."

Abigail nodded. "Kaylah and I have some things to discuss. Will you take Rachael for an hour now? I'll show you where her diapers are."

"Okay." The princess bounced up and down on her heels, eager to start.

My cousin grinned at me, and then turned to Abigail. "I think you just made her summer."

⊰ 14 ⊱

I'd already been up four times during the night when I rushed to the bathroom again. My bladder didn't burn yet, but the persistent itch that preceded a urinary tract infection was growing. I got the bottle of antibiotics out of my tote, threw on a robe, and walked down to the kitchen to find a glass. The smell of fresh coffee greeted me. Aunt Elizabeth was up. Mom had told me to eat something before taking antibiotics, so I fixed myself a bowl of oatmeal. After breakfast I set the bottle of pills on the counter and filled a glass with water.

A noise startled me. My aunt stood in the kitchen, smiling. "Good morning. How are you doing?"

"Okay."

"What are those?" she asked, with a bit of concern.

"Antibiotics. I have a urinary tract infection." I picked up the bottle and took out a pill.

Still smiling, my aunt held out a hand. "I'll take those."

Polite as could be, I shook my head. "I need them for my UTI."

She held up her index finger.

Ooh! The elfin princess stared at the digit as if it might strike. I hadn't seen my aunt do that since I'd left Oswego. Someone was gonna get switched. Argue and the count would only increase. Surely my aunt wouldn't switch her seventeen-year-old princess. "These are okay. Mom gave them to me."

Two. I stared at the two fingers, remembering the red welts she'd so often left on my legs. I studied my aunt's face, trying to figure out what to say.

Three. In a rush, I put the pill back and handed her the bottle. "Please let me take them. I have a UTI."

Aunt Elizabeth shook her head. "My sister sends her children drugs, but my daughters consult a physician when they're ill."

"I hate going to doctors." I especially didn't want to go to one while wearing a dress.

Elizabeth sighed and tilted her head. "Kaylah has your mother's power of attorney. You two can go as soon as you're dressed, but first…"

Until that moment, I hadn't noticed the short willow branch lying on top of the refrigerator. My aunt used to explain, using Scripture verses, why you were being disciplined. Her eyes insisted that switching was as painful for her as for the person she was punishing. Sometimes the explanations hurt more than the welts she left.

I glanced at the branch and swallowed, but my aunt just nodded her head toward the stairs and said, "Go get dressed."

* * * *

All it would have taken to make me a boy would have been minor surgery and a few years on testosterone. That's what Dad always said, you know, but whenever I looked in the mirror I saw an elfin princess. And the shots would only have turned her into a hairy little monster.

My cousin grinned at me as she pulled the door to Dr. Cameron's office open. She seemed amused by my discomfort. I stopped in the waiting area and turned around. "Please let me see him as a boy, Kaylah."

She put a hand on my sleeve, serious for a moment. "You agreed to the rules when you came here. You're my sister for the duration. You should be happy Mother's treating you like her own daughter. Would you rather take testosterone?"

"Hmpf."

"Well, there you are." She nodded in emphasis. "Mother wants us to go along with whatever Dr. Cameron recommends. She also forbids either of us to ask for any treatment related to your gender issues. All right? The less you argue or complain, the sooner we'll be through."

Kaylah spoke with Skye, Dr. Cameron's nurse. She was blonde and tall, taller than Sharon. She wore a pretty cotton dress that looked comfortable in spite of the heat.

Skye smiled at me and turned to my cousin. "Since this is her first visit, Dr. Cameron will want to do a complete physical." She handed me a hospital gown. "The restroom is halfway down the hall on the right. The urine specimen bottles are on a shelf in the corner. Leave the bottle on the sink when you're finished. After you change, wait in the end room on the left. Dr. Cameron will be with you presently."

A gray overcast rolled in, hiding the sun's warmest rays. Acid butterflies flew around in my stomach. What would the doctor do when he found out I wasn't a girl?

The elfin princess frowned at me from the mirror. "I'm sorry," I whispered. "I don't like being examined down there either."

The doctor was a young man with a warm smile, dark red hair, a short beard, and brown eyes that sparkled. "I'm Dr. Cameron. Most people call me Graeme." He helped the little princess up on the examining table. I sat, shivering and all, but he only smiled. "Well, lass," he said with a Scottish accent, "Why don't you tell me what I can do for you?"

I studied my hands, wondering if a complete exam meant he was gonna examine me between my legs. "I have a UTI."

"Indeed. A UTI now is it?"

"Yeah. A urinary tract infection."

"Yes. Yes. I was wondering how a young lass like you might know she has one."

I smiled in spite of myself. He was charming for a doctor. "I get them several times a year."

"Well, what does your physician think about that?"

"I never went. My mom…" Mom didn't make the little princess go to doctors. She knew how scared I was of them. I glanced at my cousin, who was standing on the other side of the small room.

She nodded. "Graeme, this is a bit awkward. Her mother kept her from doctors. She's seventeen and has some gender issues."

"Seventeen. What sort of gender issues?"

Kaylah rolled her eyes. "Her parents insist she's a boy."

"Ah. How were the UTIs treated?"

"Her mother gave her antibiotics. Mine thought she should come here, since she's staying with us now."

"Jamie, is it?" Graeme pulled up a stool and sat in front of me. "You're seventeen?"

Doubt clouded his handsome face. I didn't think he believed I was a seventeen-year-old boy. I put on my best Pollyanna smile and nodded my head. "Yes, sir."

Dr. Cameron took my blood pressure and listened to my heart. He checked my lymph nodes—all the usual stuff. Then he turned to Kaylah. "Would you mind asking Skye to assist?"

She nodded and stepped out of the room.

Graeme turned back to me then. "Your UTI is what concerns me, not your gender, but I still need to examine you. All right?"

Biting my lip, I nodded. At least he asked my permission first.

"Well, when Skye gets here, we'll take a look at you then."

When Skye walked in, she handed the doctor a piece of paper. He glanced at it and nodded. "Jamie, I'd like you to put your feet in the metal stirrups and slide toward this end of the table. Good. Now, knees apart. Good."

Sharon told me the stirrups were for girls. Boys got to stand up. Would the doctor have asked me to do the stirrup thing if he thought I was a boy?

Dr. Cameron glanced at Skye. She nodded, pencil and paper ready. "All right, now. Prepubescent hair. No darkening of the genital skin. Perineal urethral opening, somewhat elongated. Fused labia. Prominent clitoris. Gonadectomy scars. Appendectomy scar." Graeme stood up straight and smiled at me. "You can sit up now, lass."

He turned toward my cousin. "Jamie's faie. Intersex if you will. Given her short stature and feminine face, my guess would be Mixed Gonadal Dysgenesis."

Faie. It figures. I told them I wasn't a boy. I grinned at Kaylah, but my cousin seemed only mildly surprised. She sat for some time before replying to Dr. Cameron. "Can we concentrate on the UTIs for now?" My cousin made a sad face at me and mouthed, "Sorry."

Dr. Cameron nodded. "The urinalysis came back positive. I'll give her something for the pain and a cranberry sugar called D-Mannose to help her body fight off the infection."

"Very well." Kaylah looked at me again, her eyes still sad.

Graeme scratched his chin and glanced at me. "She should be on hormones. Her puberty has already been delayed longer than is healthy."

My cousin shook her head several times. "We can't."

"The child's a girl, Kaylah."

Ooh! A doctor who's on my side. I opened wide my puppy-dog eyes, locked them on my cousin, and pleaded for my girl puberty.

Graeme put a hand on Kaylah's shoulder. "Hormones are necessary for good health. Her low estrogen levels may be why she gets UTIs."

My cousin kept her mouth straight, but her eyes grinned. "All right."

I hopped down off the examining table, ran to my cousin, and hugged her. With my face pressed against her no one witnessed my tears. When I let go, the doctor was grinning. "Lass, I'm going to give you an estradiol injection and a prescription for Premarin. You'll take a pill once a day. Estrogen will give you breast development. Is that all right?"

I didn't need to say anything. I spun around on one toe—a perfect pirouette—then grinned at Dr. Cameron and hopped back up on the examining table.

"One more thing," he said, turning back to my cousin. "In about two weeks she needs to come back for a voiding cystourethrogram."

"Very well." On the way out, Kaylah leaned close and whispered, "Not a peep about this to anyone."

* * * *

Mrs. Gillespie poked her head into the bedroom again. "Are you certain you're well, child?"

The urinary tract infection had cleared up, but she'd seen me throw up and I was still a bit nauseous. "Yes, ma'am. I'm better now." I tried my best to give her a Pollyanna smile. The first week had been the worst. Every morning I'd gotten sick. Kaylah said it was from the hormones.

"Well, why don't you have some tea, dear? Perhaps that will help settle your digestion."

"Thank you, ma'am. I would love some. Are there any scones?" My empty stomach rumbled, demanding to be filled again. No matter how much I ate, my hunger wasn't satisfied.

Mrs. Gillespie glanced at Rachael, who was asleep on my lap. "You sit right there, and I'll send you a tray. No need to wake the little one."

Rachael stirred, so I picked her up and held her against my shoulder. She promptly coughed up sour drool down the back of my dress. Dirty diapers. What might as well have been morning sickness. Baby vomit. So why was I still smiling?

∝ 15 ∞

Three weeks after my first visit Kaylah and I returned to Dr. Cameron's office. A week earlier we'd gone back for a cystourethrogram. My cousin said the test showed I needed a minor surgical procedure. I was too scared to ask how minor.

Skye smiled and handed me a hospital gown. "Graeme is in the last room on the right. You can go in as soon as you've changed."

In the center of the room stood what looked like an oversized dentist's chair with stirrups where the footrest should have been. Counters and cabinets lined the walls. A moveable light hung from the ceiling. The air glowed, thick and hazy, brighter than a summer day.

Kaylah sat in a chair beside the door, talking with Dr. Cameron. The pounding of my heart drowned out whatever they were saying. I took a step back when I noticed a second doctor standing on the other side of the room. One hand searched for the door handle behind me.

Dr. Cameron smiled at me. "What's up, lass?"

All my life my parents had told me the doctors would someday move my urethral opening to the tip of my little post. That would let me stand up when I went to the bathroom. Was Dr. Cameron's talk about my being a girl just a lie? My heart struggled to break free from my rib cage. I turned the door handle, wondering if he'd keep me from leaving. "I'm okay with sitting down when I pee."

Graeme chuckled, a warm grin spreading across his face. "I should hope so. You'd make a mess otherwise."

My shoulders tightened. *What then?*

Kaylah took both of my hands in hers. "Relax. Graeme says the procedure is safe and he'll explain everything to us first. We don't even have to do anything today."

"Oh...Okay."

"You remember the test we did to map out your urinary tract?"

I glanced at the door. "Yes, sir."

"You know your genitals are a bit different from those of other girls."

I stared at him for a few heartbeats, before I nodded again. He was still calling me a girl. My muscles relaxed a little. "Yes."

"Before we start, I'd like to show you what we propose to do. All right?"

My breathing began to slow down. "Okay."

On a pad of paper he drew an illustration. "This is what your genitals are like now. Your labia are fused together. There's a little pocket behind them that collects germs. We'll cut them apart along this line. All right?"

What difference would that make? They still wouldn't be right. I stared at the drawing and nodded. When I glanced at Kaylah, her eyes were the size of saucers. *Ooh!* My heart came right up my throat. Why was my cousin so shocked?

"Splitting them is the easy part," the doctor continued. "We need to make sure their appearance is correct. Dr. Mason is a reconstructive surgeon who has experience with this procedure." Graeme tore off a sheet and drew a second illustration. "This is what your genitals should look like when we're through. These are your labia. This is the introitus to your vagina."

Vagina. Darkness closed in. I put a hand out to steady my spinning world. Had I understood him right?

Graeme's face clouded over with concern. "Are you all right?"

I scanned the room in wonder. It was all so strange. Doctors wanted to open my vagina? I admitted to having an out-of-control imagination, but this left me doubting my sanity. "Vagina?"

"Yes. You'll be pretty much like other girls once we've split your labia."

A girl! Vindication left me beyond tears or laughter. Speechless, I clung to my cousin, yearning for the childhood I'd lost. Why couldn't I have seen Dr. Cameron when I was nine?

Kaylah held me tight and patted my back. "We always knew, didn't we?" she whispered.

A sad frown on his face, Graeme took my hand. "Perhaps we should wait and do this—"

"No!" Both Kaylah and I yelled at him.

"You're sure?" Graeme held my hand while he studied my face.

After calming myself, I glanced at my cousin again. She was grinning. I nodded and said, "Yes."

"Very well." He motioned toward the chair. "We'll use a local anesthetic. You shouldn't feel a thing."

I put my feet in the stirrups. Dr. Mason raised the chair, tilted it back, and pulled the overhead light into position.

Kaylah held my hand and smiled down at me. My heart fluttered faster than a hummingbird's wings.

When they finished, Graeme helped me stand. "Wash yourself every day, but don't soak the stitches. They'll come out next week. Your vagina is only a small pouch right now. We'll talk about dilation once you've healed."

On the way home the anesthetic wore off. The little princess was a bit sore down there, but the pain didn't matter at all.

* * * *

The next day I was well enough to sit for Rachael again. The toddler wobbled as she stood next to the bookcase, one hand gripping the bottom shelf. I sat a few feet from her and reached out my arms. "Hey, pumpkin. Come here."

Rachael took two steps, sat down hard, and started crying, so I picked her up and held her. "That was good. My little princess will be walking in no time." I stood her next to the shelf again and sat beside her on the rug.

Much of my life I'd hidden behind a mask, days drifting downstream, all the unpleasantness happening to someone else. Now a pretty girl played with a toddler, but part of me refused to believe I could experience such simple joys. Embracing the illusion would shatter it, and the elfin princess would wake to find herself half boy once again. What was so wrong about this dream that my parents couldn't let it be my life?

The next time Rachael cried, I sat on the rocker and bounced her on my knee. She gurgled and promptly spit up. I wiped her face clean, changed her diaper, fed her, read her a book, and let her sleep on my lap. That was the drill. Every day. But I never tired of caring for her.

⊱ 16 ⊰

It was certainly a strange way to celebrate Rachael's birthday. Kaylah and I didn't wear makeup in church, or anywhere else most of the time, but she insisted we stop by a salon and have our hair and makeup done for the party. Like the toddler would even notice.

Going home meant leaving Rachael. Dad wasn't gonna let me stay on Saint Andrew's forever, and he for sure wouldn't let me keep taking estrogen. Would my parents tell me to go back to Miami as Jameson or make me stay home and take testosterone? Only a couple of weeks remained before school started again. I pressed a hand against Tyler's ring, seeking reassurance.

Kaylah's eyes grabbed mine. Her face serious, she held out a hand. "May I?"

"What?"

My cousin frowned at me until I pulled the gold chain out from under my blouse. She examined Tyler's ring for a long while, quiet as a church mouse. "Your soldier-boy gave you this?"

"Yes, ma'am. Right before he left for Vietnam."

Kaylah grinned. "Come on." She grabbed my hand and strode down the street.

Ten minutes later we stood before a storefront that was all glass and wood frame. *Francesca's*. The dresses in the display were all formal and beautiful—the kind of clothes that were neat to shop for, but you'd never wear more than once or twice in your lifetime. Even a real elfin princess might not own something as fancy as some of the gowns in the window.

After a moment's hesitation Kaylah dragged me inside. Wide-eyed, the little princess searched through the racks, occasionally running her fingertips over the fabric or examining some small detail of a gown. A green satin dress caught my fancy. "Isn't this one pretty?" I scanned the area, but didn't spy my cousin anywhere. I almost panicked, but Kaylah wouldn't drop me off at a store, and then leave. So I browsed.

Kaylah returned with a middle-aged woman in an elegant silk dress. With her blonde, curly hair, she reminded me of a 1950s movie star, maybe even a real princess like Grace Kelly. A glance at me, and a nod of her head, and she disappeared. Kaylah grabbed my hand and followed the woman to a back room. Along one wall stretched a rack of gowns, all white or cream. The woman selected one, handed the dress to Kaylah, and walked out, pulling the door closed behind her.

"Well, put it on." Kaylah grinned.

The princess took a closer look at the dress. The bodice appeared to be satin, the full skirt layers of tulle. An elegant design. A wedding dress? I shook my head and handed it back. "I'm not interested in trying on dresses I'll never wear."

She frowned and held out the dress again. "Humor me, will you?"

I changed clothes and let my cousin lead me to a large mirror. A beautiful lady stood in front of me, her face growing radiant.

"Here's the point, my little princess," said Kaylah with a warm smile. "We'll correct your birth certificate. Your parents will have to let you be a girl then. And when your soldier-boy comes marching home, you can marry him." She nodded. "So there you are."

Little pink flowers started budding somewhere deep inside me. In the mirror, Tyler stood next to me, grinning from ear to ear. I grinned back at him, longing for the day we'd be together again.

The elfin princess jumped out of the taxi and waited while Kaylah paid the fare. Bursting into song seemed appropriate. The air itself crackled with excitement, anticipating our talk with Uncle Stephan. Kaylah said that once he understood how happy I was, he'd talk to my parents.

I danced up the stairs, singing under my breath. Kaylah opened the front door for me and bowed. The elfin princess sang aloud as she waltzed over to the kitchen and filled a large glass with cold water. I raised it to my lips, still dancing, but froze mid-turn. Kaylah stood motionless in the doorway, face ashen, eyes wide. I turned my head, following her gaze.

The glass slipped from my hand and tumbled in slow motion to the ceramic tile floor. A thousand glittering shards exploded across the room, but the heartbreak in my father's eyes cut deeper than glass ever could, bleeding my happiness away.

"Are you that scared of me?" he asked, voice as sad as his eyes.

Too late, my defenses snapped into place; a poison arrow had already pierced my heart. I put a hand on the counter, trying to steady myself, back turned to my father's displeasure, and stooped to gather the broken fragments of my life.

One large sliver demanded my attention, a shiny scimitar, sharp as a surgeon's blade. A gentle hand enclosed my wrist. Worried eyes held mine until I nodded. The darkness had already passed, the danger gone. God wouldn't let me give up yet.

With her other hand Kaylah opened a cabinet door. She took out a broom, so I stood with my handful of shattered hopes and waited. A shaking hand wiped at my tears. It wasn't the best time to be wearing mascara. As soon as a path was clear, I ran up the stairs to the bathroom. By the time I walked back down, the floor was clean and someone had pulled an empty chair up next to my father. One deep breath and I sat beside him with my head down.

"You looked better when you were smiling," he said, lifting my chin with his hand.

I focused anywhere but on those mournful blue eyes.

He dropped his hand and turned his head away. "I spoke with another doctor last week. In Boston. He said changing genders at your age is a bad idea. Too many issues. Should have raised you female from birth. Too late now." He grimaced. "Perhaps at nine, but not seventeen."

"What gender change?" Kaylah bounced up out of her chair, livid. "She's a girl!"

I ducked as silent laser rays from my father's eyes crossed the table. Uncle Stephan scowled, lightning flashing around his head. "Sit down! We're not debating Jameson's gender again." Kaylah glanced my way and sat down, arms crossed, murder written across her face.

Dad touched my arm, recapturing my attention. "Your mother says you were only pretending." He pursed his lips and glanced out the front window at some passersby. "Have you ever tried being a boy?"

Avoiding his deadly eyes, the little princess examined her hands. I never had, so I gave him the barest of headshakes.

Dad lifted my chin again. "If you'll try, if you'll put your heart into this, I'm sure you can do it. Your mother and I want you happy. Not this play-acting, dancing-and-singing euphoria. Real-life contentment. Give it a year. If you're still miserable, we'll talk, okay? We'll find some other way. Perhaps the doctors are wrong."

A year? Might as well have been a century. The lifeblood seeped out of me, down my legs and across the floor. I glanced at Kaylah, but my cousin turned her head away.

Dad stood, a sad smile on his face. "We should go. Our flight leaves in a couple of hours."

The princess panicked, you know, thinking about her little one. "What about Rachael?"

He shook his head, sad eyes locked on mine. "I'm sorry, but she has to get along without you eventually."

"I need to pack," I whispered, hoarse.

My father shook his head again. "Pack what? Dresses? Your boyfriend's picture? Your doll?" He sighed, shame dragging his shoulders down. "Leave everything here, Jameson. Put it all behind you."

In desperation I glanced at Kaylah one last time. My cousin's eyes were closed, tears streaming down her face. Numb, I rose and followed my dad outside.

∾ 17 ∾

The small craft sailed on, well on its way to prison. Reflected in my father's eyes, the elfin princess sat quietly in her fetters. Her eyes dripped with a sorrow made worse by the realization that my father had condemned her, not out of hatred, but because of his love for a son who didn't exist.

Dad touched the fine gold chain on my wrist. A muscle twitched, but I didn't pull away. He held up my hand, appearing to study its delicate features. My fingers were long and thin, much like Mom's. Shame filled his voice when he spoke. "Did your soldier-boy give you this bracelet?"

I glanced at him for a fraction of a second. "No. Sharon."

As gently as he might with my mom, Dad pushed the hair back behind my ear. I flinched, but held still as he ran the back of a finger across my face. The elfin princess had soft skin and more freckles on her cheeks than the stars in the midnight sky. She liked her face that way. Dad's fingers brushed against my gold hoop. "He gave you the earrings?"

I nodded, a slight bobbing of the head.

Dad clasped his hands in his lap. "Tell me about him. What was he like?"

Was? My glance lingered an instant longer this time. "He was always smiling, always trying to make me laugh. He read the Bible to me. We prayed together. He loves me, Dad, and I love him. He knows what I am, and he still loves me."

"He volunteered for 'Nam?"

"Yeah, but he wasn't all gung ho." I sniffed. I wasn't crying, but my nose wanted to. "He hates the war, Dad. He went because he had to. Not like Scott." Dad stared at me as a renegade tear rolled off my lashes, down my cheek, and off my chin. My brother had died three years earlier while trying to rescue his wounded comrades. My dad still grieved for him.

He wiped a tear from my cheek. "I'm sorry, son. I hate the war too. A number of good men have died for nothing."

He hated the war? Because Scott had died? Dad closed his hand over mine. "I'm sorry I wasn't home more when you were young. Maybe things would be different now."

"You were home every day until we moved to Springfield. It's not like I'd be any bigger or stronger. My body isn't like Scott's. You can't expect me to be him."

"No, I guess not...I can't tell you how to be a boy. I realize you're not Scott, but I wrote down some things he did at your age and some other things you should try. Work through them. At least try, and if you still want to be a girl, we'll find a doctor who can help. Okay?"

I'm sitting right here. Can't you see that I'm already a girl? If I told you about taking estrogen, would you free the elfin princess? No. You'd only be that much sadder. You'll never understand. After considering my situation, I nodded. What other options did I have? I was only seventeen. What would I do if I ran away from home?

When the pilot announced our approach into the Port of Miami, Dad leaned close. "We'll take a taxi and eat lunch at the airport. I have a meeting in Washington tomorrow, so you'll need to fly to Greensboro by yourself. Your mother will be expecting a call from you this evening. She and Alicia will pick you up."

"My clothes are all at Sharon's."

"We don't have time to stop in Miami to pick up your things." He shrugged. "You'll only be in North Carolina for a week or two anyway."

I grimaced, thinking about Mom's reaction to my arriving in a dress. Dad glanced at me and smiled, like he thought I might be ashamed of Mom seeing me as a girl.

When they finally made the boarding announcement for the flight to Atlanta, my father checked his wristwatch and shook his head. "Looks like you'll have to get a later flight home; you're going to miss your connection."

A short layover in Atlanta, a connecting flight to Greensboro, and a long shuttle ride to Winston-Salem lay ahead of me. My stomach churned as I waited for his parting instructions.

Dad drew me aside and handed me his list of *Things Boys Do*. The document was formatted like some technical specification, orderly down to the small check box next to each item. His secretary must have typed it.

Go back on hormones. My heart froze. Mom would know an endocrinologist in North Carolina, but there would only be time for one poisonous shot before I returned to school. Did they expect me to take injections while in Florida? How could I go back to being a girl if I let them wreck my body? *Lord, please send Tyler back to me. I need his help and I miss him so.*

Cut your hair short. Nervous, I wrapped a golden lock around one finger, and then glanced at my dad's balding head. Would testosterone do that to me? I closed my eyes and took deep breaths, my body trembling.

Dad held me by the shoulders, no doubt trying to encourage me. "You'll be fine."

The elfin princess, reflected in the airport window, stared at me, mournful eyes pleading for help. She clenched the iron bars of her prison cart as it lurched into motion, starting its long journey to Despair. One hand sought mine as the wagon rolled past. Even now she might recover if I set her free. A single word would suffice, but my heart couldn't find the courage to stand against my father.

"I—" Words escaped me. The whole situation was surreal. How long could the elfin princess hold out? Her shorn hair would eventually grow back, but the shots would mar her beauty and transform her body. *What will Tyler do when he—*

Dad's eyes! My defenses slammed into place, chilling my emotions, even as he reached into his pocket. Part of me screamed in agony, sure of what was coming, but my body refused to react.

Dad slipped a chain over the head of the elfin princess, sealing her doom. It fell down around my neck and settled into place, dog tags clanking together against my breast. "Your soldier-boy died a hero," Dad whispered. "I'm sorry, but I suppose it's for the best. Mourn for him, but leave the boys behind you now."

With what tenderness still survived, I took hold of the remains of my love and lifted them to my lips. Never more would I see his smiling face this side of Heaven. Frost crystallized on the dog tags and spread down my arms, chilling me to stone. My love would never come rescue me.

I meant to say goodbye, but only a blast of frigid air and a rasping whisper came out, so I turned and walked down the boarding ramp.

⚚ 18 ⚚

Woodberry Drive curved back through the trees adjoining Wake Forest University. With the rustling branches and the birds singing, it reminded the elfin princess of home. The Kirkpatrick residence lay up the hill, away from the road, snuggled between birch trees and a copse of tall evergreens. Behind the house, purple and deep red sky filtered through the branches. Darkness approached as I walked up the path.

Alicia answered the door, went wide-eyed, and waved me in. "You look fabulous!" A grin lit her entire face. "I see you've gotten the whole gender thing out of your system."

"Who—" Mom walked into the living room. "Jameson, coming home in a dress wasn't one of your options. Go unpack your bags and change."

I slumped in a chair and tried to look apologetic. "Sorry, Mom. I didn't bring any." What did it matter anyway?

"What?"

"My clothes are all at Sharon's. Dad wouldn't let me stop to pick them up."

"Why didn't you take them to Saint Andrew's with you?"

"Kaylah said not to, and besides, Dad didn't let me bring anything back from Saint Andrew's either."

Alicia snorted, clearly enjoying Mom's discomfort. "She can wear my clothes, Mom."

My mother and I both glared at her. I didn't want Mom any unhappier with me than she already was. The best thing to do was go along with the plan and hope my parents would change their minds. "We'll go out tomorrow and buy some jeans and a couple of T-shirts."

Sometimes Mom let her emotions overrule reason. Hands on her hips, she shook her head. "You've worn dresses all summer; another two weeks won't hurt you." Then she turned her wrath on Alicia. "You two can share a room."

Behind Mom, I made wide eyes at Alicia. In the little house in Oswego we had shared a bedroom. Whenever a storm had come through, she had crawled into bed with me so she wouldn't be scared. Why would my mom think putting us in the same room was punishment?

She turned toward me again, her forehead wrinkled. "Why did you fly up here for two weeks anyway?"

Both hands held up in front of me, I shook my head. "Dad handed me a list of stuff to do and put me on a plane home." Hysterical laughter bounced around inside my skull, trying to force its way out. Dad had let me carry my money and *Things Boys Do* in my purse because my dress didn't have any pockets. And all I had on Saint Andrew's were dresses.

Mom shook her head a couple of times as she scanned the list. Then she nodded and shoved it back at me. "All right. I guess we'll start in the morning."

Alicia elbowed me in the ribs. "This'll be like old times."

"You're six inches taller than me now, Ali."

"Don't worry." She winked. "I'll find you something to wear."

* * * *

Mom, and Alicia, and I ate snacks and played several games of Spades before I excused myself. After a long shower, I changed into one of Alicia's nightgowns and crawled into bed. Ten minutes later my sister opened the bedroom door and turned on a lamp. "Are you asleep?" she whispered.

"No."

She sat on the bed and put a hand on my arm. "I'm glad you're back to your old self. I missed you."

"Huh?" I sat up and leaned against the padded headboard.

"You don't act like Jameson anymore. You're like you were before we left Oswego."

I studied my sister's eyes. They said we had the same emerald color. My hair was lighter, though, especially with so much Miami sun in it. "Jameson's gone, Ali. He was only pretend. I need to learn to be a boy myself now."

"Why? Talk to Mom. This list thing's stupid."

"No. Dad's right. I never really tried. I was only play-acting."

"So what? I never tried either. Besides, I thought you had a boyfriend."

An overwhelming tide of sorrow swept over me. Tyler's dog tags were in my purse. I shut my eyes and, without thinking, touched my chest to make sure his ring was still underneath my nightgown. I jerked my hand down, but it was too late. Alicia had seen. She slid the chain out. Her eyebrows shot up when she saw Tyler's ring. "You're married?" she asked, her voice a squeal.

"Shh! Mom will hear you." My chest heaved as I fought back tears. "No. Tyler asked me to hold it for him while he was in Vietnam."

"So you're engaged? Awesome!"

"He's dead, Ali."

"Wow." She dropped the ring and put her arms around me. I held the flood back as long as I could, but when the levee broke, I pressed my face against her shoulder and let all the tears go.

My sister pulled me tight. "Does Dad know?"

"Yeah. He gave me Tyler's dog tags."

Letting go, she frowned at me. "Just like that?—He's dead. Goodbye?" When I nodded, she narrowed her eyes, her face contorting with rage.

How could I explain Dad to her? I wasn't sure I understood him myself. "Don't hate him, Ali."

"It's not right," she whispered, head down.

I pulled her chin back up and tried to smile. "When Millie died, Dad held you and wiped away your tears. She was only a hamster, but he understood your grief." She nodded, a bit of the anger gone. I bit my lip, thinking about my brother. "You remember when Scott broke his leg?"

"Yeah. Dad held his hand while they set the bone."

"He knew what Scott needed."

"And for you he does nothing."

"He can't, Ali. How do you give your son what a daughter needs?"

"Did you tell him that?"

"No."

"You should."

"The words all go away when I'm around him. How would Jameson say something like that anyway?" Dad and I never did communicate well.

"Talk to Mom."

"She doesn't listen."

"She will," Alicia snapped and stalked out of the room.

"Ali, no," I whispered, rushing to follow her. A confrontation wasn't what I needed.

When Alicia pushed the master bedroom door open, Mom looked up from reading a book. "Yes?"

Alicia glanced at me. "Jamie has something to tell you."

Mom's intense gaze made me squirm. I broke eye contact and struggled to find the courage to speak. In the bedroom mirror the elfin princess seemed nothing more than a frightened little girl.

"About her boyfriend, Mom." Alicia unclasped my necklace and handed it to our mother. Her eyes grew large as she studied the ring. Then she turned pale. "You can't—boys—" She got out of bed, picked up a photo mailer from the dresser, and slid out an enlargement. I walked over so I might glimpse the photo. Mom directed her gaze at me again. "This ring is gorgeous."

"Tyler's great-grandmother left him her wedding ring to give to his bride. He asked me to keep it for him while he was in Vietnam."

"He gave it to her?" she asked, pointing at me in the photo.

"Yes, ma'am."

"He knows about you?"

"Yes, ma'am."

Mom picked up the photo again. "You two look so happy together, but two boys can't—you know that."

"Sharon thought she could convince you and Dad to let me be a girl."

That raised mom's brows. "Do you think we let Alicia be a girl?"

"That's different."

"Yes. Your birth certificate says male."

Alicia stepped between us and put a hand on my arm. "Mom, there's something else." My sister stared at me, emerald eyes on fire. "Tell her."

Lightning crackled around Mom's eyes, like she thought I had caught VD from him or something. I stared at the photo of my love. "Tyler's not coming back, Mom." Storm-driven waves beat at the levees again. My legs wobbled, threatening to give out.

"Are you going to give his ring back?"

Alicia exhaled a sound of frustration. "Her fiancé's dead, Mom. Dead! Dad told her yesterday."

Mom glanced at Alicia and me and examined the photo again. Tears filled her eyes. She hugged her little princess and pulled my head against her shoulder. "I am so sorry, honey. You should have said something." As I wept, Mom held me, swaying back and forth. When I finally let go, she drew in a deep breath and exhaled, a long sigh. "Grieve for him, dear, but let go. God will use this for your good somehow. He didn't want you to marry that boy. He does want this experience to drive you closer to Him, to make you more like Christ. He has something else in mind for you. Find out what."

Two days and I missed Rachael already. "I want to be a mom."

"At the expense of knowing your Savior?"

"No." *Why did you have to put it that way?* I wanted to obey God, but that didn't mean I was capable of being a boy. It wasn't like I was shaking my fist in His face and saying I wouldn't.

"Good." She brushed a tear from my cheek. "Trust Him to provide for your future. Even if it means growing up to be the man your earthly father expects."

☙ 19 ☙

Sunday in church a distinguished-looking man greeted me. "My name is Jim Nyquist," he said, holding out his hand, "and you must be Jameson."

I smiled up at him, trying to sound pleasant. "My name's Jamie, sir."

"All right, Jamie." He smiled. "I'm the pastor. Your father asked us to counsel you. He made an appointment for Tuesday afternoon. This morning I just wanted to welcome you to the church."

I watched Pastor Nyquist as he walked away. He seemed like a friendly enough man.

Mom, and Alicia, and I sat together. Although I'd attended the Methodist church with Tyler and Sharon, and the Presbyterian church with Kaylah, I was glad for the opportunity to worship with my family.

After the service we ate a potluck dinner. I sat between Alicia and Mom, staring down at my plate. The food was okay, but I felt like I didn't belong. Nobody was rude, but people seemed nervous. No one said anything bad; they didn't say much of anything at all. One or two stared. Had they been expecting Jameson? They were polite, but I still had a strong sense of being alone in a crowd.

* * * *

Tuesday afternoon I arrived a few minutes late for my appointment. I smiled at the church secretary. "I'm supposed to meet with the pastor."

"He's in his office, down the hall on the right. He's expecting you."

"Thank you, ma'am."

After greeting me, Pastor Nyquist motioned me toward a chair.

He opened in prayer. After speaking in generalities, he told me the reason for my appointment. "Your father asked us to counsel you regarding your gender issues." The goal of counseling, he explained, was sanctification. Biblical counseling involved using Scripture to confront people about their sins and exhorting them to repent. Counseling involved prayer and depended on the work of the Holy Spirit.

Why was I the one who needed counseling? I was fine with my body and my gender. "I'm spending the summer as a girl. I'll try to be a boy when I go back to school. Dad gave me a list of things to do."

Pastor Nyquist nodded. He paged through his Bible until he found a passage and read, *"The woman shall not wear that which pertaineth unto a man, neither shall a man put on a woman's garment: for all that do so are abomination unto the LORD thy God."* He glanced at me. "Another verse is in the New Testament—*'Does not even nature itself teach you, that, if a man have long hair, it is a shame to him? But if a woman have long hair, it is a glory to her: for her hair is given her for a covering.'* Those two passages should help you understand a boy shouldn't live as a girl. I'm sure your parents know these verses. What makes you think they would approve?"

Condemnation for being a girl wouldn't help. I needed to figure out how to be a boy. "I'm a girl. My family wants me to be a boy. I'm going to an endocrinologist tomorrow. He'll give me testosterone, but I don't want to wear boy's clothes until I look like one."

"I don't think your appearance matters. A girl shouldn't wear boy's clothes just because she looks masculine, should she?"

"No, sir. I shouldn't wear boy's clothes until I'm a boy."

"You're already a boy."

I rolled my eyes, but didn't say anything.

The pastor furrowed his brow. "We'll come back to that later. Your father was pretty sure you had sexual relations with a man. Would you like to tell me about that?"

An emotional tsunami blindsided me. *Sex with Tyler?* At that instant, I wanted Tyler's baby so badly that I'm sure my denial sounded like a lie. I smiled, holding on to the time spent with my love. "My boyfriend and I kissed but that was all."

"How long was he your boyfriend?"

I shook my head, recalling the day he left for Vietnam. Images, like pages turning in a book, rushed by. Such a short time we'd spent together. "Not nearly long enough."

Pastor Nyquist flipped through his Bible again. After a moment, he read, *"Thou shalt not lie with mankind, as with womankind: it is abomination."* He frowned at me. "Is it right for two boys to kiss?"

Whatever. "No, sir, but I'm a girl."

"Your father says you're a boy. Is he lying?"

"I'm sure he believes what he told you." What did it matter? He wasn't going to believe me anyway. "I'd be happy to submit to a physical."

"I don't think a doctor's necessary. Your father had a copy of your birth certificate." Pastor Nyquist shook his head. "You're male."

Was there any point in arguing with him? "Sir, I was born with one testis and one ovary. They had to put something on my birth certificate."

"God created male and female and pronounced it good. Regardless of a person's physical shortcomings, they're still either male or female."

"Then I'm female."

"That's not what your birth certificate says," the man insisted.

Someone knocked, so I stood and pulled the door open. The church secretary poked her head in. "Jim, your next appointment's here."

Pastor Nyquist stood. "I'm sorry, Jameson. I guess we're finished for today. Why don't you meditate on the passages I read you? We'll talk again next week. Meanwhile, you should stop wearing dresses and get a more masculine haircut."

Was that what God thought of me? A homosexual and a transvestite? How was I supposed to be a boy with such a girl body?

* * * *

Soft noises elsewhere in the house told me Mom was up and about. I rolled over, yawning. My shots had been delayed for a year. *Maybe I should have stayed home. At least Jameson would still be here.*

Mom stuck her head in the door. "You should get up, dear. You don't want to be late for your appointment."

"Thanks, Mom." I yawned again. Sleep had eluded me.

An hour later the little princess sat in Dr. Stewart's waiting room. She was pretty in Alicia's dress, with her hair all braided, and she was going to ask the doctor to poison her. Would he think me insane?

"Jameson Kirkpatrick?" said a nurse, standing in the doorway between the waiting room and the rest of the doctor's office. She stared at me with raised eyebrows until I shrugged and followed her. After she weighed me, she left me in an examination room. I sat on the padded table and waited. I might have cut my hair short, you know, but a buzz cut and a dress together, well...

A middle-aged woman in a lab coat entered the room. "Miss Kirkpatrick? I'm Dr. Stewart. What can I do for you?"

"I'm supposed to go back on male hormones."

"Oh? Why were you taking testosterone?"

"To give me a puberty like a normal boy."

"Why would you want to virilize?" She frowned. "You're a beautiful young woman."

"I was born between the sexes. My parents want me to be a boy."

"Perhaps they should adopt one instead," she snapped.

After I had changed into a gown, the doctor examined me. She kept muttering to herself. When she finished, she shook her head. "Surgeons could remove your vagina and perform hypospadias repair surgery, but testosterone's not going to give you a normal male height and build, let alone an adequate penis. You're certain you want to take it?"

No, actually! I couldn't help but wince, thinking about the shots, so I turned my face away from her and lied. "Yes, ma'am."

"How long have you been on estrogen?"

"Huh? The summer."

"Come back after you've lived as a boy for a year and we'll talk."

Ooh! Dad is going to love this. "I'm only living as a girl for the summer."

Dr. Stewart fingered a lock of my hair, which was past shoulder length. "Did you grow this over the summer?"

"No, ma'am."

"Testosterone makes permanent changes. You can't be cavalier about taking it. I'm not giving male hormones to a well-adjusted girl. Come back after you've lived as a boy for a year. Without estrogen. Without the dress. Without the hair. Show me you're serious and we'll talk."

It wasn't funny, you know, but I grinned at Dr. Stewart's back as she stomped out the door.

* * * *

The next morning I was reading when my mother opened the bedroom door. "I brought you a bottle of antibiotics to take with you." She set them on the dresser.

"Thanks, Mom. I appreciate your concern, but I won't need them."

Mom's eyes pinned me to the bed. "You won't?"

"No. I don't think I'll get any UTIs this year."

"Why not? You had several last year."

"The doctor on Saint Andrew's took care of everything for me."

Mom frowned. "Oh, really? What did he do?"

If I could convince her, maybe she'd talk to Dad. "He split my labia so my vagina wouldn't retain urine."

"You don't have a vagina, Jameson."

"Whatever."

"Don't you whatever me."

"Mom." I got out of bed and stood in front of her. "You got mad at me because I couldn't talk to you and Dad about my gender issues. Well, I'd like to talk. Will you listen?"

She relaxed a hair and tilted her head. "I'm sorry. I'm listening."

"I have a vagina." How difficult was that to understand?

Mom sighed. "Jamie." She was finally going to call me Jamie instead of Jameson? "Sit down for a minute and listen to me. All right? We didn't split your labia because the doctors thought a vagina might confuse you."

I grimaced, but held my peace. Mom's eyes held a sadness I'd only seen before in Dad's. "I know how feminine your body is; I'm reminded every time I see your face. But your vagina isn't real; it's only a small pouch."

"They could do surgery."

She shook her head, vehement. "Vaginal surgery's expensive, extremely painful, and would mean you'd need to dilate every day or your vagina would shrink. If they cut your clitoris, they'll destroy nerves." She shook her head again. "Surgery's not a good answer." Mom shifted her position to face me. "God gave you a feminine body and a heart to match, but you're still a boy." The melancholy that pursued me pounced and ripped its claws through my heart. Mom pulled me close. "Honey, I'm praying that God will send someone your way who'll love you as you are. All right?"

I sniffed, wondering how Rachael was faring without a mother. Mom raised my chin with her hand and smiled. "A woman who's going to be a doctor might let you be a stay-at-home dad. You could afford to adopt a house full of children."

"Oh, please! Sharon would want to plan my entire life."

"And you'd bring spontaneity to hers. Would that be so bad?"

I closed my eyes. "Mom, Sharon loves Frank, and Tyler loved me the way I was."

She hugged me again. "Be careful, all right? Most men won't be as understanding as Tyler."

* * * *

In the hallway mirror, the elfin princess smiled and brushed a bit of lint from her sleeve. Alicia had given me a pretty navy blue skirt and jacket set with a white satin sleeveless top. The ensemble was sort of a forties style—soft and feminine. Mom had told Alicia the flared skirt was too short for her, but the length was fine for me. I braided my hair, sort of a last hurrah, and tied it with a white satin bow. Mom walked up behind the princess and put her arms around my small waist. "Don't tell your father, but I think you're beautiful."

I grinned. "Be careful, Mom. You'll confuse me."

"Dr. Stewart called. Seems you've been on estrogen for a while."

I sought out her eyes in the mirror, but didn't detect any anger on my mother's face. "Yes, ma'am. I started taking Premarin in June, but my pills are still on Saint Andrew's."

"You've put on weight. Do you like what estrogen's done to your body?"

Warmth spread across my cheeks, and my grin proved impossible to suppress. "Yes, ma'am."

"Dr. Stewart agreed to put you on testosterone next summer if you see her as a boy."

The elfin princess wilted, smile fading, shoulders drooping. I turned my face away, afraid to let my mother see my pain.

Mom hugged me a little closer anyway. She brushed a wayward strand of hair away from my eyes. "Are you really going to live as a boy until you finish your father's list?"

"Yes, ma'am. As soon as I get to Miami."

"You'll cut your hair?"

"Alicia trimmed it for me."

"That's not what I meant."

"I know…Yeah, but I'm not sure how short. Plenty of boys wear their hair long."

"Perhaps Sharon will like it the way it is."

"Sharon has a boyfriend."

"But she's letting you stay with her."

"She thinks I'm a girl, Mom, and it's only until the dorm opens."

"All right, dear. I'll be praying for you."

I hugged my mother. "Thanks, Mom. Would you tell Pastor Nyquist I can't make my appointment? I'll be working on Dad's list. I cut my hair. I'm wearing a suit when I leave."

Mom smiled, arching a brow. "A suit?"

I nodded and gripped my jacket. "This is a skirt suit, isn't it? And Alicia trimmed my hair. Please, Mom? I don't want to be in trouble with them, and I'm gonna try to be a boy. Isn't that what they want?"

Mom appeared to be trying hard not to grin. After a few seconds she nodded. "Say hi to Sharon for me. And call when you get settled in."

Alicia's voice came from the front room. "Jamie! Your cab's here."

I kissed my mother on the cheek. I was going to miss her.

♥ 20 ♥

At the end of her long journey the elfin princess climbed down out of her prison cart, stretched her aching muscles, and breathed in the scented tropical air. Her emerald eyes feasted on the brilliant colors, surveying the trees and flowers attending her. Even the butterflies had come out to bid her farewell.

I raised one hand, palm skyward, and smiled as a monarch touched down and fanned its wings in greeting. Each sight, each sound, I filed away, hoping to cherish my final day forever. The tropical sun danced across my skin. Too hot already, jacket over one arm, I glanced up at the corner window that used to be my room. Forever and a day had passed since Jameson had lived in the dorm.

On the lake side of Eaton Hall my honeysuckle remained faithful. The princess pressed her face into the blossoms and breathed deep of its wonderful fragrance. Would anything smell as sweet tomorrow?

"Jamie?" Behind me stood Lisa, as beautiful as ever. "Oh, let me look at you," she exclaimed, one hand on each of my arms. She stepped back, grinning. "You should say hi to Sean. He's over on the bench. Come on."

When I hesitated, she grabbed my hand. "Don't be shy. He'll be glad you're back."

Sean stood to greet me. The unexpected warmth in his eyes distracted the little princess.

"Jamie! Are you living as a girl now?"

"Unh. Just over the summer." I bit my lip, trying hard to appear brave. "Back to boy land today."

"Bummer," said Lisa, graceful brows tortured into a frown.

I forced a smile. "I'll be okay. Good to see you both again."

Lisa grabbed her camera. "May I take your picture next to the magnolias?"

One final portrait of the elfin princess surrounded by her favorite blossoms? Award her an Oscar for her smile. "Sure," I said with what I hoped was a casual shrug.

"Is makeup okay?"

"Yeah. Why not?" I shrugged again, staring at the ground and wondering if a picture would be all that remained of the princess. Would I grow old clinging to a photo and a ruined set of dog tags?

"Sis, why don't we all go to Wolfie's first?" A gray overcast darkened Sean's steel-blue eyes as they embraced mine. My mom and dad had always told me I had an overactive imagination, but I would have sworn he was sad the elfin princess had to go away.

Lisa's eyebrows shot up. "Oh! I'm sorry. I entirely forgot." Facing me, she smiled, rueful. "I promised him we'd have lunch before I dropped him off at work. Why don't you join us?"

Anything to give the elfin princess one more breath of freedom. "I'd love to."

We climbed into Lisa's Firebird and headed across the MacArthur Causeway and up Collins Avenue to Wolfie's. I couldn't help but think of the time Tyler had taken me there so long ago. His grin seemed to be fading from my memory. I pulled out his ring and held it up to the light. It sparkled like new. But I'd never wear it.

After we ordered, I asked Lisa how her photography was going.

She waved a dismissive hand. "I spent the summer taking work-shops."

"So tell me about them."

Lisa's excitement when she talked about her summer put a smile on my face. She'd known me as a boy. Now I sat with her at a table in Wolfie's, dressed as a girl, and she acted as if it were the most natural thing in the world. I had known she would befriend the elfin princess. Too bad it was only for a day.

"—but let's talk about your summer. You're Kodachrome now! What happened?"

I laughed at that, wild and free, like sunshine breaking through the mist.

Sean glanced up, his steel-blue eyes alive with fire. What had him so —my laugh?

In spite of her impending doom, the elfin princess flashed him her brightest smile. I glanced at the mirrored wall tiles. A hundred emerald eyes sparkled back at me. I was more alive without Jameson, even with my beloved Tyler gone and me under sentence of death. "You remember the play last spring? The guy who kissed me was Sharon's brother." I glanced at Sean, but couldn't read his face. "I was a girl over the break so we could spend time together." Sweet memories left drifting rose petals, soft sorrow, and the faintest touch of Tyler's hand on my cheek. "When Mom found out, she told me to stay with relatives until I was willing to go back on testosterone. While I—"

"Testosterone?" Anger disfigured Lisa's beautiful features. "Why?"

"Huh?" *Ooh!* Too late I realized what I'd said. Well, better they understood everything. "I'm not really a boy, you know. I was born with one testis and one ovary. The doctors took them out because I got cancer."

The waitress brought our food. I put a big dollop of sour cream on my *latkes* and corned beef. Wolfie's made the yummiest potato pancakes. As soon as the waitress left, Sean reached out his hand toward me. "We hold hands when we pray," he said, with a warm smile. So I held their hands while he asked the Lord to bless our meal and our conversation.

Sean kept my hand until I glanced up at him again, and his eyes captured mine. A muscle in my shoulder twitched. Okay, so I'd just told him I was a hermaphrodite and all, but he got way more than that out of it. The little princess squirmed under his gaze. All she could think to do was throw another smile at him and yank her eyes away.

I had only taken three more bites when Lisa's intense eyes bored into me. "What do the doctors call your condition?"

"Um. They—Sharon says I have Mixed Gonadal Dysgenesis."

She nodded as if she were an expert on all things faie and turned toward her brother. "What are the odds?" He nodded, and her piercing gaze returned to me. "Testosterone's absurd. You should be on estrogen."

Sharon studied this stuff because she was a med student. I got that part. But how in the world did a nineteen-year-old photographer know anything about MGD? "I took Premarin most of the summer."

"You stopped? Why?"

"Dad came to Saint Andrew's and put me on a plane home." I pulled *Things Boys Do* out of my purse and handed it to her. "He says I can be a girl after I try everything on his list."

Anger grew on her pretty face as she scanned the document. "He can't be serious!" Sorrow blossomed in her eyes, and she shook her head. "Tell him no."

"He's my father. I'd lose my family and have to quit school."

"I thought you had a scholarship."

"I do, but he pays for my room and board. I have some money, but not enough."

"So stay with me."

Could I do that? I told Dad I would try. "Thanks. That's really sweet, but I gave him my word. I need to at least try some of the things on his list."

She passed *Things Boys Do* back to me, frowning and shaking her head.

Lisa and I waited outside while Sean paid the tab. Her face still suffered from emotions that didn't belong there. "I thought you had a boyfriend."

My lower lip trembled as I fought to hold my emotions in check. "He died in Vietnam."

"Oh! I am so, so sorry." She hugged me, her hand lingering on my back until Sean returned. "Sean, her boyfriend died."

He took my hands in his and held them. "I'm sorry for your loss, Jamie. I remember how happy the two of you were in that photo." Then he kissed me on the forehead, and we headed for the car.

Lisa dropped me off at the Pierson residence. Sharon had left a key under the mat, so I let myself in. A note on the guest room door said Kaylah had dropped my things by the house.

Sofie greeted me as I entered the room. I sat next to my old friend and held her, wondering if I were allowed to keep my only doll.

My dresses were all clean and hanging in the closet. My other girl clothes were stacked on the dresser. The bag with my boy clothes still sat on the floor.

I opened my tote and dug to the bottom, but couldn't find my picture of Tyler. There was only the Bible that Uncle Stephan had given me and a large manila envelope. I sat down and dumped the contents beside me on the bed. Tyler's photo was there. So was a sheaf of official-looking documents. I picked them up and began reading.

The first sheet was an affidavit signed by Dr. Cameron. The paper said Jamie Kirkpatrick was female and described her condition, including the presence of a small vagina. She might have a uterus. My heart didn't know whether to laugh or cry. I set the papers down and examined the other items—a large bottle of Premarin pills, a tube of estrogen cream, and a box of plastic rods with a manual labeled *Vaginal Dilation Protocol.*

The papers caught my attention once again. The last several pages were certified copies of an Illinois Birth Certificate for a girl named Jamie Iseabail Kirkpatrick. At one time the elfin princess would have danced around the room. Instead, a sea of emptiness swallowed me. Legally female now, I'd committed myself to being a boy. Acid churned in my stomach. A girl would be ashamed of doing some of the things on Dad's list.

Jameson's clothes smelled all musty when I unpacked them, so I dumped them into the washer. While waiting for the laundry to dry, I sat in the wing-back chair and opened *Vaginal Dilation Protocol.* I was still reading when Sharon walked in.

She stared at me, mouth open.

I grinned, thinking how I must have seemed to her when she last saw me—a mute little girl. "Thank you. I had a wonderful summer. I'm happy to be back."

That earned me a smile. "I worried about you. You seemed…"

I jumped to my feet. "Yes. I missed you, too." We hugged like we'd actually been friends.

Sharon fingered my jacket. "That's a cute outfit. Did you get it on Saint Andrew's?"

"Alicia gave it to me. The skirt was too short for her."

"So everything's all right with your family now?"

"All right? Hardly. Dad gave me a *Things Boys Do* list. If I do them all I can be a girl." When Sharon's eyes glassed over, I shrugged. "Yeah. Crazy. Guess he thinks I'll find something I like I can't do as a girl."

"What about your mother?"

"She thinks we should marry and adopt a bunch of kids."

Sharon dropped her purse. "You? My husband?"

I laughed. The thought of the two of us together was too scary to take seriously. "Don't worry, Sharon. You're not exactly my type."

"So, how long is this list?"

"A dozen items, but some are pretty long."

"Like?"

"Hunting—track, kill, prepare, and eat an animal."

Sharon waved a hand. "Pff. That one's easy."

"Easy?"

I glanced toward the laundry room when the dryer started buzzing.

Sharon nodded. "I'll go change. Then we'll go hunting."

The elfin princess glared at me from the dresser mirror. She was used to wearing dresses and didn't want to switch back. I shrugged at her and apologized. When I tried to put on Jameson's old clothes, I discovered his jeans no longer fit. They were too tight on my hips.

"You've put on some weight." Sharon stood in the doorway, an approving smile lighting her face.

"Yeah. Maybe ten or fifteen pounds."

"I think it all went to your hips."

I grimaced. "Yeah. I was on hormones most of the summer."

"You should keep taking them."

"No. I'm supposed to put my heart into this. Can we go to Burdines and buy some bigger jeans? I have to wear boy's clothes now."

"Not tonight. Here. I'll measure you and pick up some jeans over my lunch break tomorrow."

Sharon disappeared and then reappeared with a tape measure. After she finished she nodded. "You're a junior size one now."

"Junior?"

Sharon smirked. "Yes. Junior for boys."

‰ 21 ‱

I shook my head, studying the tank. "I don't know, Sharon."

She grinned, clearly enjoying herself. "We had to hunt through five stores before we tracked down our quarry. You still need to catch one."

"What?"

"Reach in and grab one. Florida lobsters don't have claws."

I squinted at the tank again, grabbed one, and handed the struggling creature to the clerk.

Sharon nudged me. "We need two."

I reached in and snagged another.

"Now you prepare them and eat one."

"What? Boil water?"

"Yes. Boil or broil them. Melt butter. Split the tail open and pull out the meat."

"Eat the thing?"

"You never had lobster?"

"I'm from Illinois. They have crawdads, but I don't think anybody actually eats them."

"You'll love the taste."

Dad and Scott had been all smiles whenever they dragged back a bloody deer carcass. I frowned at my catch. "Are you sure this qualifies as hunting?"

"Yes. Now put a check in the box."

On the way back to the car Sharon was quiet. I studied my friend's sad face. "Would Frank teach me to ride a motorcycle?"

She stopped and stared at me. "Frank's in Chicago."

"Well, when he gets back."

"He's living with his parents while going to school. Fewer distractions."

"Oh. Wow. I'm sorry."

"You're going to buy a motorcycle?"

"Yeah. I can't afford a sports car."

Sharon rolled her eyes. "You'll get yourself killed on a bike."

"I'll be okay."

* * * *

The next morning I lay on my side in a sleeping bag and studied Tyler's dog tags, trying to work up the courage to tell Sharon. She'd accepted her brother's death, but the proof still might hurt her. A soft rustle of the flap gave me just enough time to close my hand before Sharon stuck her head into the tent. "How are you doing?"

How was I? Not bad after a sleepless night. I rubbed my eyes, hoping my vision would clear. "Didn't you hear me screaming?"

"No. What happened?"

"Something the size of a rat ran across my face during the night."

"Probably just a palmetto bug."

"And these little red ants keep biting me."

"Why do you think I wouldn't sleep out here with you?"

"Why didn't you warn me?"

"I told you camping was no fun."

Something biting me again drove me out of the sleeping bag. "That's enough. I'm done." I pushed past Sharon and stood in the back yard, brushing more ants off my legs.

Sharon chuckled and nodded toward the back door. "Go on in. I'll put everything away later."

Inside, she put a hand on my arm. "I'd like to ask you something before you get dressed." Her eyes said I was about to get another of her big-sister lectures. "Last time we spoke, you loved Tyler. Camping is one thing, but how can you be thinking of living as a boy again after falling in love as a girl?"

"I will always love Tyler." I wasn't the best at breaking bad news, but I was determined not to make the same mistake Dad had made, so I made eye contact with her and took a deep breath. Sharon nodded twice, a faint smile on her lips. "You never were any good at hiding your emotions. Tyler's been dead for months. Do you finally have closure?"

I placed the dog tags in her hand and hugged her. "Dad says he died a hero."

She held them up to the light. "Your father gave you these?"

"Yes. He has contacts in the military." Sorrow seemed permanently etched across Sharon's face. I wondered if my friend ever laughed anymore.

Her eyes focused on someplace far away as she spoke. "All his life Tyler wanted to be a hero. He understood the risk and still chose to go to Vietnam." Her eyes met mine then, boring into me. "My brother loved adventure. Tyler could have gotten a student deferment, but he wouldn't sit still long enough to stay in college." Sharon sat on the couch before continuing. "He always said he wanted to marry but never settle down. He wanted a wife who would join in his adventures and travel the world with him. He wanted a life full of excitement and continuous motion."

"What about children?"

"They would have tied him down, but you couldn't get pregnant. That's one reason he changed his mind and decided to date you."

"No children?"

"I told him most girls with your condition are born with a strong maternal instinct." She shook her head and let out a sigh. "I think he would have adopted out of love for you, but being tied to one place would have crushed him."

There was nothing to say. The Lord had spared me a sorrow greater than Tyler's death. How would I ever have chosen between my love and having children? Time to let go, at least in part. I undid the clasp of my necklace and handed her Tyler's ring.

"What's this for?" Sharon looked more surprised than I'd ever seen her.

The memories were precious to me, but I could never bear to put Tyler's ring on my finger. The heirloom belonged with the Piersons. "This should stay in your family."

"You *are* family, Jamie. There is only you and me, and I don't think I'll have any children to pass it down to."

"You don't want any kids?"

"I do, but by the time my practice is established..." She shrugged. "I don't know."

"I thought you and Frank were getting married when he graduates."

"Frank's having a rough time in school and we've been drifting apart."

"God will send you someone else."

"Perhaps, but not until I finish medical school and my residency. I don't have time for anything or anyone else."

"You need to take the ring, Sharon."

"Why?"

I flashed a mischievous smile. "Mom would be really happy if I gave you a wedding ring."

Sharon rolled her eyes and laughed from her belly. "Tell you what. Let my grandmother buy it from you. She can give the ring to one of my cousins."

"I won't sell it, but there's a charity on Saint Andrew's that takes care of orphans. She could send them a donation."

"All right."

"Thanks, Sharon." I studied her face. She'd already told me she wouldn't help with anything else on the list, but it wouldn't hurt to ask. "Can you give me a haircut before you leave?"

She glanced at her wristwatch. "Sure. Go ahead and shampoo. Be quick, though; there's not much time."

"Do I need to wash my hair for a buzz cut?"

"A buzz cut?"

"Dad wants my hair short."

"Then he can cut it."

"How about a pixie cut?"

Sharon's eyes burned into me, storm clouds gathering above her brows. "That won't make you look like a boy."

"But I can at least say I cut my hair short."

A short, sharp nod from Sharon and I hurried to the shower. The elfin princess glared at me as I rushed past the mirror. I ignored her; what else could I do? She loved her long locks, you know, but short hair was on Dad's list. "Sorry," I whispered as I dried off.

Sharon began by shortening my hair all over. When she noticed my eyes leaking, she set the shears down. "I can't do this with you crying."

"I'm sorry." I wiped away my tears and kept my eyes closed until she finished. Then I went to my room and washed my face. The girl in the mirror wore the longest and cutest pixie I'd ever seen. The style emphasized her pretty elfin features. My fingertips touching hers, I tried to reassure the girl. "You're almost a real elfin princess with your hair that way, you know, and now we can check the haircut box. Everything will be okay. You'll see." I had to cut my hair shorter before school started, but I didn't have the heart to tell her yet.

Things Boys Do sat on my dresser with some other papers. I ticked *Cut your hair short* and scanned the other items again. *Get a motorcycle* might actually be fun. The fine print said I could drive a sports car instead, but I couldn't afford one. No license, anyway. For that I needed—*Ooh!* I ran to the dresser and snatched up my birth certificate. One hand on my hair, I ran to the bathroom. "Iseabail!" I tapped on the mirror to get her attention and held up the document. "You need a birth certificate to get your driver's license."

I had to be Jamie to get my license. She understood right away and started bouncing up and down. Then her brows shot up and she grinned.

"What?" No time to learn to ride before classes started. Did I need to register for school as Jamie?

In the mirror the elfin princess swayed as if she would start dancing.

"No!" I shook my head several times so she would understand how serious I was and pointed to the list. "Boys. Things *boys* do."

Her smirk reminded me of the face Mom made whenever I told her an obvious lie. I exhaled a long sigh in defeat. "Okay, so maybe I'm not a boy." Dad said the list was stuff Scott had done and some things he thought I should try. So Scott and Dad were the boys in *Things Boys Do*, not me. It wasn't my fault I had to do some of the things as a girl.

The elfin princess executed a pirouette and bowed to me from her mirror. I smiled and popped a tablet from my Premarin bottle. Maybe Lisa would still help me check off *Move in with a girl*.

ɔ3 22 ଚଡ

I didn't have Lisa's address, but I found an Alexander on Alhambra Circle in the phone book. Since I wasn't quite sure how to explain everything, I decided to stroll on over to the house while I thought about what to say.

Low gray clouds scooted across a bright blue sky. Leaves and flower petals caught up by the wind swirled through the air. The elfin princess grinned at the palm trees doing their slow ballet. They turned to bow as she passed. The Student Union building offered her temporary shelter from the wind as she watched scraps of paper race across the concrete walk. Back in the elements, I raced the length of Miller Road across campus and crossed San Amaro Drive.

I'm not sure what I had expected, but large trees shaded the two-story stucco and wood structure. Their rustling branches whispered of a quiet contentment. The princess imagined little Rachael running across the yard, the toddler laughing and screaming in delight. I waved at her and rang the doorbell.

An oriental woman in a blue and white kimono answered the door. "*Yōkoso. Omatase shimashita,*" she said with a slight dipping of her head.

I imitated her little head bow and clasped my hands behind my back. "Is Lisa here?"

She nodded and waved me in. "*Dozo ohairi kudasai.*" In the entryway she indicated a chair. "*Dozo osuwari kudasai.*"

Lisa wore the same style kimono—white cotton with an indigo flower pattern. She would probably have looked good in a sweatsuit, but she seemed the type to never dress that informal. "Oh! I love your new hairstyle. So you've changed your mind?" It might have been getting gloomy outside, but Lisa was all sunny.

"A reprieve is all."

"Oh." Clouds blew across her fair face, revealing her disappointment. "Well. Take off your shoes and come in."

She brightened again when I explained the change in my situation and mentioned my new birth certificate. "I'm going to be a girl this semester so I can get my driver's license. You said I might be able to stay with you?"

"Sure, but I have some conditions."

"Oh."

"Don't be sad. They're good ones."

When the elderly woman brought us green tea and almond cookies, Lisa's eyes went wide. She jumped up and said something to her. Then she turned to me. "I am so sorry. I've forgotten my manners. Jamie, this is my mother."

The little princess bounced up out of her seat and did her best curtsy, at which Mrs. Alexander laughed. Cheeks burning, I whispered, "Glad to meet you, ma'am," and sat down again. Lisa and I both stared as her mother walked back toward the kitchen.

"My mother," said Lisa, "survived Nagasaki. She lost everything she had and everyone she knew. She got deathly ill. Her hair fell out and it never grew back. One can understand why she's a little sensitive about some things." She glanced toward the kitchen and sighed. "She married a Scottish soldier, but she still likes to hold on to some of her traditions. One is no shoes in the house. Another is the *yukata*." She fingered her robe. "This type of kimono is made from cotton and has a gauze lining. I wear mine as you might a bathrobe."

"Where do you get them?"

"*Okaa-san*—Mother—will make several for you."

Lisa scanned me as if she thought I might object. I shrugged. There were worse things a mother could demand of her daughter's houseguests. My own mom didn't appreciate anybody sitting around in PJs.

"No boys in the house unless we're both here—and then only in the living room."

"Okay."

"My parents spend most of their time overseas. When they're home, *Okaa-san* owns the kitchen." Lisa grinned, eyes alive with amusement. "I hope you like Japanese food."

"As long as it's not raw fish or something."

Lisa shook her head. "She only makes sashimi on special occasions. Usually it's tempura or *oyakodon*. You like rice, don't you?"

"Yeah."

"All right then. There's only one other thing." Her face got all serious, and she picked at the fabric of her *yukata*. "I have a small circle of close friends, a sort of sorority. We don't keep any secrets from each other. I want you to join."

She wanted to be a closer friend? "Sure."

"You'll have to share your secret with them."

"Oh." I stared at Lisa and trembled. Fear and excitement battled within me. Would they be my friends, too? I nodded and drew in a deep breath to calm my nerves. "How do I join?"

"I sponsor you for membership. You tell them your story. If no one objects, they tell you theirs and you're in."

"Sounds okay to me." Was that excitement or apprehension that ran up my spine?

"Oh. I almost forgot. The girls in the group aren't Christians. I'm not either. Sean preaches at us; I'd appreciate it if you didn't. All right?"

The elfin princess usually said what was on her heart, but she rarely criticized anybody. Kinda hard when you couldn't even get your own sex straight. I put on my best Pollyanna smile for her. "Well, give me the evil eye when I mess up, okay? I'll apologize."

That earned me a chuckle. "So when would you like to move in?"

* * * *

The girl in the mirror swayed to some internal music, a slow-dance beat. Behind her on the floor lay a futon that unrolled into a full-sized mattress. The only other items in the small room were a nightstand with a lamp, a couple of photos on the walls, and a bamboo mat on the floor. The mirrored closet doors concealed a built-in dresser, shelves, and a place to hang clothes. My dresses and tops didn't take up much space. Moving everything I owned had taken less than half of the Firebird's small trunk.

A soft knock on the frame of the rice paper door and Lisa poked her head into the room. "Do you like it?"

The princess hugged Lisa and did a little dance with her bare feet. "It's neat! Thanks so much for letting me stay here."

Lisa chuckled. "*Okaa-san*'s almost as excited as you are. Now I won't be alone in the house when they leave. She was worried. Sean lives in the guest room attached to the carport, but he's out of town for the rest of the month." She glanced at her wristwatch. "Want to help with dinner?"

"Sure. Mind if I call home first?"

"No. Go right ahead. There's a phone log on the stand. Write down the calls you make so we can divvy up the bill."

"Okay." I picked up the receiver and dialed home. My mother answered.

"Hi, Mom."

"Are you at the dorm?"

"No. I decided to rent a room from Lisa this semester. You remember her. She's the photographer I told you about. Dad's list says to move in with a girl. We're only friends, you know, but I figured..."

"What happened with Sharon?"

"Her parents are spending the winter down here, so there's really not any room."

"Well, your father should be happy you're taking his list seriously. Since you're not staying in the dorm, I'll get him to send you a check to pay for the room."

The little princess swayed to her inner beat and winked at Lisa. "Thanks, Mom. Tell Dad and Alicia I love them."

☙ 23 ❧

The only team sport I'd ever played was volleyball. Well, I played some softball, too, but only with kids my own size. Jameson had tried to play intramural volleyball, but other kids hadn't wanted him on their team. He couldn't compete with the boys.

The coed teams were always seeking girls willing to play, though, so I thought I might be able to check off *Play a team sport* by playing volleyball as a girl. I loved the game and determined to put in the practice time necessary.

After supper I walked past the cafeteria to the intramural fields. Teams were already forming, so I hung out at the volleyball courts and played whenever anybody let me. I was used to being the shortest, but the number of tall girls surprised me. Height was good for a volleyball team, but not everybody needed to be tall. I could dig and set, both important skills. Not all tall people did those well. My serve wasn't powerful, but I sent the ball floating over the net most every time.

"Hey, shrimp." I glanced up from the sidelines. One of the tall girls —she must have been close to six feet—pointed to the open spot in the front row. "Here. Five-one. Set a little behind me. *Capisce?*"

Five-one meant always moving to front and center after the serve, regardless of the rotation. I stood with my back to the net, waiting for the other team to serve. No point in my trying to block. The first three times our back row returned the ball. Tall Girl scowled at them. The next time they passed the ball to me, but way off-center. She started her jump even as I reached the ball. I thought the set would be too late, but she connected on the up-arc and spiked.

The boy on the other side of me didn't play nearly as well as Tall Girl. He kept getting called for carrying. She scolded him a few times, and then threw up her hands. The other girl on the team played okay. She was almost as tall as Tall Girl, but not as aggressive. She smiled more, too.

At the end of the game Tall Girl walked to the sidelines and spoke with a boy who had arrived during our practice. She pointed at me, and the boy nodded his head. She beckoned to me, so I went to find out what they wanted. "Gary's our team captain. Rules say we need three girls. You're our third."

I put on my friendliest grin. The team wasn't the greatest, but I kind of liked Tall Girl. "Thanks."

Gary narrowed his eyes and shook his head. "You're Jameson, aren't you?"

"My name's Jamie."

"We need three girls. We already have four boys."

Tall Girl didn't appear to understand. She scowled at him, hands on her hips. "I want her on the team."

Gary shook his head. "No. He's a boy. He lived in Eaton Hall last year. We need three girls."

Her darkening eyes scanned me again. "That true?"

I shrugged and walked away.

* * * *

Dark clouds hovered over the elfin princess in the entryway mirror. She scowled at me as I kicked off my shoes and nudged them to the side. "I'm sorry, okay?" I wasn't a boy, but I had no experience being a girl either. Sometimes reality didn't quite meet my expectations. I went to my room and waited until I had cooled down before making my way to the kitchen.

Lisa stood by the pantry, putting groceries away. She smiled in greeting. "Sean's back. Would you mind making spaghetti sauce tonight?"

Ooh! Now I could ask him to teach me to ride. I washed my hands in the kitchen sink. "I don't mind. Do we have everything?"

"I think so. You use wine in your sauce, don't you? Is Chianti all right? There's half a bottle left. Otherwise I'll need to open something else."

"Chianti's okay." I smiled and pulled ingredients out of the refrigerator, humming to myself.

After a month of living with Lisa, I was still sensitive about my gender issues. She never got on my case, but she appeared to find it all amusing. "Do you find cooking soothing?" she asked, peeking over my shoulder.

"Yeah. I guess so."

"I'm not fond of it, but I think most women are."

I frowned at her while opening a can of tomatoes. "Please don't start with the gender nudges today. I have enough problems already."

Her face snapped from teasing to genuine concern in an instant. "I'm sorry. What happened?"

"Dad says my IQ tested out at one-sixty-something, but the minute I'm a girl no one thinks I have a brain." I twisted open a jar of mushrooms with a snap and set it down a little harder than I meant. "And I was mad and not paying attention, so I walked into the men's room."

Lisa's face contorted. She put a hand over her mouth, but didn't quite laugh. "I'm sorry." She grabbed my elbow. "Come on. Let's talk."

"How can I keep my grades up if everyone assumes I'm stupid?"

"You actually want my opinion?"

"Yeah."

"You wear jeans every day. You look younger than you are. No one gives a hoot what a twelve-year-old tomboy thinks."

"Okay. So…"

"So we need to mature you a bit. Wait here." She disappeared into her bedroom and returned with her makeup case and a lighted mirror. After she'd unpacked some things and set up, she motioned for me to sit down. "You wear lipstick and a little mascara, right?"

"Yeah."

"Subtle is good, but you're fading into the woodwork. Let me show you seventeen."

In the mirror I watched Lisa remove my makeup and start over. As she worked, she explained how each item was used. The transformation amazed me. I wondered how long it would take me to learn to duplicate her work.

Lisa packed her case and put away the mirror. "I have a sundress that's too small for me. The top is smocked, so the bust should fit you."

The hem of the dress, as it turned out, didn't quite reach my fingertips. "Pretty, but way too short."

Lisa smiled and shook her head. "You can't replace something with nothing. To break your old habits you need to leave your comfort zone. If you're self-conscious about your clothes, you won't be walking into the men's room." She smiled and leaned against the counter. "By the time you're comfortable with short skirts, your new habits will already be established."

"And my grades?"

"Your clothes, hair, and makeup are as important as what you say. A smart girl nods her pretty little head and agrees with the professor."

"Lisa, that's disgusting."

"That's the way life is, Jamie. Learning the material isn't enough for a woman. Most professors care more about how you look than what you think. Swallow your pride. Once you graduate, you'll forget all about them. You're pretty. Use that to your advantage." Lisa winked at me. "Remember to smile and your grades will be fine." She patted my arm and walked away.

Rather than change out of the dress, I threw on an apron and went back to my spaghetti sauce, wondering what Mom would say if Alicia wore a dress so short. I'd gone from *Things Boys Do* to short skirts and fancy makeup. Was I capable of putting my heart into being a boy?

The front door opened as I arranged the last of the silverware. With several days' growth of beard and a dark tan, Sean might have passed for a castaway only recently rescued. Eyes of steel-blue fire flared in surprise and, I thought, joy. He was only a friend, but happy little butterflies swarmed in my stomach and fire burned on my cheeks. I opened my mouth, no doubt to insert my foot, but Lisa rushed to the rescue, running to hug her brother.

"I'm so glad you're back!" She grabbed his hand and pulled him toward the kitchen, grinning. "Let me introduce my new roommate."

When I walked out from behind the table, a long-legged elfin princess reflected in those steel-blue eyes.

A cool draft against my legs brought warmth to my cheeks. I stepped back behind the kitchen counter, but Sean walked around it. "Don't hide. You're rather fetching in that dress." He hugged me, and then stood back. "That hairstyle suits you perfectly—changed your mind, then?"

Had I changed my mind? It's not polite to stare, but those blue eyes refused to let me go.

"Shall we talk over supper?" Lisa nudged Sean over to a seat, and then drained the spaghetti. I put the sauce on a trivet and got salad and sodas out of the refrigerator.

Sean blessed the food. His hand lingered on mine until Lisa grinned and passed me the salad. "Why don't you tell him what happened?"

"I—" Had I forgotten my love so soon? How could Sean slide so easily into that place in my heart only Tyler should occupy? "Some things I can only do as a girl." Sean grinned in a way that made my pulse throb, and my cheeks heat up again. *Ooh!* I shut my eyes to avoid his. "Dad's list says to get a motorcycle." I passed *Things Boys Do* across the table to him. "My birth certificate says Jamie, so I need to be a girl to get my license."

"You're legally female, then?"

"Yeah. They corrected my birth certificate. I was hoping you would teach me to ride a motorcycle."

His blue eyes shone like a clear summer day. "This says you can drive a sports car instead. I'd be pleased to help you find one."

"With insurance and all, a car would be too expensive."

"I might be willing to help you with that."

Lisa glanced at her brother, clearly as surprised as I was. What would I do at the end of the semester if Sean helped me pay for my car? I sighed and shook my head. "I can't."

"So you're set on a motorbike, then?"

"I have to, Sean."

Azure eyes locked on mine again. "I'm pretty busy. How long do you have?"

"I want my license before the semester's over."

His warm smile fled, leaving only sadness. "Then back to boy land, I suppose."

"Yeah."

"What if I say no?"

I closed my eyes, hoping to head off tears. "I'll teach myself. It can't be that hard."

A heavy overcast dulled his eyes to gray. "You're right, there. Riding's easy. Staying alive's the difficult part."

I pushed a bit of spaghetti around with my fork. The last thing I wanted was to argue with a friend. I forced a deep breath in and a long exhale. "Please, Sean."

"You'll do exactly as I say?"

Such intensity emanated from his face, I had to look away. "Yeah."

A hand rested on mine, forcing my eyes back to his. "I want your word."

It wasn't like it was a marriage vow. Why the formality? "Yes, sir."

"Very well, then. If you're finished eating, let's have a look at my bike."

"I'll clear the table and put on some jeans." I pushed back my chair, grabbed my plate, and took a step toward the kitchen.

"You're fine as you are."

I glanced back, but Sean was already headed for the door. "Sean, wait."

Lisa grinned and shook her head. "I'll get the dishes. You go ahead."

I hurried after Sean, struggling to catch up. He led me to the carport. Sitting on his Harley, he demonstrated the brakes, and clutch, and gear shifter, and all, while I leaned against the side of Lisa's Firebird and watched.

Faded images of Tyler, like wayward ghosts, echoed through the carport. The two of us walking hand-in-hand along the beach until my skin stung from salt and sun. My arms encircling my love's waist, holding tight as his Kawasaki raced the wind. Handsome in his uniform, my soldier-boy kissing me and turning to go. "I miss you," I whispered as he faded away. A single errant tear ran down my face.

Sean brushed a sad memory from my cheek and kissed the wet trail my sorrow had left in its wake. "Here, now." His arms drew me close, a hand pulling my head against his shoulder. Drops of sorrow I shed, longing for my father to hold his little girl so, to brush away my tears. Arms around Sean's waist, my heart cried to God for comfort.

When the storm of my emotions had passed and the clouds parted, Sean brushed the wet hair from my eyes. I meant to kiss his cheek, you know, but he turned his head and the elfin princess pressed her lips against his, a light touch of innocence that left us both without words.

Amused blue eyes smiled. His hand brushed my side, electric in its gentleness. I stepped back and studied his face. He'd always been kind, but the depth of his tenderness captivated me.

"Go change and we'll ride out to Crandon Park," he said.

I shook my head to clear away the cobwebs, and headed for my room. By the time I returned, Sean had a helmet waiting for me. I strapped it on, climbed on the seat behind him, and wrapped my arms around his waist.

The elfin princess wasn't stupid, but sometimes her heart led where her mind refused to go. The clatter of Tyler's dog tags still echoed in my ears. Another boyfriend would be utter foolishness. I leaned my head against Sean's back and savored the ride.

⚘ 24 ⚘

Lisa told me five women belonged to her little sorority, but only three could show up for my interview. The rest would meet me some other time. Too nervous to do much else, I sat with my nose in a book, reading the same page again and again, comprehending nothing. I glanced at the elfin princess in the living room mirror. She smiled at me, her face pale.

Voices in the entryway alerted me to the ladies' arrival. With one last glance at the mirror, I rose to meet them.

One of the women I recognized from volleyball. I didn't remember her name, but Tall Girl was one of the most assertive people I'd ever met. Sharon introduced her as Donya.

"Hi. I think we met on the intramural field."

Donya appeared surprised and more than a little peeved. She brushed right past me, frowning. "You can't be serious, Lisa. Gary says this kid was a boy last year."

Lisa grinned and put a hand on Donya's arm. "Chill. I met Jamie her freshman year, when she was living as Jameson. She meets the qualifications."

"Doesn't seem much like a boy to me," said the other woman.

Lisa glanced at me and extended a hand toward her. "This is Aiko."

Lightning danced through the dark clouds between Donya and Lisa. Donya scowled at me. "No, Lisa. No boys. No girls who used to be boys."

I took a step back and glanced toward my bedroom door. Confrontation always made me want to run and hide. "That's okay, Lisa. I don't want to cause any—"

Lisa grabbed my arm as I turned to flee. "No. Wait." Then her voice turned harsh. "I'm sponsoring her. You can't vote before you hear her story."

"I don't need to vote. The rules say no." A low rumble of thunder rolled through the room. Donya plopped down on the couch and crossed her arms.

Lisa sighed and turned to the other woman. "Aiko?"

Aiko scanned the ceiling as though searching for the answer. "The rules state that an applicant must identify as female. There's nothing about past gender changes. Or future for that matter."

Lightning still charged the air around Donya. "Let's get this over with then, so I can go home."

Lisa slid open the glass door to the Florida room and turned to me. "Shower and go sit in the hot tub. I'll join you as soon as I put out some refreshments."

Interview in a hot tub? Whatever. Wide-eyed, I studied the women for a moment before I headed for my room. Behind me the air continued to crackle.

At the door to my room I turned back. "Can I borrow a swimsuit?"

"No clothes!" Was that Donya, or had Lisa run out of patience?

Well, I could always wait until they all left before I got out, or turn my back and wrap a towel around myself.

The shower in the guest bath was the kind that could drown you if you weren't paying attention. The torrent of water massaged my tense muscles until I was ready to fall asleep before I even got into the hot tub. After I showered, I grabbed a *yukata* and walked to the Florida room. The tub appeared to seat six people. I climbed into one end and eased down into the water. It was comfortably hot, the jets gently stirring the surface.

A moment later Lisa walked into the room, so I closed my eyes and rested my head. She laughed, a clear, high-pitched musical sound. "You can look now. This is a ritual of sorts that helps us bond. There are no secrets between us."

When I opened my eyes, she was seated across from me, shoulder deep in water. She'd said my membership required a unanimous vote of the women attending. Why sit in the tub if Donya had already made up her mind? How could telling her about my condition make things any better? "Donya and me bond?"

Lisa chuckled. "She's always like this. Don't worry about her."

Aiko took a seat next to me. Donya joined us last of all, dark clouds still trailing her. As soon as Donya settled in, Lisa nodded. "Well. Let's get started then," she said in a light, musical voice. "I'm sponsoring Jamie. She has a genetic condition called Mixed Gonadal Dysgenesis. It resulted in short stature, a triangular face, and a certain amount of sexual ambiguity. Go ahead and stand up, Jamie."

She was so nonchalant. Did she mean to calm my nerves or give me a heart attack? My eyes pleaded with her for a way out, but she shook her head. "We have no secrets here." Then she stood. "Look at me," she commanded in a gentle voice.

Lisa had a gorgeous figure, but what I saw as the water dripped away, were the scars, one on either side of her abdomen. My heart convulsed in my chest. She had two little white lines like mine. Then I noticed she had only a small wisp of pubic hair. A muscle in my leg twitched. Ripples expanded across my vision. I trembled as my world fought to establish a new equilibrium. As different as our bodies were, I understood, for the first time in my life, that other people like me existed.

Lisa appeared to be amused by my discomfort. She continued as if discussing the latest fashion trend. "Everyone thought I was a normal girl. Even my doctor. At puberty I developed like one, but at sixteen I still hadn't gotten my period, so my mother took me to a specialist. He discovered that the lumps in my abdomen were testes. My condition is called Testicular Feminization. My body's androgen insensitive, so even though I had testes, my genitals turned out female." She held out a hand and helped me to my feet. "My body converted enough testosterone to estrogen to give me a normal female shape at puberty. Finding out I was intersex was too much for my boyfriend; he left me. I freaked out and ended up seriously depressed for several months. Even now I find my condition hard to accept sometimes. You don't have the same thing, but it's still comforting to meet someone else—and find you're just a normal person."

"I'm normal?" A bit hysterical, I laughed the tears out of my eyes.

"You know what I mean," she said with a warm smile and sat down again.

Donya stood then. She had the same little white lines, but almost as much pubic hair as me. "I have a partial form of Testicular Feminization, so instead of being born with normal male genitals, I had a small phallus

—more than what you've got—with the urethral opening on the side of the shaft near the base." Lightning and hail surrounded her head as she spoke through clenched teeth. "The doctors removed it and performed vaginal surgery."

My eyes went wide. When she sat down, I stood still, my mouth working, but no sound coming out.

Aiko stood and nodded. "Testicular Feminization is related to the X chromosome. When it's not a spontaneous mutation, it's inherited from a mother who's a carrier. Lisa and I are sisters. We're both androgen insensitive. We also have two sisters who are XX. Either one may be a carrier." She smiled and sat down again.

In the glass wall of the Florida room the elfin princess stared at me, eyes wide and glassy. She didn't believe in hermaphrodites. I didn't have the heart to tell her elfin princesses didn't exist either. Would five mythical creatures in one spot be too much for the space-time continuum?

"So, kiddo, why were you living as a boy?" Wisps of cloud still hung over Donya's head, but the storm had passed.

"My parents want me to be a boy. The doctors keep telling them it's too late to be a girl."

Donya said something not nice about doctors. Nobody said anything else, so I sat down.

"Without objection, membership is approved," whispered Lisa.

I leaned my head back and studied Lisa's face. It was great that I wasn't alone. The other ladies were friends. They weren't freaks; maybe I wasn't either.

A sudden ray of sunshine burned a hole through the clouds, lighting Donya's face. "You still wanna play volleyball?"

"Yeah."

"Gary's pretty good, but the other guys on our team suck, and he's not willing to do anything about them. The other two girls would stick with me if I left to form a new team."

"I'm in." I smiled and glanced at Lisa.

Both she and Aiko eventually nodded. Donya's sunshine burned bright. Kind of scary, actually.

I studied Lisa. How could I tell myself I wasn't a hermaphrodite now that I lived with one? Every time I saw one of my little circle, I was going to be reminded of my own condition. Eyes closed, I let my muscles relax. Friends were worth their cost.

"Did you win the Kramer case?" I popped my eyes open. Lisa appeared to be talking to Aiko.

Her sister shook her head. "No. I tried to tell them months ago what evidence they'd need if they ended up in court, but they wouldn't listen. She lost custody because she was too lazy to keep records."

"Oh! I'm sorry. She's really sweet."

"Yes, but judges don't care about personality."

Lisa's eyes turned to me. "She's a law student. Tell her about your father's list."

I shrugged, not wanting to talk about it. "My dad gave me a list of stuff he wants me to do is all."

Lisa's brow twisted down in anger. "Her father wants her to have sex with a girl. Isn't that child abuse?"

Aiko tilted her head back, as though studying the ceiling. "No. That sucks, but it's not abuse. The law's pretty weak about that. Her only option is to leave home. Sitting in a hot tub at a friend's house has got to be better than being a runaway."

* * * *

"Class dismissed. Miss Kirkpatrick, please see me before you leave."

Professor Pennington had walked in at the beginning of class and announced that she was our new instructor. At registration I'd made sure to avoid any of Jameson's old teachers, but I hadn't counted on Professor Bledsoe getting sick.

"So you took your own advice," she said as I walked up to her.

"Ma'am?"

"Weren't you a boy last year?"

Professor Pennington liked to hand out embarrassing assignments. The previous year she'd made me give a speech explaining why being a girl was better. In the weeks after Tyler's helicopter had gone down, I hadn't cared much about school, or even life, so I'd given the speech as a girl— hair in pigtails, earrings, dress, and all. Got an A. I grinned at her and shrugged. "Words are powerful. You should be more careful what you tell people to write."

She nodded and smiled at me. "Are you happier now?"

"Yes." I shrugged and walked out the door, smiling at the sun's warmth on my face. The weather in Miami never got old, not even with the heat and humidity. My next period was free and Sean was meeting me, so I found an empty bench and started reading.

A while later a shadow interrupted my concentration. "Weren't you in Creative Writing?"

A guy with black-rimmed glasses stood in front of me, holding a book in one hand. He looked older than Frank, and I didn't remember his face, but I tried to be polite anyway. And besides, the notebook sitting next to me on the bench said Creative Writing right on the cover. "Yes."

"You're good with English rules and stuff?"

"Yeah." Okay, so I should have enunciated a little better.

"Would you mind taking a quick look at my term paper?"

He seemed like a nice enough guy. "Sure. Why not?" I held out a hand.

"I'm sorry, but I left my stuff at my apartment."

I thought about showing him one of Donya's *What kind of moron are you?* stares, but I wasn't sure he'd get it. "Drop by tomorrow. I should be here."

"My paper's due in the morning. The apartment's not far… Please?"

"I have to meet someone in about fifteen minutes."

"You'll be back in time."

He sounded like he was gonna whine for the next ten minutes if I didn't go with him. "Okay." He took off, and I struggled to keep up as we headed toward Ponce. I glanced at the paperback in his hand. "Is your book any good?"

He stopped and leered at me. Well, that's what it looked like. "*Lolita?* Have you read it?"

Now why would I ask if I'd already read the book? I decided to go ahead and give him one of Donya's stares. "No. What's it about?"

"A girl like you."

"Like me?"

He glanced at me. "I'll explain when we get to my apartment."

A vehicle heading south on Ponce whizzed by, slowed, and circled back as we crossed the street. The car looked like Sean's Cortina, so I stopped and waited. The guy I was following grabbed my hand. "Come on. South Dixie's clear. Let's get across."

I shook my hand free when I recognized Sean. "Let me find out what he wants first."

Sean pulled up to the curb, so I walked around to the driver's side. He was sweet, but he treated every stranger like a potential threat. "Who's your friend there?"

I glanced at the guy in the black glasses and blinked when I realized I hadn't asked his name. "I was only gonna check his term paper. We'll be back in a few minutes."

Those steel-blue eyes of his turned three shades darker, almost a solid gray. "You were leaving campus alone with someone you don't know?"

Black Glasses stood by the crossing, fidgeting. Lisa had warned me to be more careful. "Any guy worth knowing will understand when you refuse to be alone with him," she'd said. I couldn't think of anything better to say, so I made a sorry face.

Sean nodded, blue eyes happy again. "Let's go get your license."

I yelled to Black Glasses, "I'll check your paper first thing in the morning if you'll meet me at the same bench," and climbed into the driver's seat.

The Cortina brought a smile to both of our faces every time I drove it. Outside, the car was an old compact Ford your grandmother might drive. Inside waited a Lotus, longing to be raced. I picked up on driving a stick right away, even learning to shift without the clutch and all. Sean said I was born to it.

He didn't say that about me when I drove his Harley. Sean didn't close his eyes, but he didn't smile either. I never pranged his XLCH, you know, or dumped it. Well, I did lay the bike down on the grass once, but it wasn't running or anything. The kickstand sank into the ground and I couldn't hold the bike up.

Most of the time we just rode places on his Sportster, me on the back, arms wrapped around him. He said I needed to build up my confidence, and balance, and all, but I think he just liked spending time together. I know I did.

You only needed one driver's license in Florida, and when Sean pointed out that *Things Boys Do* didn't actually say I needed to own a sports car, I agreed to take my test in the Cortina instead of on his Harley. Sean smiled like he thought I might have killed myself on his bike. Even the examiner smiled when I passed my test. As Kaylah would say, "So there you are."

* * * *

Sharon's Toyota in the driveway meant she should be home. I pressed the bell again. When she finally answered the door, she apologized. "Have you been out here long? I was using the blow dryer."

She waved me in and over to the kitchen table. "Have a seat for a minute." She picked up a manila folder and flipped through some papers. "My father asked me to talk to you about Tyler's estate."

Had he actually been gone only six months? Tyler had drifted so far away. Fondness for him still held a place in my heart, but the pain of loss had receded, and the fire had cooled. A new love had replaced the old, heedless of my brain's objections. Where bamboo shoots had once exploded with life, a young oak put down deep roots. I dreaded the day when my newfound love kissed me farewell and put me on a bus for boy land. The dream had to end soon, but did he actually believe it? I prayed that Sean and I would part without too much sorrow when the semester ended.

Sharon picked up a set of keys lying on the kitchen table and placed them in my hand. Before letting go, she said, "Tyler left you his motorcycle. Promise me you'll sell it."

An odd mix of fear, excitement, and adrenaline welled up out of my gut. Sean's XLCH might have been as fast as Tyler's Kawasaki, but something about the scream of a Mach III induced an addictive rush of terror that the Harley's rumble didn't. Sean would kill me if I rode it. If I didn't kill myself on it first. My trembling hand dropped the keys on the kitchen table. "Can I leave it here for now?"

"Sure!" Relief swept across her face. Why didn't anybody trust me on a bike?

⚛ 25 ⚘

I shook my head at Sean and dabbed at my runny nose. "I'm not really up to going out right now. I've got a virus or something." My futon beckoned. Home was the best place to be on such a dreary day, anyway. Outside, the wind blew dark clouds across the sky, threatening rain.

"Come on. The fresh air will do you good, and you need the experience of riding in bad weather."

So I climbed on the bike and rested my head against his back. A few days earlier he'd said we'd ridden more than a thousand miles together. I closed my eyes and let dreams overtake me, sure I could ride in my sleep.

The rain came and Sean pulled into the shelter of an overpass and shut the engine off. Low cumulus clouds had turned from gray to black and green. "We'll wait out the storm here." He led me up the cement incline to a spot clear of debris and out of the wind.

My head against his shoulder, I closed my eyes. "Wake me when the war's over. Okay?" He leaned back against the embankment and pulled me closer. I imagined the two of us together as I drifted off to sleep.

An arc of fire outside the window lit the room; thunder shook the house. The elfin princess hopped up out of bed and checked on Rachael to make sure she was okay, but like her mother, the child had learned to sleep through thunderstorms, content in the hands of a merciful God. Mommy returned to bed, resting her head on her husband's shoulder, one leg and one arm sprawled across his body. Gliding my fingers across his chest, I lay awake and prayed for my family, telling God about my longing for another child. My husband stirred and the little princess stroked his face with her fingertips. "Can we have another baby, Sean?"

He gazed at his princess, eyes twinkling with amusement and whispered, "Of course."

Another flash-crack-boom overwhelmed sight and sound. Dazed, and hair alive with static, I sat up. Beyond the shelter of our overpass, angry black clouds boiled, throwing rain and lightning bolts earthward. Sean's Harley stood guard on the blacktop shoulder below us. *Ooh!* I bit my lip and eased my head around. Amusement frolicked with fondness across Sean's lips and eyes. "Another, is it? How many children do we have then?"

The heat in my cheeks spoke of a bright red face. *Akane*, as *Okaa-san* would say. "Only one. Rachael's fifteen months old."

Sean put his arm around me when bits of dirt blew into my eyes and they started tearing up. "She's the toddler you took care of on Saint Andrew's?"

"Yes."

Sean pulled me closer. "Why don't you go visit her then?"

"My cousin says it's not right for me to disrupt her life. She needs stability."

"And they won't let you adopt until you're married," he whispered into the silence between thunderclaps.

I wanted to do a number of different things right then, but I closed my eyes and listened to the rain soak into my soul. My life seemed to be stuck in somebody else's tragedy.

He brushed the hair away from my eyes and kissed his little princess right on the lips. "I'm going back to school next term. To finish my degree."

My eyes popped open. "That's—" Blue patches had begun to appear in the distant sky, but steel-blue eyes reflected rain. "Here?"

"Edinburgh."

"As in Scotland?"

"Aye. I wish I'd known you were so fond of me." He kissed me again, with more passion. "Married, were we then?"

Only weeks remained before I had to move back to Eaton Hall and work on *Things Boys Do* as a boy. At least Sean might hurt less if he were the one who said goodbye first. "Yes. When do you leave?"

"Next week."

I worried about the little princess, you know. She cried way too much.

* * * *

Whatever I accomplished in a day, working on Dad's *Things Boys Do* list, whatever I learned about being a boy, each night before I went to bed, I followed the *Vaginal Dilation Protocol* that Dr. Cameron had written. His instructions specified how many days for a particular step and how long to hold the dilator in place each day. On my back, with my legs spread apart, I applied a bit of KY Jelly to the tip of the rod and slid it in. As much as I tried not to think about what I was doing, the increasing diameter and depth of penetration whispered "girl" straight into my soul.

A soft knock on the door and Lisa poked her head into the room. "You're awake. Good."

Ooh! My legs twitched, my hand slipped, and a muscle spasm spit the dilator out. "Unh!"

"Donya's coming over. She needs to talk. Would you mind staying up?"

I laughed. Six months earlier I'd roomed with Frank and thought I was a boy. Now I lived with a girl who didn't even blink when she discovered me with a plastic rod stuck up my vagina. I cleaned myself and the rod with a washcloth and threw on my robe. "Is she okay?"

"She gets stressed out by doctor visits. A little hand-holding and she'll be fine." She walked to the dresser and touched my box of dilators. "May I?"

"Yeah."

She picked up the box, looked at a few of the dilators, and examined the *Vaginal Dilation Protocol* instructions. "Which one did you start with?"

"The smallest." Even that one was larger than my little post.

"Outstanding. I'm so glad you didn't need surgery." She set the box back on the dresser.

"Yeah. Mom says surgery sucks."

"Donya had a McIndoe procedure. The doctors used a skin graft to line her vaginal canal. Her vagina wants to shrink, so she needs to be aggressive about dilation."

"Is she?"

"No. She doesn't like dilating, and if she shrinks much more, she'll need surgery again. Her doctors are always on her about that and keep pushing her to get a boyfriend."

"Boyfriend?"

"Yes. She's not as feminine as they'd like, either. I guess they think a boyfriend would solve both problems."

Ooh!

Lisa grinned at my embarrassment. "You'll find it much more pleas-ant to let a boy dilate you." She picked up one end of the rod I'd been using and let it fall back into the box with a clunk. "My brother's fond of you. I think he's still a virgin, but he might be willing to help you now that you're far enough along. For medical purposes only, of course."

Ooh! I glanced at the mirror. Green fire smoldered in the eyes of the elfin princess. The fact that Sean and I couldn't have intercourse had always sort of reassured me, allowing me to flirt without worry. I didn't have a strong sex drive, but having intercourse would make me a normal girl—or at least a normal bad girl.

"Would you like me to talk to him for you?"

I tried to sound nonchalant, but my eyes went wide, and I swallowed. "No," I whispered. I certainly didn't need Sean thinking about sex.

* * * *

British Racing Green. That's what Sean said anyway. The elfin princess didn't call the color that, but she liked it. Well, in satin, at least. It reminded her of the first buds on a young laurel tree. The flouncy sleeves of my dress brushed the insides of my elbows. The hem just reached my fingertips. I spun around to see how the skirt would fly.

Lisa did my French braid, and makeup, and all, so I only needed a final check. Everything had to be perfect for Sean's going-away party. I grinned at the girl in the mirror. I liked being pretty, but I didn't dress fancy very often. Too much work. Lisa called it my gender bounce. Tomboy in jeans one day. Princess in a short skirt and makeup the next. She didn't think Donya's doctor would approve. Like I cared.

The phone rang while I was touching up my lipstick. We didn't need to leave for a while yet, so I answered it. "Wow. Dad. Hi!"

"Jameson? You sound like your sister."

"I'm still a soprano, Dad. Dr. Stewart won't give me testosterone until summer."

"You went to her in a dress. What did you expect?"

Well, whose fault was that? "Are you home for long?"

"A month unless something comes up. *Détente*'s been messy lately. The folks in DC are nervous—Is your hair short?"

The elfin princess smirked at me from the mirror. Her hair was past shoulder length again, at least in the back. "Lisa promised to cut it when we get home tonight. She trims it for me every six weeks. Hey, Dad, we're going to a banquet tonight. Sean's company is throwing a party in his honor."

"See? I thought you could do it."

"Do what?"

"Go out with your roommate. Dating's on the list I gave you."

I glanced at Lisa. "*Date a girl*. Yeah. Okay." Lisa pointed at her wrist. "Dad, Lisa says we gotta go now. Love you."

As Lisa walked past, she grinned. "A date, hmm? I'll keep that in mind tonight."

While sitting in the front seat of Lisa's Firebird, I thought about how much wearing skirts had changed my habits. You couldn't get in and out of a car in a dress the way you did in blue jeans. Or sit on a couch. Or pick something up. I might not have worn short skirts every day, but my body had learned to act like I did. How long would *that* take to fix when I went back to being a boy?

Sean greeted us in the lobby and led us to a large room overlooking the ocean. As people arrived, he introduced his sister and me to them. After the third small group had chatted with us and moved on, Lisa elbowed me and nodded toward the hall. I followed her to the ladies' room, wondering what was bugging her.

"What is your problem, Jamie? You're acting like the Ice Queen out there." Anger and concern struggled across her face.

In the mirror, Lisa stood next to the elfin princess. Both stared at me until I turned away in shame. "I'm sorry, but my coach will be a pumpkin again soon."

That brought a sad smile to her face. "Be sure you leave a glass slipper for him then."

"I'm supposed to be a boy, Lisa."

"Midnight is hours away."

"It's only a fairy tale."

"Yes. Let your imagination run free while you can. Give him something to cherish. I don't think you'll have another chance."

"Thanks, Lisa." I hugged her and headed back to the party.

I found Sean chatting with some old guy. The little princess walked right up and snuggled, slinking an arm around Sean's waist inside his coat. "You're not talking about work again, are you?"

Steel-blue eyes studied mine as my heart thumped in my throat. Reflected in his sea of blue, an elfin princess smiled emerald green, eyes only for him. More than his eyes smiled, you know. "Jamie, I'd like you to meet Sheldon Steinburg. He oversees hotel operations."

I tore my eyes away from Sean long enough to take in Mr. Steinburg's wavy silver hair and dark tan. He had the sort of face that made you want to be polite. When he kissed my hand, I bobbed my head and pulled Sean tighter. "Good to meet you, sir." Relief swept through me when his eyes dismissed me, and he continued his conversation with Sean.

Some time later, a man in a chef's hat whispered to Mr. Steinburg. After a quiet conversation, the two men left. Blue eyes met mine again. "What changed?"

"A friend reminded me the night is still young."

He kissed me, lightly. "Come with me."

Parting wasn't going to be so easy. "To Scotland? I can't."

"Why not?"

Lisa interrupted, nudging us toward the buffet. "Come on. Let's eat. You two lovebirds can talk later."

The three of us gathered at a small table off in one corner. After Sean prayed for our food, his eyes found mine again. "No more dreams of us together then?"

"I'm not allowed, Sean. I have to be a boy next semester."

"A boy, is it?" Mirth brightened steel-blue to aqua. He brushed his fingertips up my bare leg, his tenderness sending a warm tsunami through my body. "My touch has no effect on you then?"

All my senses went on full alert. Words got all caught up in my brain, so the little princess shook her head several times and made big eyes at him.

"I have one semester of school left and an internship to complete. Then we'll marry and adopt a house full of little ones."

"Dad would never let us marry."

Sean put a hand on my cheek and kissed me. "Scotland will let us marry without his consent."

"I gave him my word."

"You've completed a number of things on his list."

"Sean, do I look like I've tried to be a boy?"

He gripped me by the arms, anger flaring across his face. "There's nothing—you hear me?—nothing you can do to be a boy. All you'll do is ruin your life, and I don't want to witness that."

I bit my lip until I tasted blood, struggling not to cave to what he—what my heart—wanted. Keeping my promise to my father would cost me all I cared about.

❦ 26 ❧

Farewells at the airport were quiet. Sean kissed me goodbye, but we stared at each other in silence until the final boarding call. Lisa hugged me and followed her brother. She was spending a few weeks in Scotland with her family. "You should be the one going with him," she whispered.

I turned away before I could agree with her, afraid I'd end up on the plane.

Back at the house I sorted through my things. The girl clothes I left in the closet with a note to Lisa saying she could give them to the Salvation Army. The photos of Rachael, Sean, and the circle I placed in a box with my schoolbooks.

Sharon had thrown out all my Jameson clothes. They were hopeless anyway, so I set out the jeans and tops I thought a boy might get by with wearing. I'd buy something more masculine later, maybe some loose-fitting jeans and shirts that wouldn't show my curves.

I picked up Sofie and held her, remembering the day I had gotten her. As long as I kept my doll, as long as I cherished memories of a girl's childhood, I'd never be a boy. A wastebasket sat in the closet; it was as simple as leaving her there. I set Sofie on the dresser and straightened her skirt. Lisa could give her to the Salvation Army after I left.

After I finished packing, I flopped down on the couch and opened *The Left Hand of Darkness*. Some books took forever to read, not because of their poor quality, but because they struck too close to home. In the Hainish Cycle, Le Guin had captured at least some of the sense of otherness that overshadowed my life, that drove me away from acknowledging my condition, even to myself at times.

I read a few pages and set the book on the coffee table. *Darkness* was too much, what with me being days away from living as a boy again. I picked up the tattered *Things Boys Do*, instead. Already etched into my memory, I scanned the list again anyway. *Date a girl, Sleep with a girl, Drink,* and *Smoke* were all that remained. Except *Register for the draft* and *Go back on hormones*, of course, which they wouldn't let me do yet, and *Cut your hair short*, which was due again. Depression enfolded me as I lay down.

I'd almost dozed off when the doorbell chimed. Not expecting anybody, I ignored it. Twice. Three times. Somebody started pounding at the door, so I got up.

A young woman stood on the porch. Tall and beautiful. Hair in an upswept style, makeup, high heels, and a pretty dress, like she was going on a hot date. "Donya?" I stared, having never seen her in a dress.

"May I come in?" She brushed past me, strode into the kitchen, and set a brown paper bag on the counter.

"You have a date? You're pretty, you know, with makeup and all."

"Thanks. I do clean up nice, don't I?" Donya transferred several items from the bag to the refrigerator, folded the bag, and stuck it into the pantry. "I figure if you can pretend to be a boy for a semester, I can be a normal girl for one night." She sat on the living room couch and picked up *Things Boys Do*.

Not wanting another lecture, I sat next to her and reached for the list. "Don't you have a date?"

She grinned, holding the list out of reach. "Yeah. I do... When you finish this stupidity, you'll come back to your friends and be a girl?"

Her soft tone threw me. Did she care? "Yes. If I still can...Why?" What was she up to?

"So let's put the list to rest tonight."

A last-minute attempt to talk me out of being a boy? Both hands raised in front of me, I shook my head. I didn't want to argue. "I don't—"

"Come on, Jamie." Donya grimaced, thrust the list in my face, and pointed to *Sleep with a girl*. "Don't play stupid. You and me. Tonight. Let's check off the rest of these boxes."

My brain was still somewhere between *The Left Hand of Darkness* and inviting a friend into the house. The girl who ridiculed me whenever I talked about being a boy wanted to sleep with me? "Why?"

She flashed me a *What kind of moron are you?* scowl. "I'm trying to keep a friend from ruining her life. Do you wanna do this or not?"

I stared at the *Things Boys Do* list, trying to think. Even though I put on a brave front, in all honesty, I really didn't think I'd ever finish the list. At the most, I would cut my hair and chug down a few beers, hoping Dad would relent before I started taking testosterone injections again. If I had all the other boxes checked off, perhaps I could avoid the shots. Sleeping with a girl wouldn't kill me; the shots might as well. From under my brows I gazed at the wall mirror. The elfin princess stared at me, eyes full of anger. "*Bás thar easonóir*," she hissed.

I tore my eyes away. She was right. Dad's little princess should have told him she had to obey God rather than man. My heart lacked the courage to refuse my father to his face, so my only choice was between spreading the list out over the year, and completing it in one night. Either way, I'd have to live with my shame forever. With Donya's help I might at least avoid the shots. "I'll go get the clippers."

"Your hair can wait 'til morning. If I'm gonna be your girlfriend tonight, you gotta be yourself."

Would *Sleep with a girl* count if Donya treated me as a girl? I would still be a boy, right? Who was I kidding? My faie-girl body having sex as a boy? It struck me that I might finish the list, but none of the items would be checked off by a boy. So what was the point?

Donya was smiling, but she seemed as nervous as me. She arranged my hair just so. Then she nodded toward the Florida room. "Come on. We'll smoke out there."

"I get nauseous around cigarettes," I protested.

She rolled her eyes, closed the sliding door behind us, and sat on the wicker couch. "This blend actually helps get rid of nausea." When I sat next to her, she put a hand on mine and said, "It'll help you relax. All right?"

Donya pulled a long-stemmed pipe out of her purse. Its ornate wooden bowl, carved with elk, reminded me of an elfin hunting pipe Kaylah had shown me once. Donya packed the bowl from a small zippered pouch and lit the pipe, drawing several quick mouthfuls of air and smoke through it. Leaning back on the couch, she closed her eyes and drew in a deep breath. She blew the smoke in my direction and smiled. "See? Totally mild."

To me it didn't smell much like tobacco. An experimental puff didn't leave me gagging, so I drew in the hot fumes and held them in as they cooled. That led to a fit of coughing, but the next time was better. After passing the pipe back and forth, I began to understand why people enjoyed smoking. It made me feel wonderful. "Dad's gonna ask me what brand I used," I said, blowing smoke in Donya's face and grinning.

"Jamaican Red. I have a friend who…imports a key…a package once in a while."

"They raise tobacco in Jamaica?" I asked, incredulous.

"Yes, actually." She started giggling and shook her head.

Something about her laugh made the whole situation hilarious. She closed her mouth, but her jaw kept working. Small puffs of smoke leaked out between her lips. I filled my lungs one last time, held it, and tried to blow smoke rings. When I handed the pipe back to Donya, she knocked the ashes out into one of the potted plants.

With the back of her fingers, Donya stroked the side of my face. "None of the girls want you to leave." She leaned toward me like she was going to kiss me, but paused and grabbed my hand instead. "Come on, kid. Enough smoke. Let's move on to drinks."

Back in the kitchen, Donya set the pipe on the counter and opened the refrigerator. She pulled out orange juice, vanilla ice cream, and a bottle of vodka. After blending them, she poured the mix into a pitcher and filled two tall glasses with ice. "Will you set these out by the hot tub?" When I returned, she put her arms around my waist, pulled me close, and put her face against mine. We both laughed when a muscle in my arm twitched. "You're still nervous. Go sit in the hot tub and pour yourself a drink. Relax. I'll be out in a few minutes. I'm going to order pizza." She pulled the belt of my dress loose and we both started giggling again.

I grabbed a *yukata*, left my clothes draped over the back of the couch, and eased into the tub. Donya's orange creamsicle drink tasted smooth and sweet, especially with hot jets of water massaging me. I grinned and waved at the elfin princess sitting in her own hot tub behind the glass wall of the Florida room. She toasted me with her drink.

Donya walked into the room wearing one of Lisa's robes. We both laughed when she pretended to be a stripper. She threw the *yukata* across the room and joined me in the water. I watched her pour herself a drink, wondering if she was as nervous as me. As the water bubbled around us, I studied her face. *We don't need to do this.* "Dad would probably count this as a date—even without kissing—if you want to stop now."

She chuckled, sad eyes meeting mine. "Two naked girls in a hot tub, drinking alcohol?"

"No." I sat upright, frowning. "Don't you get it? His son with a girl, naked in a hot tub. What's the point of any of this if I'm a girl?"

She snorted and gestured toward my chest. "His son has breasts."

Six months on hormones and a twenty-pound weight gain had given me hips, pubic hair, small breasts, and a rounder face. I loved what estrogen was doing to my body, but wondered what Dad would think. I set down my drink, crossed my arms over my chest, and sank down into the water up to my nose.

"Oh. Come on." Donya poured herself another drink, took a long swallow, and grinned. "Is the boy ticklish?"

"No." I tried my best to keep a straight face, but when she started giggling again, I joined her. We'd used up all the tobacco, but smoke still lingered in the Florida room, curling around the lights and mixing with the mist rising off the hot tub.

When she turned toward me with an evil grin, I backed away. "No. Really, I'm not," I said.

"I think the boy lies," she whispered, inching closer.

The doorbell chimed. Donya jumped up out of the tub. "Pizza! I am so hungry." She threw on the robe and ran into the living room, leaving the sliding door open.

The elfin princess frowned at me as I poured myself another drink. "I'm sorry," I told her. "If I drink enough, maybe I won't remember how the boxes got checked."

"*Gu leòr,*" whispered the elfin princess.

I pursed my lips and stared at her. *Enough? Yes, Iseabail.* The time had come to end the charade. *Lord, my entire life has been consumed by my gender issues. Please forgive me for letting it become an idol. I want to obey Mom and Dad, but the list isn't right. Please show me what I should do. I want to love you and obey your law. Please help me.*

When Donya returned, she set a box of pizza on the side of the hot tub. "He is such a jerk!"

"Who?"

"Russell. The pizza delivery guy. He actually asked me for a date just now." She stepped into the water and back out again. "I'm going to put on some music."

I didn't have a record player or a radio, so I wasn't familiar with much rock and roll, but I did recognize Procol Harum. *A Whiter Shade of Pale* fit my mood well. The smoke lingered, but the laughter had migrated to someone else's party.

Donya sat beside me again and we both munched quietly on pizza. Trying to lighten the mood, I smiled at her and said, "Well, you've made an honest woman of me."

"Huh?"

"I'm going to tear up Dad's list."

"Yeah? Why?"

"It's wrong." I didn't have the courage to tell her I still had to try to be a boy. Okay, so I could be stupid, but I kept my promises. That's one reason I didn't like making them.

She stared at me with puppy eyes. "You don't want my virginity?"

I raised an eyebrow and bit my lip to keep from snickering. "You?"

"Yeah. I had vaginal surgery. Dilation isn't pleasant; I don't think intercourse would be, either. They cut off my clitoris, so I've got no feeling there. I…"

"There's no shame in being a virgin," I said, contemplating the water swirling around me.

"I know. You won't tell anyone though, will you?"

We sat for some time, both of us quiet, while the hot tub kept right on massaging my weary soul.

"Jamie?"

"Hmm?"

"Look at me."

When I turned my head, she kissed me, quick as that. "Now I can at least tell Parker I kissed a boy." She winked and reached for her drink again.

⁓ 27 ⁓

The elfin princess frowned at me from the bathroom mirror, silent accusation clouding her emerald eyes. I set the scissors on the counter and touched my fingertips to hers. "I don't like this any more than you do. Dad's list is wrong, but that doesn't mean I don't have to obey Mom and Dad on other stuff."

She raised her brows at me, but I shook my head. "No. The birth certificate's just a piece of paper. Dad can change it." *What kind of moron are you?* I'd seen quite a few of those looks in the past several days. She didn't think my boy impersonation pleased God. I didn't either, but what could I do? I'd promised my father I'd try.

So the little princess cut her hair—a short shag, not a buzz cut. I wasn't brave enough for that yet. I cleaned up the mess and apologized to the girl in the mirror.

Before I made it out of the bathroom, she scowled at me again and shook her head. I was going to try riding Tyler's motorcycle, and she expected me to kill myself on it. I stopped and tried to reassure her. "No, Iseabail. I'll learn to ride the Kawasaki on the intramural field first. Grass is soft, right? I won't get hurt."

I tied Tyler's dog tags to the handlebars, so I could pretend he was with me, and walked his motorcycle over to the school. The bike threw me a dozen times before I decided I was ready to ride it on the street. As I limped into my room, I smiled, proud that I could do something—anything—to show that I'd tried.

* * * *

The drive down South Dixie Highway proved uneventful. Lisa and I had spent so much time in Burdines that riding to Dadeland required no brain activity at all. Rather than shopping, however, I continued on North Kendall Drive. I wanted to find out how fast Tyler's Kawasaki would go. *Things Boys Do* only hinted at speed; but my brother had collected tickets when he was seventeen.

Out past the turnpike I opened it up and was going eighty-five when I braked hard for the west end bend. Fortunately, the curve was long and the road wide because the brakes on the Mach III weren't the best and the bike kept wanting to go straight.

Turning north on Krome Avenue, I leaned down against the tank, shifted into fifth, and held the throttle wide open. Krome was the perfect place for speed—lonely and straight as you'd ever want. From Route 27 all the way down to Homestead, you could run flat out and never see a cop car.

The speedometer needle oscillated between one-ten and one-twenty, with the wind and the engine noise screaming in my ears. The motorcycle wobbled and gyrated, like a bucking bronco. The Blue Streak might have been the quickest accelerating vehicle on the highway, but riding one implied a death wish.

Out on the road, at high speed, a bit of gravel could end it all. Wouldn't that be nice? They'd cry about losing their son in a motorcycle wreck, all right, but Dad would consider it a boy way to die. Would he grieve for me the way he did for Scott? The police might not tell him I had breasts. My driver's license said female, but they certainly wouldn't grieve for their dead little girl. No. They'd probably make the corpse look like a boy. The Bell Star was a pretty cool helmet, but not the best for crying in. *Oh, great! Now my nose is running.*

Killing myself wouldn't solve anything. I eased off on the throttle and coasted in near silence. Well, my life was over anyway. I was a total failure as a boy.

A tractor-trailer approached, so I veered a little to the right to avoid his pressure front. Some large bug struck me in the neck and began dancing around. The little princess loved nature, but creeping things gave her the shivers. Frantic, I clawed at the intruder. He went down my T-shirt, so I yanked at the fabric until he crawled out on my lap and blew away. When I looked up again, I discovered that a second diesel rig had pulled into my lane. The front grille filled my vision. An emblem at the top read *Peterbilt*.

Lord, please don't let me die like this!

For a heartbeat and a half, death inched closer.

The elfin princess rode one of the fastest and most agile stallions in all of the fairie realms. She dug her heels into his sides and screamed, "Ruith leis!" He reared up, mighty hooves pawing at the air as he sprang forward. Too late—the troll was upon them. His ax breached the steed's silver armor, wounding his flank. The battle-horse spun in mid-air, screaming in agony, and lumbered away, unsteady and bleeding from the gaping wound. The elfin princess pleaded with him to jump, to be away, but he stumbled and knelt, crashing into an old stone wall and sending his rider headlong into the moat beyond.

My body hit the water in the canal at an angle and rolled, skipping across the surface, like a flat stone thrown by some boy, like a rag doll, limp arms flailing. When the world stopped spinning, I lay face down in the water and felt the murky green liquid seep into my helmet until, in a panic, I yanked it off and gasped for air.

I'm still alive. Trembling, I took several deliberate breaths. "Thank you, Lord!" I screamed.

One boot gone, I shed the other, along with my jacket. Heart pounding, the princess crawled through vile green slime, the likes of which could only be found in the heart of Hell itself. No shoreline here, only a gradual thickening of the goo.

By the time I squirmed my way to dry land, I was exhausted. I slumped against a mound of dirt and squeezed my eyes shut. Why should God have spared me? I'd grown up in a church that thought it had all its doctrine right. So had the Pharisees. My faith was in Christ, but my life didn't provide much evidence of it. I hadn't been to church since North Carolina. I hadn't read the Bible at all since leaving Saint Andrew's. I couldn't even work out in my mind which sex God wanted me to be.

Even if He expected me to be a boy like my brother had been, I hadn't the slightest idea how to get there. My parents wanted a son, but Dad's list read like the seven deadly sins. Being myself meant defying my parents. Would I be defying God, too? Life had been simpler when I had Jameson, but pretending wasn't God-honoring either.

On Saint Andrew's I hadn't thought much about gender. Taking care of Rachael had consumed most of my energy. Pastor Gillespie had led his wife, and me, and the other girls in prayer and Bible study. The Gillespies had held me accountable without any gender pressure. My last Sunday on Saint Andrew's, the pastor had preached from First John. *If we confess our sins, he is faithful and just to forgive us our sins, and to cleanse us from all unrighteousness...*

I tried to wipe the slime off my hands, but it only smudged further.

And if any man sin, we have an advocate with the Father, Jesus Christ the righteous: And He is the propitiation for our sins…

"Lord, thank you for having mercy on me. My gender's become an idol. The desire to be a boy or a girl consumes my every thought and dictates my actions. The obsession nearly cost me my life just now. Please forgive me and release me from my chains. Please show me who you want me to be and what I should do now."

I staggered up to the road and sat on the guardrail. The canal stretched off into the distance, but I couldn't tell where I'd hit the water. No way to find Tyler's dog tags now. All I had left of him was gone. It occurred to me that he would have wanted me to go to Saint Andrew's. "Lord, I'll go back home and find out if Dad will let me go to Saint Andrew's. Take care of Rachael and forget about gender for a while. Thank you for forgiving me."

"Y'all want a lift, missy?"

I glanced up at the old Chevy pickup. "*Gu leòr,*" the elfin princess whispered to no one in particular. Even with short hair and covered in swamp mud and all, I was still a girl to the old farmer. Okay, so the soaking-wet clothes didn't help any. "Yes, sir."

"Well, hop in back. I'll drop y'all at the Sunoco on Southwest Eighth. They got a pay phone."

The sun touched the western horizon and exploded into streaks of purple and red. In the east, the night's first stars peeked around high cirrus clouds. A beautiful end to a miserable day. I crawled into the bed and sat next to an old spare tire. Nothing like a brush with death to focus your life. "I tried, Lord, but I can't be a boy. I'm just not one."

At the station I dialed my cousin's number and leaned against the wall next to the restrooms.

"Hi, Kaylah. Can you come get me?"

"What happened? Are you all right?"

A vile green substance, half-dried in places, streaked my arms. The same goop discolored my soaking-wet T-shirt and jeans. The stench would have embarrassed a cesspool. "Bring a plastic tarp to wrap the body, okay?"

"Say what?"

"I took my bike swimming."

"Bike?—Why?—Where are you?"

"A gas station—the Sunoco out on Calle Ocho, near Krome."

"I'll be there in half an hour."

I stood and tried to rub some of the gunk off. It smelled putrid and stuck to everything. "Lord, I'm sorry I wasted so much of my life dreaming and pretending. I want to obey my parents, but I'm not sure how."

I sat down again and waited for Kaylah. My skin began to itch as my clothes dried. Would I ever be clean again?

My cousin shook her head, eyes growing dark with anger. "Where's your bike?"

"Most of it's in a canal somewhere. We'd never find it." I climbed into the car and slumped in the rear seat. Neither of us said a word the entire way back to her townhouse. When we arrived, she handed me a bucket, a sponge, and some soap. Then she turned on the garden hose and slammed the door as she went inside. After I washed, she handed me a towel and made me put my clothes into a trash bin.

I put on the robe she threw me, sat at the kitchen table, and waited, anxious for her to speak, praying I was mistaken about the dark clouds of shame marring her face.

Kaylah had stood up for me my entire life. She'd taken my side against Mom and Dad, insisting I was a girl, even after Aunt Elizabeth had switched her good for it. She'd somehow even gotten my birth certificate fixed.

When I glanced at Kaylah again, her brown eyes burned almost golden. "What are you doing to yourself?" My cousin the attorney didn't sound like I was her client anymore.

"Ma'am?" I blinked, a slow terror clenching my stomach.

"Didn't you tell your father you're legally female?" Brown eyes held mine, demanding.

My father had bled the little princess to death with his sad eyes. "I was scared, okay? Dad wants me to be a boy. He would just get them to change my birth certificate back."

"He can't, Jamie. The paperwork has to reflect reality. Are you a boy, then?"

All the *Things Boys Do* stuff I did was as a girl. "No, ma'am," I whispered, shoulders slumping. The little princess shrank down in her chair. If she were small enough, maybe nobody would notice her. "I'm going home. I'll tell Dad I'm a girl."

Kaylah leaned close to her little princess, her voice gentle. "What will you do then?"

No doubt where I'd be if I had my druthers. "I'll go back and take care of Rachael."

"Would that glorify God more than what you've been doing?"

"Yes, ma'am."

"Why don't you go home for Christmas then? Do your makeup and wear your best dress. Your father should see how pretty you are…" She tousled my hair. "Even with a short shag. Tell them you're a girl, and you're going to Saint Andrew's. Don't back down this time. All right?"

"Okay."

"Pray and trust God to work it out. All right?"

"Okay."

"There you are."

❧ 28 ❧

The elfin princess pulled up the hood of her forest green pea coat and braced herself against the wind. North Carolina winters didn't chill to the bone as fast as the bitter cold of northern Illinois, but after a year in Miami, my blood ran thin. I studied the house, all strung with Christmas lights, and imagined my father waiting right inside the front door. For years I'd been afraid of him, or at least afraid of making him sad. For months my anger had smoldered. His displeasure would still cause me pain, but not like before. Some part of me insanely expected him to be proud of his little princess for refusing to further sully her honor with *Things Boys Do.*

I opened my Bible and read in the dim afternoon light, sheltering the book against the wind. All the calculations based on genetics, gonads, genitals, and gender came down to one thing—how to play the hand I'd been dealt. The chief end of Man was to glorify God and enjoy Him forever, but thus far my life had been consumed by questions of gender. I longed for God to make something out of what remained.

"Lord, please make Dad see that I'm a girl. Help him understand how much it would mean to me if he told me it was okay to be his daughter. Please grant me favor in his eyes so I can go stay with the Gillespies." The little princess dabbed at her eyes. She didn't want to walk in with her mascara all ruined. I wiped my eyes again and started up the drive. "Please give me the courage I need to stand my ground. Please grant me peace, Lord. Thank you for making me Your child."

As I walked up to the house, one of the garage doors opened. A moment later our Skylark backed out into the turn-around area. Dad got out and began walking back toward the house, leaving the car running. His head swiveled my way when the gravel under my shoe crunched. "You should be inside, honey," he said.

His tenderness threw me until I realized he had mistaken me for my sister. Even in the twilight he should have at least noticed my height. Way too short to be Alicia. "It's Jamie, Dad."

"Jameson?" I stood still while my father studied me. "Have you no shame?" Disgust filled his face and his voice.

Shame? Me? What about your stupid list? I bit my lip hard and counted heartbeats, trying to hold back my anger. "No, Dad. I gave that up when I started on your list."

A short, sharp bark of a laugh burst from my father's lips. "Right. I can tell you've been diligent. Dress like a whore. That was item seven, wasn't it?"

Godliness with contentment is great gain. Peace and warmth flooded me. I was still frightened of my father, but some tipping point had passed. In a softer voice I said, "I did more of the list than was right. Would you ask Alicia to go to bed with someone?"

"She's not a boy."

My father professed to being a Christian, but even an unbeliever should have seen the hypocrisy in expecting your sons to be promiscuous and your daughters to be virgins. "Neither am I!" I didn't exactly yell, but Mom would have slapped me for the tone of my voice.

Dad only stared, anger smoldering in his eyes. "I should never have allowed you to go to school before having surgery and at least a year on testosterone."

Surgery? You can't be serious. "Dad, I—"

"No, Jameson. As of now you're grounded. Ask your mother to give you a buzz cut and find you some decent clothes. You'll stay home until we get this straightened out. I'll find you another doctor." He nodded as if everything were settled. "We'll get you back on track."

"No, Dad. I'm a girl. And I'm not going to talk to any of your stupid doctors."

Dad didn't lose his temper, but his face grew taught. "Do as I say and go in the house. Now." His voice was even, but his eyes burned.

Lord, please grant me courage. I took a deep breath and exhaled slowly. "No, sir."

Smoldering blue eyes studied me as he pulled off his belt. He'd strapped my brother once. I'd forgotten why. Scott had run off and joined the Army afterward. He had never come back.

Sad emerald eyes battled Dad's blues, raining pity down on this stranger with the belt. *My* dad would never punish me for being a girl. I met his stare for as long as I could, but when the tears started, I squeezed my eyes shut and waited, legs shivering.

The breeze picked up, rustling the branches and chilling me. The evening was turning cold, but my cares and fears drifted away on the wind. I might not embrace the pain, but I would bear it.

Lord, please reconcile us. Even now.

Dad grunted. "Go inside before you catch pneumonia."

My eyes popped open in time to watch him buckle his belt again. He glanced at the darkening sky. "If you don't change your mind by morning, you're on your own." He walked back to the Skylark and drove away.

After the car passed out of sight, I shouldered my tote and walked up to the door. My sister answered. Her reaction was pure Alicia. "Wow! I can tell you put your heart into that outfit. Are you trying out for Miss Florida?"

I laughed and hugged her tight. "The war's over, Ali. No more stupid list." I stepped past her and glanced out the picture window. "Dad just left. You know how soon he'll be back?"

"No." My sister pursed her lips. "Some emergency. Mom said they want him at Site R. Stat."

"You're prettier when you smile," Mom said, walking into the room.

"Hey, I gotta study. We'll talk later." Alicia hugged me again and headed toward her room.

I unbuttoned my coat and hung it in the closet, refusing to let anger overwhelm me. "I talked to Dad about his list. I've done all I'm gonna."

Mom chuckled, a soft musical sound. "I can tell. Did you complete any of it?"

"More than I should have," I snapped. "I'm a girl, Mom." My anger wouldn't help, but it was hard to let go.

I expected argument, but she only nodded. "I know, dear."

"Any idea when he'll be back?"

"Apparently there's some trouble that's not in the news yet. He thought it might be a month or two." Mom hugged me, stepped back, and frowned. "Don't you think your dress is—what happened to your legs?"

The bruises from my motorcycle wreck were visible with the short skirt I was wearing. "I'm okay, Mom." I sat on the couch, leg next to a pillow, and put my hands in my lap, hoping to cover the worst of the discoloration.

Being away so long, I'd forgotten my mom liked more direct answers. The clouds above her turned dark gray. "Jamie?" Mom didn't like repeating questions, either, you know, so it was best to answer right the first time.

"Sorry, Mom. I was in a motorcycle wreck about a week ago."

My mother shut her eyes. Her storm clouds turned thick and black. "Was your boyfriend injured?"

"No, Sean—No, ma'am. He's in Scotland. He went back to school."

"You bought your own motorcycle?" Her voice went up a notch in intensity. Not a positive sign.

"Tyler left me his," I whispered, studying my knees.

"That kamikaze five hundred thing you were telling me about?" Mom's voice went right off the top of the scale. "Pull up your dress and lie down."

"Mom, I'm—"

"Now!"

I slid my dress up and lay on the couch. On my left side, from my knee to my armpit, stretched a mass of purple and green blotches. Mom shook her head and began poking around my abdomen and under my ribs. I gasped when she pressed my side. "What did the doctor say? Did you crack a rib?"

"I, um…didn't go to a doctor."

Mom's green eyes caught mine and held them, her anger flaring. She probably looked like that when she exiled me to Saint Andrew's. "Sell the bike," she hissed. "Your reckless days are over. You understand me?"

I couldn't sell the Kawasaki anymore, but with Mom there was only one acceptable answer. "Yes, ma'am."

Mom studied my face as the clouds above her dissipated. She shook her head and glanced toward the kitchen. "Did you eat yet?"

"No, and I'm starving."

After a snack of soup and sandwiches, I asked to speak with her in private. "I'd like to leave some things here with you." I followed her into the master bedroom and closed the door. Out of my tote I got my set of vaginal dilators. "These are dilators."

"I'm aware of what they are."

Surprised, I paused for a moment, studying my mother. "I'm sorry, Mom. I didn't mean to sound snippy. I finished dilating is all." I opened the box and removed the largest one, holding the plastic rod in front of her. "This one fits in this far," I said, indicating length with my other hand. "That should be enough for intercourse, don't you think?" I replaced the dilator, closed the lid, and handed her the box. From my tote I pulled a manila envelope containing the affidavit from Dr. Cameron and several copies of my birth certificate.

My mother put the box on the dresser and sat down on her bed, arms crossed. "We should never have let you go to school so far from home. It's not been good for you."

I wanted to scream so badly that I clenched and unclenched my hands several times, my whole body trembling. "What is wrong with you people?" I hissed. Okay, so I messed up big-time on the honor your mother thing, and my conscience kicked in. "I'm sorry, Mom. I'm a girl. Okay?"

Mom stood, eyes narrowing. I was gonna get slapped or switched, maybe both. Her lower lip trembled, but her anger faded and she tapped the envelope in my hand. "What does it take to get a birth certificate corrected?"

I stared at the envelope, wondering how she knew. Had Kaylah told her? "I have no idea."

Mom smiled. "One physician and one parent. All Dr. Cameron required was that you demonstrate a credible desire to be a girl and that he verify what was between your legs." She tousled my hair and walked over to the dresser.

"You signed?" My voice slid right up the scale. Yeah, I was more than a little surprised.

She raised both hands in front of her and shook her head. "Oh, no. Not me. Your father would divorce me if I did something so foolish. I had nothing to do with it. Perhaps giving your cousin a power of attorney was a lapse in judgment, but who could have foreseen the way she'd use it?"

The little princess used to work logic problems with her mother. Home school wasn't always about books, you know. Sometimes Mom told me stories and made me guess what came next or figure out who had done what.

Of course Kaylah would use her power of attorney to correct my birth certificate. Once she knew. Someone had pointed her in the right direction. "You were counting on my getting a urinary tract infection. Aunt Elizabeth sends me to the doctor, and he tells Kaylah what to do."

The doctor and the power of attorney would have been pointless, though, without a credible desire to be a girl on my part. Mom had sent me to Saint Andrew's after Sharon mailed her the picture of me with Tyler. Sharon, who'd encouraged me to be a girl. Sharon, whom Mom had made me stay with after my surgery. Had Sharon been acting as Mom's proxy all along? "Sharon?"

Mom squirmed on the bed while I was still trying to figure out what to say. "I'm sure the other girls at your school wear fancy makeup and short skirts, but I expect my daughters to be more concerned with modesty and chastity than fashion. Your sister looks up to you. When you wear a miniskirt, she wonders why I won't let her wear one."

The dress I was wearing wasn't my shortest, but it was well above my knees. I didn't think I'd ever wear anything that short again, with it so cold outside. My heart softened when I realized where she might be taking the conversation.

Mom took one of my hands in both of hers. "My seventeen-year-old daughter just told me she's prepared to have sex with a man. She has no experience being a teenage girl. She's naive about boys. She hasn't had time to develop sound judgment regarding clothes and makeup, let alone dating. How's a mother supposed to feel? I'm terrified for you."

My mother's words were gentle, even kind. They made it past my defenses and tore into my heart. I hugged my mom and blurted, "I was planning to spend next semester on Saint Andrew's. I'll be staying with the Gillespies and taking care of Rachael for them."

"Pastor Gillsepie and his wife?"

"Yes."

"Living with them?"

"Yes, ma'am."

"What about school?"

"I'm putting my education on hold for now."

"Honey, you can't—" Mom paused, studied my face, and nodded. "All right. The Lord will provide a way to go back when He thinks you're ready." She chewed on her lip, eyes scanning me. "You'll throw away that outfit?"

Everybody said I looked cute in the dress. I'd miss it. "Yes, ma'am."

"And the makeup?"

That hurt. "Is it that bad?" I'd tried my hardest to improve my skill with cosmetics.

"Your makeup's beautiful, just not appropriate for a daughter of mine."

Somehow, I should have seen that one coming. My mother was treating me the way she treated Alicia. Wasn't that what I'd always wanted? I went to my sister's bathroom and washed my face clean. "Welcome to my world," quipped Alicia, grinning at me. When I changed into my bell-bottoms, she shook her head. "No jeans."

I shrugged, grinning back at her. "Can't blame me for trying."

When I showed Mom, she hesitated. "You didn't bring another dress?"

"No, ma'am."

"Get your sister. We'll go buy you one. That can be your present."

"It'd make Alicia's Christmas if you bought her a pair of bell-bottoms."

Mom pursed her lips. I thought I could see the gears grinding. "All right. Get her, and let's go."

The elfin princess danced across the living room to Alicia's bedroom and shared the happy news. We both grinned all the way to the Rich's store on Silas Creek. Mom dropped us at a dressing room and went back out into the store. As soon as she was out of sight, Alicia hugged me. "I can't believe you talked her into letting me get bell-bottoms. That is so awesome."

It might have been a dismal winter day outside, but the sun shone inside. Mom had two daughters now. The older needed to be an example for the younger. "Enjoy them while you can. Mom expects both of us to become mature enough that we won't wear pants anymore. Especially jeans."

Alicia snorted. "Like that'll happen."

"I'm going to stay on Saint Andrew's next semester. The Gillespies don't allow their girls to wear pants, so I'm leaving mine behind."

A grin split my sister's face. "Maybe you should tell them you're a boy."

The little princess stuck out her tongue at Alicia just as Mom returned. She chuckled and handed me a slip. "Try this on first."

I took off my bell-bottoms and peasant top, put on the slip, and stepped out of the booth.

Mom stared at me, and her eyes narrowed. "Where's your bra?"

Seven months on hormones had given me breast development. Not exactly cleavage, but you could tell I was a teenage girl. "I don't wear one. I figured I'd wait until—"

"No seventeen-year-old daughter of mine is going to run around without a bra." Mom turned on her heel and stalked out of the dressing area.

Alicia snickered while I stood there with my mouth open.

Several minutes later, Mom returned. The sales lady with her walked right up to the little princess with a measuring tape. "Your first bra! Aren't you excited? How old are we, dearie?" I gaped at her, mortified.

"She's twelve," piped Alicia, ever helpful.

"Twelve. Wonderful! You're almost a B cup." She turned to my mom. "We sell some beautiful padded bras that should fit her. Wait a moment and I'll get a couple."

Mom showed me how to put on a bra without having to be a contortionist. I stood close to the mirror, staring at myself. *Slaughterhouse Five*, a twelve-year-old for the moment, living life in some random order. A coming of age delayed five years. A single tear broke free, glided down my cheek, and dripped on my chest. Why should buying a bra be such a big deal?

Alicia grinned, but Mom's smile hinted at sadness as she handed me a dress. "Try this one first. I suspect you'll like the style."

A minute later I gazed at myself in the mirror. On the front of the dress, a row of buttons ran from the Peter Pan collar down to the waist. On either side pin-tucks ran parallel to the buttons. The dress zipped up the back. A cloth belt tied in a bow. The full skirt hung several inches past my knees. Was this Mom's way of saying she was sorry? Just pick up where we left off? I chuckled to myself. At least this one didn't have a scratchy crinoline petticoat like the dresses I'd worn when I was young. "This one's fine, Mom. Let's find Alicia her bell-bottoms."

Alicia led us to a pair of corduroy jeans she'd apparently been eyeing for months. When she tried them on, Mom frowned but held her peace. I hugged my grinning sister. "Those are awesome on you."

I studied my mother, wondering how long she'd hold out. Not long. A smile touched her lips. "You look good in those."

Alicia's eyes went wide. She grinned at me and hugged Mom. I closed my eyes and thanked the Lord for His goodness.

Once we were back home, Alicia ran to her bedroom with her new pants. She wasn't often so excited. I glanced at Mom, nodded, and followed my sister into the bedroom. Might as well take off my jeans before I regretted giving them up.

Five minutes later, wearing my new dress, I found Mom at work in the kitchen. "May I help?"

"Are you certain you're not going to do any more of your father's list?"

"Yes, ma'am. Dad gave me until morning to change my mind, but I'm not backing down. I'll leave right after breakfast. I love you both, but I can't be a boy for you."

"You know what God requires of a Christian woman?"

"Uh. Not exactly."

Mom's wan smile warmed my heart. "Then I have a list of Scripture verses for you."

"Thanks, Mom." I studied my hands until she made a face at me. Mom could always tell when I was trying to find the right words.

She hugged me tight. "Forgive Sharon. And me. We deceived you, but we wanted what was best for my little princess." She smiled and put a hand on my cheek. "If you tell your father, we'll all be on our own. Give him a chance to get used to your being a girl. Meanwhile, take the time you need to find out who God wants you to be."

"Why didn't you just let me be a girl when I was nine?"

For a while I didn't think she would answer. Her eyes got all distant looking and glistened with unshed tears. "Home schooling was illegal back then. When we were charged with truancy violations, we asked Dr. Parker to help us change your birth certificate. When my jaw dropped, she nodded. "Yes. Him. But he wouldn't unless you had surgery. We didn't want to send you to public school as a boy, so we found a district near Springfield that would let us home school under close supervision. Meanwhile, we kept searching for a doctor who would help us change your legal status to female." Pain blossomed across her face and she turned away. "By the time I found Dr. Cameron, your act had convinced your father you were happy as a boy."

I hugged her tight and let her cry on my shoulder. "I'll be okay now, Mom. I promise."

∽ 29 ∾

Watching the ocean swells, the elfin princess rejoiced to be airborne. The breakers off Government Cut had been brutal, forcing the seaplane to taxi out a considerable distance before takeoff. Still a little green, I leaned back and closed my eyes. Raindrops pelted the window next to me, providing a staccato counterpoint to the droning engines.

Like a foster child, completely dependent on my new family, I'd left everything and everyone behind. Even Sofie. She sat on the dresser in the Alexanders' guest room. Little girls played with dolls. A time for growing up awaited me on Saint Andrew's.

Not even Kaylah understood what her little princess needed, and maybe I didn't either. I glanced at the dark clouds outside and noticed the elfin princess smiling at me. My fingertips touched hers. "God will make it all better. You'll see."

When the thrumming of the engines lessened and the plane banked, the sun broke through the overcast. An island peeked through the clouds, welcoming me to a new life.

* * * *

The streets were even busier than on my first trip. The small bus crawled through surging crowds. Walking would have been faster. No matter; there was no hurry.

Street vendors and children tried to sell their wares to the passengers. They walked beside the bus as it crept along the road. I gave in to one little boy who promised to bring me an ice-cold soda. Even though he charged me three times the normal price, I smiled when he brought back a bottle and opened it for me. Two blocks later he grinned when I handed him the empty.

As soon as the bus turned on Fairfax Avenue, the traffic sped up, leaving behind the vendors, the noise, and the clouds of dust and diesel fumes. Soon enough, the bus dropped me off in front of the old kirk. I strolled across the kirk yard to the old fountain, where I washed my hands and splashed water on my face. A couple of barefoot kids ran around, screaming and laughing. Birds in the ancient trees called to one another. A gentle breeze rustled the branches of the old oak.

"Jamie?" Startled, I spun around. Pastor Gillespie was hurrying toward me, grinning like a little boy. "Welcome back. How was your flight?" He walked right up and hugged me.

"Thank you, sir. I enjoyed the trip." Happiness bloomed in me, filling my heart with joy. I wondered how much of my mood stemmed from my fondness for books like *Pollyanna* and *The Boxcar Children*. Shouldn't I have been happy around my own family?

Pastor Gillespie picked up my tote and led me across Martin Lane to the manse. Mrs. Gillespie waved at us from the front door. "Welcome back, Jamie. We were about to have tea. Won't you join us?"

"Thank you, ma'am. Tea would be delightful," I said, thinking about Mrs. Gillespie's yummy scones.

Halfway down the hall we met Heather coming out of one of the bedrooms. She rocked back and forth as she stepped into the hallway, one hand on her belly. "Jamie! I'm so glad you're here."

I hugged her with care. "I'm happy, too. You must be close now."

"My due date's three weeks away." With one hand she pushed against her back. "I can't wait. My back's been horrid." She glanced at Mrs. Gillespie.

The elderly woman nodded. "Jamie, Heather hopes you'll take Rachael right away. The wee one gets on better with you than anyone else."

Little Rachael. She was special, that one. If you were pregnant and had back pain, keeping the toddler would be difficult. "I'll take her whenever you'd like." I put on a happy smile, wondering what seven months of caring for Rachael would do to me. I liked the toddler, but Rachael had insisted on being with me every minute of every day, wailing when I tried to leave. Babysitting the orphan was neat when I had a chance to get away for a while each day. How would I do with no breaks? Well, I said I wanted to be a mom, didn't I? This was my chance to discover what motherhood was like.

Mrs. Gillespie nodded toward the sitting room. "You can fetch her when she wakes from her nap. Let's have our tea in peace."

The pastor led me to a bedroom with two twin beds and a crib. "This is your new home." He set my tote on one of the beds. "Let's go have some scones."

My eyes surveyed the room. The Ainsworth girls had stayed there the previous summer, but Kaylah said they'd been taken in by relatives. I ran my hand over the cotton bedspread. The furnishings were plain, the beds small, but this was my home now. *Lord, thank you for giving me exactly what I need.* I nodded to Pastor Gillespie and followed him down the hall.

Changing diapers wasn't one of my favorite activities. I wiped Rachael clean, dusted her bottom with a little talcum powder, and pinned a fresh diaper in place. At least Rachael had the sense to lie still while being changed. With some of the other babies, I'd been afraid of sticking them with their own diaper pins. I kissed Rachael on the forehead and set her on her feet. "Let's get dressed. Okay, pumpkin?" Rachael picked up her jumper. She got the dress over her head, but struggled to get her arms through the right holes until I helped her. "Good girl! Want to read?"

"Goldie, Mommy!" Rachael ran to the bookshelf and grabbed *Goldilocks and the Three Bears*.

My smile remained in place in spite of an inward groan. I worried about Rachael's insistence on calling me Mommy. I'd been correcting her for a month. "Not Mommy. Jamie. Okay, pumpkin?"

"Mommy!"

Rachael's interest in books was wonderful, but we'd already been through *Goldilocks* a hundred times. Time to find her some others. I sat in the rocker and pulled the toddler up on my lap.

* * * *

I wasn't sick, but the Gillepsies insisted all their girls get an annual checkup. After Graeme finished the examination, he wrote me a new prescription for Premarin and told me he wanted me to have a hysterectomy. "You should have had one last summer."

"But why?" Having a uterus was something I clung to whenever I doubted my sex.

"I'm sorry, lass. I wish you could carry a baby to term, but you can't. Taking estrogen alone may cause uterine cancer. Progestins can cause other problems. Rather than risk future issues, I think it's wiser to remove your uterus now."

Dr. Cameron had always been straight with me. I decided to trust him no matter how much it hurt. "Okay."

"I'll have Skye call Abigail to schedule the surgery. That's it—unless you have any questions."

"You know my mom." I searched his eyes for a reaction. Mirth blossomed there.

"Is that a question?" Dr. Cameron's grin made me think of Tyler. "Yes. I kept her apprised of your situation last summer."

"I wasn't living as a girl, you know, at least not until Mom sent me here. But you changed my birth certificate anyway."

"Your cousin did." His smile returned to normal, but his eyes still sparkled.

"That's not a credible desire to be a girl."

"No. But you seemed eager to take estrogen. You didn't complain about the side effects."

"So you went ahead and split my labia?"

"It was the least invasive procedure." His eyes searched mine before he continued. "There are a couple of things you should understand—most children who are born with your condition want to be boys. The doctors remove their vagina and uterus and perform hypospadias repair surgeries to move their urethral opening to the tip of what becomes their little penis. Nothing we did to you is irreversible. Surgeons can still make you a boy."

Unreasoning fear welled up in me. I took a step back before getting myself under control.

Dr. Cameron nodded. "Your reaction is exactly why I signed the paperwork. It wasn't that you had a vagina; it was how you reacted to having one. My goal, and your mother's, was to see how you'd do as a girl, while still preserving your options." He held out a hand. "You've become a lovely young lady. Your mother had no doubts. I don't either, now."

* * * *

The things Pastor Nyquist had said had been eating at me for months. I didn't want to be bad, but I didn't know how to be a boy. Pastor Gillespie had always been nice, even the times he'd scolded me. Would he have been so kind had he known what I was?

I longed to be a member of a church that would help me. Even if my gender wasn't sin, I was still messed up in other ways. Plenty of them.

What good would it be to join the kirk if I had to hide who I was from them? I had to talk to somebody.

Butterflies raging in me, I poked my head around the door of the study. What would he say? "Pastor Gillespie?"

The pastor glanced up from his book and smiled. "Yes, Jamie. What may I do for you?"

"Are you busy?"

"I always have time for my girls. What's on your mind?"

In and out, I forced patient breaths. "What does God think of people who are faie—you know—born between the sexes?"

He removed his reading glasses and set them on the desk. "Intersex is rare, but I've heard of a few cases. Do you know someone who's faie?"

A muscle in my leg twitched. I studied my hands. "I am."

Clouds of doubt rolled across his eyes. "You are? Who told you that?"

"Dr. Cameron."

He nodded, and then seemed to study my face. "The Bible doesn't speak about intersex much. God created mankind male and female and said that was good, but sin corrupted everything, even sexual development." He turned his chair toward me. "Since mankind fell, some people have been born between the sexes. Dr. Cameron says you're one, does he?"

I relaxed a little. He didn't seem too upset with me. "Yes, sir."

"Well. Long ago the issue was brought before the General Assembly." He pursed his lips, eyes still on me. "The Americans allow doctors to determine the sex of these children, based on guidance from a man at Johns Hopkins University." He shrugged, tapping his pencil on the desk. "After much study, prayer, and deliberation, the assembly recommended simply that faie children consider how best to glorify God with the body he's given them."

Hope rose in my heart. "I'm allowed to adopt?"

The pastor grinned. "You'll probably do exactly that. And I suspect you'll find a young man who'll love you and not care whether or not you're faie."

"I can marry?"

Pastor Gillespie nodded. "So long as he knows about your condition before you're betrothed."

I could marry! Hope budded like young roses.

* * * *

I sat next to Kaylah in the back pew, gazing up at her and thinking about how much my life had changed. Rachael, my own little princess, sat on my lap, playing with my bracelet.

Pastor Gillespie had said my membership vows would be administered near the beginning of the service. Kaylah touched my arm and nodded when the time came for me to go forward. I smiled at my cousin and set Rachael on the pew next to her. Her mommy took a single step toward the aisle, and the toddler started screaming, so I walked back and picked her up. I went forward, carrying the toddler, and stood before the church, facing Pastor Gillespie as he administered the vows.

"Do you acknowledge yourself to be a sinner, in need of salvation by Christ, and do you believe in the Lord Jesus Christ, receiving and resting upon Him alone as He is offered in the Gospel?"

"I do."

"Have you been baptized in accordance with His Word?"

"Yes."

"Do you swear in the name of God, in humble reliance upon the Grace of the Holy Spirit, to live in a way that becomes followers of Christ?"

"I do."

"Do you swear in the name of God, to support the ministry of this church, in its worship and work, submitting to its government and discipline, while pursuing its purity and peace?"

"I do." I walked back to my seat, grinning.

* * * *

The night was stormy, but it was quiet snuffling noises and something soft moving against my face that woke me. In a panic I reached for my throat. Two small arms had wrapped around my neck. With firm but gentle pressure, I peeled them away.

"Mommy!" Rachael's high-pitched screech pierced my eardrum.

"I'm right here, pumpkin," I whispered, putting my arms around Rachael and drawing her close. The toddler quieted down again, apparently satisfied.

I lay awake, wondering how to help the girl. I'd done everything short of chaining Rachael to her crib. You didn't punish an orphan for missing her mom. Time and again I'd tried to explain that I wasn't her mommy, but all Rachael seemed to understand was that her mother was rejecting her. Rachael's anguished calls for a woman who would never answer tore at my heart. I yearned to comfort Rachael, to nurture her, to protect her. To be her mom.

I'd always wanted children, but I'd expected to wait until I got married. At least a dozen reasons came to mind why a single teenage girl shouldn't adopt, but none of them would sway Rachael. All she seemed to understand was whether or not her mommy was nearby.

Lord, this is crazy. Rachael drew me from in front while my own nature, like a traitor, shoved me from behind. My desire to be accepted as a girl paled in comparison to the hunger that drove me to be a mother.

Rachael thinks I'm her mom. I want to be. Lord, please give me the strength to do what You want, and the wisdom to understand what that is.

As I closed my eyes, I considered what to say to the Gillespies. Perhaps I should plead insanity when they asked me why I wanted to adopt Rachael.

☙ 31 ❧

The old stone fence around the manse had long ago been overrun by raspberries and blackberries. I enjoyed walking along the perimeter with Rachael, letting her eat berries. Wary of thorns, the toddler clung to my skirt with one arm and reached out with the other to grab succulent morsels from my hand. At times Rachael got more berry on her jumper than she swallowed. She wore the same stained dress as last time, but I'd forgotten how often she wanted to hold my skirt. I'd have to make sure I wore the same clothes next time. No sense in ruining more than one outfit.

I picked Rachael up and kissed her on the forehead, letting the girl get juice and pulp everywhere. She giggled. "Mommy eat berry." The toddler pressed berries into my mouth, her little hand smearing purple goo down my chin. I'd given up convincing the orphan I wasn't her mom.

"Jamie!" Mrs. Gillespie stood in the kitchen doorway. I moved Rachael to my hip, picked up the basket of berries, and headed toward the manse. The elderly woman waited for us just inside the entry. "Mr. Gillespie will be here in a few minutes. Why don't you go ahead and clean up?"

Rachael followed me to our room, where I washed her face and hands and helped her change into a clean jumper. On the way to the kitchen, I dropped off our dirty clothes in the laundry. I threw on an apron, washed the berries, and set them in a bowl on the kitchen table.

Setting up a highchair for Rachael took care. The toddler, as always, was attached to Mommy's skirt. "Okay, pumpkin, up you go." I set her in the chair, latched her in, and started helping Mrs. Gillespie serve lunch. When Rachael started wailing, I waggled my index finger back and forth at her. "No." The child squawked one more time and quieted down. Mrs. Gillespie was grinning when I glanced her way again.

After Pastor Gillespie had prayed and everyone started eating, he looked up from his bowl of soup. "Abi and I have discussed your request to adopt Rachael and have sought the Lord's face about the matter. Right now you're a bit young to be taking on such responsibility." I set my spoon down and struggled to hide my disappointment. As if reading my mind, Rachael exploded into tears. I pulled her up out of the chair and held her.

Mrs. Gillespie sighed and shook her head. "God has established a bond between you and the little one. That's for certain."

The pastor nodded, tapping a finger against his lower lip. "We have to consider what's best for Rachael. Even if you had sufficient income, we'd still be concerned about you and the wee one being off on your own. If you were married…"

Even though I understood, it still hurt. I put Rachael back into her chair and gave her some warm soup to drink, but I left my own bowl untouched.

* * * *

Sand and salt spray clung to my skin, making my face and hands sticky. I brushed at my skirt again, but keeping up with the blowing sand was hopeless. I lunged for my hat when a gust threatened to whip it down the beach faster than I could run. The day was still clear and bright, but the wind had picked up in the past few minutes. Rachael seemed oblivious to the sand, but it was probably best to leave before she got cranky.

On the boardwalk I searched for the right path through the dunes back to the street. A voice came from behind just as I was about to urge Rachael down one. "Are you girls lost?"

I grabbed Rachael's hand and turned around. A constable—what passed for a police officer on Saint Andrew's—walked up to us. I relaxed a little. "No, sir. We were headed home."

"Where are your parents?" He was polite, smiling at me like I was his own daughter.

North Carolina probably wasn't the best answer. "They're home."

He looked incredulous. "Do they know you're wandering about the beach alone?"

I put on my best polite smile. "We're not wandering, sir; we're going home."

I stepped aside to let a family pass, but when Rachael noticed a small boy with an ice cream cone, she started yanking on my skirt. "Ice cream, Mommy!"

The officer arched an eyebrow. "Mommy? You're pretty young to be a mother."

Rachael continued to yank on my skirt. I frowned at the officer and raised my chin. "I'm almost eighteen. Rachael's an orphan. We live with the Gillespies."

"On Martin Lane?"

"Yes, sir."

"You must be Jamie, then."

I stared at him, dumbstruck.

He chuckled. "I'm a member of your church. Pastor Gillespie speaks highly of you." He pointed down the path I'd been considering. "This goes through to Fairfax." He grinned and accompanied us out to the street, where Rachael added ice cream to the sand and salt already coating her.

The toddler fell asleep on my lap on the ride home. I struggled to carry her off the bus. It took an hour sitting next to the fountain before she was ready to walk the rest of the way to the manse. Rachael was getting too heavy for me to carry for long, and I hadn't brought the stroller.

I cleaned up the toddler and put her down for a nap. Rachael went right to sleep, sprawled on the bed, while I sat in the rocker and smiled at her. The orphan still insisted on calling me Mommy, but at least she was starting to let go of me for an hour or two at a time. She seemed to understand now that Mommy would be back.

The frame with the one photo I'd brought sat on the dresser. Lisa had taken a candid shot of Sean and me on his Harley, helmets in our hands. Our faces suggested a kiss was about to hide our smiles. Rachael murmured in her sleep. The toddler insisted the man in the photo must be her daddy. Who else would be in a picture with her mommy? I didn't have the heart to tell my little girl that Sean had probably already met someone else. Anyway, I'd burned those bridges good by insisting that I had to go back to boy land. A deep sigh grabbed hold of me and left me gray.

"Lord, I don't know how this will all work out, but I trust You to give us what we need."

I got up, took a quick shower, and changed into a clean jumper.

Pastor Gillespie had been encouraging me to write to my family and friends. He wasn't in his study, so I sat at his desk and pulled out some stationary. I'd already written Lisa a note to let her know what I was doing. And Alicia, to assure her we were still a family, even if Dad and I were estranged.

Sean—by now Lisa must have told you I'm not in school anymore, and Dad kicked me out of the house. I'm staying on Saint Andrew's and taking care of Rachael. She's the little orphan girl I told you about. She thinks I'm her mom and that makes my heart soar. I joined a good church here. The pastor and elders are okay with my being faie and living as a girl. God has assured my heart of His love for me. Pastor Gillespie even says I can get married and adopt someday. I would gladly spend the rest of my life here. Who needs to spend one more minute thinking about my gender? Wish you were here with me. I never stopped dreaming about us.—All my love,—Jamie

After I addressed the envelope, I decided not to send it. Why tell Sean I still loved him? No sense in opening old wounds. Eyes closed, I cherished the memories of our time together.

"Jamie. Would you help me, please?" I looked up to see Abigail standing in the doorway.

"Yes, ma'am." I jumped up and followed her, forgetting the letter on the desk.

* * * *

Eighteen candles. I made a wish and blew them all out. The Gillespies smiled at me. Kaylah, too. Only Rachael didn't seem impressed. "How many would like something on top of their cake?" Kaylah and Abigail raised a hand. Pastor Gillespie grinned and nodded. Everyone but Rachael. She didn't want any cake. I pulled the ice cream tub out of the freezer and set it on the counter in back of Rachael, out of her sight.

"Ice cream!" yelled the toddler. "Ice cream, Mommy." No doubting what her wish was.

The telephone rang as I served the last plate. I glanced at Mrs. Gillespie before walking to the sitting room to answer the call.

"Lisa. Hi!"

"How's the birthday girl?"

"Fabulous. What about you?"

"I'm well. When are you coming back?"

I glanced back toward the kitchen. "I'm not sure Rachael will ever let me leave her."

"I'm doing a photo exhibit the first week of June. You have to come. Bring her with you."

"Really?"

"Sure. We'll put the two of you in Sean's room. I'll move your dresses and things in there. I never did get around to giving away your Raggedy Ann, either. You still want her?"

Sofie? My heart warmed at the thought. "Yeah. Thanks. How's Sean?"

"He's still in Scotland. You miss him, don't you?"

The elfin princess struggled to find the right words to say. I missed him, for sure, but had given him up when I refused to go with him. "Yes. I do. Is he dating anyone?"

"I don't know. He's been kinda quiet. Oh! Before I forget. The event is formal. Buy an appropriate dress."

"Okay. I'll get Kaylah to take me to the dress shop we went to last summer. Can you pick us up at the seaplane port?"

"Sure. Let me know when."

"Sean's room. That'll be a trip. I keep that picture you gave me on the dresser here. Rachael's convinced the man in the photo is her daddy."

"Oh! You should write to Sean. He'd be thrilled to get a letter from you."

"No. He wouldn't want to hear from me now."

"Don't be too sure."

❧ 32 ❧

The bag was labeled Darjeeling. I added two scoops, poured in boiling water, and covered the teapot with its cozy. Rachael stood by her highchair, waiting, so I checked the oven one last time. Dinner was ready. I squatted down in front of the toddler and straightened her collar. "You are so pretty in your clean dress. Let's put on an apron. Okay, pumpkin?"

"Apron," Rachael repeated, shaking her hands.

"Hold still." How much longer would the little apron I'd made for Rachael fit her? The girl was growing like a bamboo shoot. "Okay. Dinner time."

Rachael squealed and ran out of the room. If she didn't find everyone, they'd certainly hear her calls.

Pastor Gillespie arrived first, Rachael riding piggyback, screaming, either in delight or in terror. Perhaps both. Mrs. Gillespie looked like she wanted to throttle her husband, but she kept silent. Kaylah grinned and took a seat.

It had taken me half a dozen stops to find lamb tenderloin. Fresh rosemary and garlic from Mrs. Gillespie's garden, a little sea salt and black pepper, a dash of olive oil and white wine—my mouth watered in anticipation of broiled lamb. Mashed potatoes were easier. Broccoli wasn't available, so I settled for the sweet peas that grew along the fence. The pastor worked on getting Rachael into her highchair while I put dinner on the kitchen table. The toddler held my hand while Pastor Gillespie asked the Lord to bless our meal. After I had fixed Rachael's plate, I sat down and served myself. Excitement grew with every bite. Mrs. Gillespie had been grinning all day, as if she had a wonderful secret she was struggling to keep.

Pastor Gillespie set down his knife and fork, groaned, and pushed back from the table. He sipped his tea and closed his eyes. I grinned at him. "There's pie."

He chuckled and shook his head. "I'll burst if I eat another thing. Save me a piece, though."

"Ice cream!"

I turned toward Rachael. "That's right, pumpkin. You can have ice cream after you finish your peas."

Kaylah and I cleared away the dishes. No one wanted dessert right away, so we moved on to our traditional after-dinner family devotions. Pastor Gillespie read Scripture. The family prayed together. Toward the end of our second hymn, I realized I hadn't struggled with gender issues for three months. The Gillespies accepted me as—well—me. Most everyone else seemed to think of me as the cute little redhead who lived with the Gillespies. Rachael, of course, still insisted I was her mommy.

Mr. Gillespie steepled his fingers and gazed at me. "The agreement Kaylah made on your behalf was for you to care for Rachael in exchange for room and board." He poured himself some tea and took a sip. "We're pleased with the improvement in the girl's behavior, and we've noticed you're maturing as well."

Mrs. Gillespie nodded and leaned forward, clasping her hands on the kitchen table. "We think you're ready to take on additional responsibility. Three new girls arrive next week. You already prepare dinner for us once or twice a week. Would you be willing to cook our evening meal every day? With a job you'd be a step closer to adoption."

"Ice cream, Mommy!"

I laughed and rose from the table. "I guess Rachael approves. Would anybody else like dessert?"

When we were finished, I cleared the table. "When would you like me to start?"

"Behind that door," said Mrs. Gillespie, pointing past the pantry, "is a small apartment. Long ago it was the cook's quarters. We'll move you and Rachael in after we've cleaned it." She poured herself a cup of tea, and motioned for me to follow.

"Although we encourage you to socialize with the girls and befriend them, you'll also be a role model. To help everyone understand that distinction, you won't be dressing like they do. The clothes you arrived in are more suitable."

"And Rachael?"

"You may dress her as you would your own daughter."

Ooh! Happy thoughts played tag through my brain.

Mrs. Gillespie led me into the apartment. The air was stale, the floor dusty. Cobwebs hung from the corners. To the right stood an ancient canopy bed. Several chairs gathered around a table. In one corner stood an old leather recliner with a lamp on a table beside it. Straight ahead lay another door to what proved to be a spacious bathroom. I strolled across the bedroom and pulled back one of the old drapes to let more sun in. The cozy room came alive with light and color. All it needed was a fresh coat of paint. Blinds on the windows. Matching canopy drapes and bedspread. On a long table in front of the window, an orchid in a black vase and the picture of Sean and me on his bike. The old armoire polished, a full-length mirror on the wall nearby. I grabbed Mrs. Gillespie's hands. "It's perfect!"

⸙ 33 ⸙

It needs salt, I thought, tasting the stew and glancing through the door into the cook's quarters. Rachael appeared to be playing with one of her dolls. After adding a pinch of sea salt to the pot, I stirred, and tasted it again.

"Jamie, dear, can you spare a moment?" Mrs. Gillespie stood in the kitchen doorway.

"Yes, ma'am." I covered the stew, turned down the flame, and followed Abigail into the cook's quarters.

"You requested a week off to visit your friends in Miami. You may go if you agree to three conditions. First, Rachael will accompany you."

My jaw dropped. I'd assumed they'd turn down a request to take my little girl with me. "Thank you!" The princess hugged Abigail, nearly knocking her down.

Mrs. Gillespie returned my grin, a warm fire lighting her face. "You're mature enough now for the two of you to be on your own for a week. Second, Kaylah will help you get Rachael a passport."

"Saint Andrew's does passports?"

"The magistrate will issue a travel document with a photo of you and Rachael on the front. The Americans will accept it as proof that you're the child's guardian. The third condition is something I'm certain you would do anyway—take no chances with her." Mrs. Gillespie handed me an envelope. "You may need these papers if Rachael requires medical attention. You can call us, but the decisions would be yours."

I stared, wide-eyed at the envelope in my hand.

"You'll do fine." Mrs. Gillespie hugged me.

"Thank you." I picked Rachael up and swung her around. "We're going to Miami!" The girl squealed and kicked her legs.

Abigail grinned and shook her head. "Robert and I are still praying you'll be able to adopt her someday."

After Mrs. Gillespie left, I held Rachael for a few minutes. It was the perfect time for our daily devotions, so I opened up *Bible Stories* and read to my little princess.

* * * *

The open-air bus squeaked as it bounced along the road to the port. I squinted, trying to keep the bright reflections from blinding me while still watching the crowds. That also helped keep some of the dust out of my eyes. Rachael didn't appear to mind. Her head swiveled in continuous motion, eyes wide, arms waving or pointing. "Mommy, look!" and "Mommy, what's that?"

At the terminal I took Rachael to the ladies' room to clean her up. I unpacked a washcloth, soap, and a towel from her diaper bag. "Go potty. Okay, pumpkin?" Rachael balked at going into the stall. This was her first time in a public restroom. I finally gave up, hoping a diaper and cover would suffice.

The airline agent sold me two tickets. Perhaps Rachael would spend at least part of the flight in her own seat. In the gate area I brushed out her golden curls so the toddler would be presentable, at least for boarding. In the humidity Rachael's hair writhed with a life of its own. Barrettes slipped right out.

Boarding the plane, I thought Rachael might panic; she seemed so overwhelmed by her new surroundings. As soon as I stowed my bags, I picked her up and went to find a pair of adjacent seats. "Hey, pumpkin. Sit here, okay?"

Rachael started crying as soon as I set her on the seat, so I sat next to her and moved the toddler to my lap. The girl clung to her mommy, tears running down her face, so I held her tight. "It's okay, pumpkin. We're going to Miami, remember?"

The girl settled down and gazed out the window for a while, but lost interest as soon as we became airborne. She slept through most of the flight, but whenever I tried to move her sleeping form to the extra seat, Rachael woke and squalled until I picked her up and held her again. You couldn't blame the child for being so cranky; this was all new to her. I gave up after a while and let Rachael sleep, stretched across my lap and the seat next to me.

The landing was uneventful. I thanked the Lord for the smooth waters off Government Cut. No one needed Rachael seasick.

Lisa met us at the port. By the time I changed Rachael and unpacked our bags, the sun had set. The toddler was asleep before we finished eating. Rachael napped on the couch while Lisa and I finished the dishes.

My friend's grin warned me of an impending gender nudge. "Motherhood fits you well. You've got a glow about you. Will you stick with that or return to school?"

I glanced at Rachael and considered the contentment I felt taking care of the toddler. Chains of love bound me to her and to Saint Andrew's. I hadn't read or studied anything other than the Bible during the semester, hadn't even thought about college. Didn't care. Maybe I'd marry someday and adopt the girl. When she was old enough, I might go back to school. God would show me my next step in His time. "God's given me five months of relative bliss caring for Rachael instead of worrying about my gender."

Lisa led me to Sean's room. A large futon bed covered most of the floor space. Against one wall were an old oak desk and a large bookshelf. I carried Rachael to the bed and left my tote and her diaper bag on the bathroom counter.

Lisa stopped near the door, her face showing some internal struggle.

I chuckled and put a hand on her arm. "We have no secrets, Lisa."

She bit her lip, her brows creeping up her forehead. "No makeup, a plain dress, your hair in a braid—you've changed quite a bit since you left." Concern laced her words.

"I'm fine. The Gillespies don't allow makeup or short skirts, but I realized a month or two ago that I didn't need all that to be me. If I ever return to Miami, I'll probably spend most of my time in blue jeans."

"Would you dress up for Sean?" Her face seemed to be asking if I still liked boys.

"In a heartbeat."

Lisa said goodnight and left, so I changed into a *yukata*. After I tucked Rachael in, I wandered around the room, trying to unwind enough to sleep.

Memories of Sean hung in the night air, taunting me—a tender touch, a kind word, the smile that brightened his eyes when we were together, our sad farewell.

On the shelves, family photos stood guard over trophies, trinkets, and books. The elfin princess examined every one. A grin warmed my face while studying a picture of Sean and his four sisters, all wearing football jerseys, faces dirty, hair disheveled. Another photo was of Sean as a young boy holding up a string of fish, his father standing beside him. A third was a dorky high school graduation shot.

On the desk were several photos of Sean and me—at the park, on the bike—and one of me playing volleyball. Against the wall rested an enlargement of that magnolia girl photo from the day Lisa and I met. At what point had our relationship become more than friendship for Sean? I was pretty sure Tyler had only loved the girl named Jamie. If I thought too much about whether or not Sean had loved Jameson, I was going to get a headache. It was enough that he'd loved me, and I still loved him.

Sean had left an old flannel shirt on the back of the chair. I found comfort in holding it close, like a child with her favorite doll or blanket. The elfin princess lay on the bed next to her daughter, curled up with her love's scent beside her, and dreamed of him.

♋ 34 ☙

The dresses probably weren't good enough for real princesses, but I liked them anyway. What else mattered?

Kaylah had gone with me to Francesca's to help pick out something to wear to Lisa's photo exhibit. After two hours of my trying on and rejecting dresses, my cousin had gotten grumpy. I'd explained that if I was going to spend money on a fancy gown, it needed to be something special, a dress with personality. Kaylah had crossed her arms and shaken her head, but then grinned. "A gown fit for an elfin princess," echoed in my ears as my cousin disappeared between racks of clothes. She'd reappeared a few minutes later with The One Dress. I'd stared at the gown, wondering where I'd seen it before.

As Rachael and I rode down to the main level I gazed at our reflection in the wall of the elevator. The gallery had provided a hotel room for us to change in and keep our things safe. The gowns were tea-length affairs with layers of white tulle for skirts, dark green satin bodices, and knit silver belts that tied in back. Both Rachael and I wore a flower on one shoulder. I grinned, glancing at the ballet slippers my cousin had pulled out of an old box in her attic. Starlight slippers—ancient memories had awakened when I put them on Rachael's feet. Once upon a time an elfin princess had worn them.

"Pretty!" The toddler exclaimed, pointing at Lisa.

"Yes. She is." I kissed Rachael on the cheek. "My little princess is beautiful, too."

Lisa stood at the door to the gallery, greeting people as they entered. Her full-length black gown hugged her figure, making her a fabulous sight. She clapped her hands together when we walked up to the door. "Oh! Those dresses are adorable!" My friend hugged both of us and moved on to the next set of guests. I smiled as she walked away, happy for her success.

Inside, rows and rows of wonderful images lined the walls. The number surprised me.

"Mommy!" The toddler laughed and pointed at a photo of Jameson sitting on his bench, reading a book. "I'm sorry," Lisa had said. "From over by the magnolia tree you looked like a…friend." Almost two years had passed. Rachael would have been but a newborn.

Other images of me hung nearby, although it wasn't clear from the photos or the titles whether or not the model was the same person. I studied the pictures, wondering if I should be bitter about being faie. At conception I'd gotten an X chromosome from my mother and a Y from my father, but sometime during the first few cell divisions, I'd lost a Y. Turner had stolen the baby boy and left an elfin changeling in his place. My condition had resulted in mild heart and kidney malformations, had trashed my reproductive system, made me short, and altered my face. The loss of a Y chromosome had made me a girl.

"What are you thinking about?" asked Lisa, a warm smile lighting her face.

I turned away from the photos and glanced down at Rachael. The toddler clutched my skirt with both hands, her face buried in layers of tulle. "I was wondering about the boy-me. Sharon says he would have been six feet tall with a more masculine face."

Lisa's eyes went wide. Then she grinned. "I never thought about that. I suppose I would have been the same height."

I took a step back and studied Lisa. I couldn't imagine the beautiful young woman as a boy. "You might have been as cute as your brother."

A sad frown spoiled Lisa's beauty. "I still feel like a freak sometimes."

I picked Rachael up so she wouldn't fall over. The toddler opened her eyes and rested her head on my shoulder. I studied my friend's face and tried to reassure her. "Am I a freak?"

Lisa's brows shot up. "No! You're—" All her loveliness rushed back in an instant when she grinned. "—enchanted."

"Is that why you took the photo of me before we met?"

Her face got all serious, and she nodded a couple of times. "I search for interesting faces. When I first noticed you—from over by the magnolia tree you looked like a girl with Turner Syndrome. I was unaware of the mosaic form—that you could have a Y in some cells and not in others—

so your gender confused me. Since then, I've learned that several different conditions can cause short stature and your distinctive facial shape— Turner, MGD, Russell-Silver."

"I'm glad you found me. You and Sean have both been good for me."

"Are you happy now?"

"This is the body God gave me. He's also the one who gave me the grace to be content with it." I glanced at the photo again. "Is that how you found Donya?"

Lisa chuckled and shook her head. "No. After I got my diagnosis, I asked Dr. Parker if I could talk to another patient. When he refused, I hung out near his office with a telephoto lens and waited. Eventually this tall girl showed up."

Someone from the gallery wanted to speak with Lisa, so I walked around for a while, studying the photos. Lisa's artistic abilities amazed me. Before the evening was night, Rachael got heavy and my arms ached. I didn't see any place to sit and rest, so I found Lisa again to say goodbye. "Hey. We're gonna take off. I think your exhibition's fabulous."

"Thanks." Lisa hugged me and kissed the sleeping Rachael on her forehead. I tucked my little princess into the passenger seat of the Cortina and drove her home.

ೞ 35 ೞ

I rang the bell one last time. Dropping by and introducing Rachael was what a friend would do, but I wasn't eager to see Sharon.

My *friend* had encouraged me to be a girl in public just to give Mom an excuse to send me to Saint Andrew's. God had used that for my good, and I understood it might have been the only way to draw the elfin princess out of hiding, but I hated being deceived. I didn't even want to know whether or not Tyler had helped set me up. Why spoil pleasant memories?

I picked up Rachael and started walking back across campus. Lisa had dropped us off, but I'd told her I'd either ask Sharon for a lift or we'd walk.

Sitting on the grass by the lake, I held out one hand so my little princess could gape at the monarch sunning itself there. "Isn't he beautiful, pumpkin?"

"Pretty!"

When the butterfly bid us farewell, and fluttered away, I led Rachael to a magnolia tree and picked her one of its large cream and lilac blossoms. We continued on our way to the Alexander residence, taking our time and enjoying the flowers.

Rachael and I sat at the edge of the intramural field and ate a snack of milk and homemade cookies before continuing. What more could a little princess have asked for? Well...a nap.

With the orphan asleep on my lap and some kids practicing their soccer moves on the field, I took out my Bible and read the book of Ruth. I loved the story of a woman who, although outcast by law, was made a child of God through grace, and became an ancestor of our Lord. It also gave me hope that one day my little princess might have a father.

Rachael stirred, rubbing her eyes with balled fists. "Mommy pray," she said, sitting up and folding her hands.

"Okay, pumpkin." I folded my hands like hers. "What should we pray about?"

"Thank you, God." She smiled and waved her magnolia blossom.

"Yes. Thank you, God, for the beauty of creation." I winked at her. "Thank you for my pretty little princess, too."

She folded her hands again. "God save Mommy. God save Rachael." Puppy-dog eyes grabbed my heart and twisted. "God save Daddy?"

"Yes, pumpkin. God, please give my little girl a father."

"Amen." Her little head nodded twice.

We meandered over to the Alexander residence, stopping to examine every flowering plant along the way. By the time we reached the house, Rachael was drooping again. She even got cranky enough that I had to scold her.

Okaa-san greeted me with an excited, "*Dozo ohairi kudasai!*"

I bobbed my head and stepped inside, carrying Rachael. "*Ojama shimasu.*" The old woman's face lit up. My long hours of patient language practice had been worth the effort.

* * * *

The *korokke* were delicious. Mrs. Alexander put ground beef and potatoes in hers and fried them golden and crispy. Even Rachael liked the taste, and she was a picky eater.

Okaa-san wouldn't let me help in the kitchen before lunch, but Lisa and I cleared the table and did the dishes while Rachael played with Sofie on the rug. When we finished, I walked into the living room, picked up the phone, and dialed home.

"Hi, Mom. Rachael and I will be staying at Lisa's for a while."

"Oh? What happened?"

"Mrs. Gillespie fractured her hip. She and Pastor Gillespie are staying with friends until she's healed. Kaylah says we should stay in Miami for now. Lisa's letting me rent Sean's room until he gets back. Anyway, I wanted to tell you where I'd be."

"Thanks, dear. I'll be praying for Abigail. By the way, your father would like you to come home as soon as you can."

"Yeah?"

"We had a long talk with Sharon. He was unaware of how much of his list you'd completed and that your birth certificate had been corrected. He'd like to help you find a gender program."

With the same idiots who said it was too late? "Okay, but I can't right now. I'm taking care of Rachael." She was all the treatment I needed.

"Bring her with you."

"No, Mom. We're supposed to stay here."

"I'll talk to Kaylah. I'm sure it's all right."

I hung up the phone, wondering why I wasn't happier about what seemed like a victory.

❧ 36 ❧

Over the weeks Rachael and I stayed in Sean's room, the Alexander girls grew attached to the toddler. Aiko gave my little princess PJs with booties and a hood with pointy little ears. She painted eyeliner whiskers on Rachael's cheeks. The toddler spent the evening crawling around on the floor, pretending to be a kitten. I put some Cheerios in one bowl and some milk in another. By evening Rachael lay asleep on the floor, curled up around her empty dishes.

She wouldn't drink regular cow milk anymore. My grandparents owned a dairy farm up by the Joliet Federal Penitentiary. I'd grown up on raw milk, and when I found a farmer in Florida who sold it, I let Rachael taste some. She refused to go back to pasteurized.

I picked up my little princess and tucked her into bed. She murmured and waved her arms, so I handed Sofie to her. Eyes closed, I prayed for my little girl, thanking the Lord for her health and apparent happiness. She hadn't mentioned her desire for a daddy lately. Well, not for a day and a half, anyway.

The clock said two-thirty, but I still had at least an hour's worth of work left to finish. Professor Pennington had arranged for me to do some proofreading and a little typing. It didn't pay much, but she let me do the work at the house and on my own schedule. Weary, I slid into my chair again, leaned my head on the desk, and rested my eyes for just a moment.

* * * *

Soft noises in the night assured the elfin princess that all was well. Moonbeams danced across the walls and floor. A cool breeze rustled the drapes. Distant voices of angels singing drifted through the room.

"Sleep well, my love. I'll return for you," whispered my husband. The tender brush of his fingertips across my cheek caressed my dreams. Passion awakened in the sleeping princess. I reached for him, but he was already gone. Fragrant flowers graced the air, comforting me, assuring me he'd be back.

Face buried in a pillow, I lay on my belly, treasuring the quiet cool-ness of morning. Bright light peeking between the curtains told me my little alarm clock had missed her early morning potty time. A fresh-cut magnolia blossom in a vase next to the futon brought a smile to my face. Too many late nights. I didn't recall picking the flower, nor even lying down to sleep the previous night.

I stretched and crawled out of bed. "Rachael?" Sometimes she tried to go potty by herself, so I drifted back to the bathroom. Bloodshot eyes stared out of the mirror. Had some idiot forgotten to lock the outside door? "Rachael!" Panic drove me around the yard, searching for my baby.

Relief flooded me at the sight of my little girl in the living room, playing with Sofie. Heart still racing, I scooped her up into my arms and held her. "Honey, you shouldn't go out when Mommy's asleep. You gave me a fright."

Her big blue eyes danced with joy as she played with the bow on my pajama top. "Daddy's home."

"I'm sorry, honey, but you don't have—"

Strong hands squeezed my shoulders and turned me around. "Let me have a look at you in the daylight." Sean's eyes embraced mine. I fell into their steel-blue ocean depths, body trembling with delight at the warmth.

My little princess giggled, legs running in mid-air. "Daddy's home!"

I set Rachael down and hugged Sean. "I am so glad to see you. What brings you back?"

His arms slid around my waist and drew me tight. "You. Lisa told me you and your daughter had moved into my room." He glanced at Rachael, who was clinging to his leg. "Is she the one you told me about?"

"Yes." I stood on tiptoes to kiss his cheek. *Ooh!* My body trembled when his hand brushed lightly over my bare back. In my rush to find Rachael, I'd left my *yukata* behind. Baby dolls weren't the most modest thing to wear when greeting an old boyfriend. "Ooh. I uh…need to…" I took a step back, pulse throbbing.

Blue eyes grinned while Sean picked up an afghan from the chair and wrapped it around me. He sat on the couch and coaxed me down beside him. "I brought you a flower this morning, but found you asleep at my desk. Only little Rachael here greeted me."

I leaned my head against his shoulder and sighed. "Well, you can't just walk in on a girl and expect her to give up her sweet dreams." The elfin princess grinned at me in the picture window, her green eyes flashing. "Now can you?"

"Oh and what might you be dreaming of, there in my room?" Those steel-blue eyes displayed a love grown deeper since I had last plumbed their depths.

He'd come back for me! My smile spun wildly out of control. "You," I whispered.

His face grew serious as he studied mine. "No more foolishness then?"

The air grew thick and warm around me. It wasn't like he was asking me to marry him, but it was clear he wanted my word. "No, sir."

"Daddy pray." The toddler climbed up on Sean's lap and folded her hands.

Blue eyes grinned, daring me to correct the toddler, but I'd learned long ago who had the stronger will. "What shall we pray for then, my darling daughter?" he said.

"Daddy's home. Thank you, Jesus."

"Yes, and Mommy can marry Daddy now."

The heat in my cheeks exploded across my soul. *What I wouldn't give to be your wife.* Some things could never be, though. Even if Dad accepted me as a girl, would he ever allow me to marry? I started to object, but Sean pressed a finger against my lips and shook his head. "You wrote that you never stopped dreaming of us together. Last night you smiled when I told you I'd be back for you. Will you deny your love, or will you trust our Lord to work it all out?"

Such terror swept over me that my body swayed. Did God intend this man to be my covering, an instrument of sanctification in my life? Running was so much easier than living. Perhaps God did want me to marry someday, but I wasn't sure I was anywhere near ready, nor ever would be. And besides… "We would need to get my parents' permission. Dad will never let me get married."

A small hand grabbed mine. "Mommy pray."

I looked down into blue eyes that dared me to trust a child's God. "Okay, pumpkin. What shall we pray?"

"Thank you, Jesus. Daddy's home."

And all things, whatsoever ye shall ask in prayer, believing, ye shall receive. I smiled at Rachael and folded my hands over hers. Could I tell her no after praying with her so many times? "Okay. Thank you, Lord, for sending my little girl a father and me a husband. We trust that You'll work out all things for Your glory and our good."

"Amen," she agreed, nodding her little head.

Sean took my hand and slid a ring on my finger. "It's not much. I'll replace it once I have a job."

Silver thistles inlaid a beautiful gold band. "It's perfect!" I exclaimed, "and you'll do no such thing."

"Ah. The submissive wife already?"

"Yes." I gave him my best Pollyanna grin. "Dad will want me to finish school, you know."

"And so you shall...someday." He pulled Rachael up on his lap again. "Right now our little girl's mother should consider sleeping in a bed at night."

As much as I enjoyed reading and marking up the mimeographed copies of manuscripts, the late hours had to end. The thought of them brought a yawn. "Okay. I'll cut back so I'm only reading while Rachael's taking her naps."

He eyed me as if he thought I was being stubborn. "You'll still be working."

Okay, so I was hardheaded sometimes. "Yes. I'd be reading anyway."

"All right. Save the money. I won't hear of you paying rent anymore."

"Okay...Wait. Don't you need your room? Rachael and I can go stay with Kaylah."

"No. I can use the master suite until my parents get back. I'd much rather have the two of you here where I can keep track of you."

I struggled upright in my cocoon. "Good. Then keep track of Rachael for me while I get dressed." I pulled the afghan tight around me and ran to my room.

I was drying off after my shower when Iseabail tapped on the mirror.

"Hmm?" I said, hanging up my towel and picking up a comb. With the fog obscuring the top of the mirror I could barely make out her face.

"Aren't you excited?" I asked, leaning close to the mirror. "I'm getting married!"

The elfin princess shook her head, emerald eyes wide.

I waved my comb at her. "Don't be afraid. You have a feminine shape. Not like a boy at all. You're at least ninety percent girl now. Maybe ninety-five."

The princess glanced down and made a scissors motion with her fingers.

I stepped back and shook my head several times. No one was gonna start cutting on my little post. Not even for my husband. "No, Iseabail. Too bad if he doesn't like the five percent boy part. I told him I was a hermaphrodite and all. Besides, it's only a little post. I can't pee with it or anything."

She stared at me with narrowed eyes, but I turned away and started combing my hair again. She worried too much. Sean loved me the way I was. Didn't he?

Another tap on the mirror and I spun around. What now? Her face was all lit up this time.

Ooh! She was right. We had no secrets. Lisa could talk to Sean about what I had between my legs and tell him I had finished dilating. "For medical purposes only," I whispered and giggled. No surprises then.

I finished combing out my wet hair as the girl in the mirror swayed back and forth. If only Jameson had known about cream rinses, he might have kept his hair in better condition. I shook my head. Boys were so stupid about some things.

The day was already too warm and humid to waste much time on my looks, so I threw on blue jeans and a comfortable top and walked back to the living room to find out how Sean and Rachael were doing.

I needn't have worried. My daughter was riding around on Mr. Horsie's back. Sean was making snorting sounds and shaking his head.

"Let's eat!" came Lisa's voice. Mr. Horsie whinnied and galloped off toward the kitchen. The rider on his back screamed, a high-pitched screech like fingernails across a chalkboard. Oh, yeah. He was gonna make a fine dad.

Was it lunchtime already? Lisa got out leftovers—turkey and potato salad. I found bread, mayo, and mustard for sandwiches. Sodas for the Alexanders. Raw milk for me and Rachael.

Silent grins surrounded me as I ate. Well, except Rachael. She scowled and poked at her potato salad with her little fork. Lisa and Aiko seemed close to laughter. Sean, for his part, was the essence of innocence. I tried my best to ignore their grins, but kept my ring under the kitchen table until Lisa asked me when the big day was.

"We still have to get my parents' permission. That might be a while." *Yeah. Like the day after Hell freezes over.* "I'll call them this afternoon."

Aiko set her fork down and shook her head. "My boss says your documents are all based on someone named Kaylah Levinson being your legal guardian, at least on Saint Andrew's Island. The travel document would result in your being treated as an adult anywhere else."

An old song my mother used to sing to me rolled through my mind. —*Today is the day we give Jamie away with a half a pound of tea.*—Had Kaylah gotten anything out of the deal? Loneliness drove me from the table. I retreated to the living room and sat on the couch. Was it right to drag Sean and Rachael into my problems?

I scowled at the phone when it rang, but picked it up anyway. "Yeah?"

"Are you all right?"

"Hi, Mom. Yeah. Just a little down today."

"Your father says he'd be happy to have Rachael here. He doesn't think the doctors will mind your taking care of a toddler. Girls do that sort of thing."

"Okay... Um, Mom, Sean asked me to marry him."

Silence. Not good.

"I said yes."

"Honey, you need to wait. Give your father a chance to get used to your being a girl. All right? And don't tell him about Sean. Your father's not going to let you marry someone who knew you when you were a boy. You need to finish college first anyway, so just sit tight. All right?"

"They're not going to let me keep Rachael forever without adopting her."

"Let me talk to Kaylah. We'll work something out."

Sean pulled me up off the couch and wrapped his arms around me. I mumbled, "Gotta go," and hung up. One of Sean's hands brushed along my waist and around my back. *Ooh!* His lips pressing against mine insisted I wasn't alone.

* * * *

A soft rapping on the door was Sean's polite way of asking me to hurry up. We were headed for the beach for a few hours while Lisa kept Rachael. Less than five miles from the university, Matheson Hammock Park provided a closer, cleaner, and quieter beach than Miami. Tyler and I had strolled around the white sand shores of its atoll pool, soaking our feet in the warm water and gazing at the Miami skyline. Iseabail scowled at me from the bathroom mirror, but I shook my head at her. "No. You worry too much." Lisa had gone with me to the end-of-summer sale at Burdines and helped me choose a swimsuit. She'd insisted I try on a bikini she'd picked out, saying a one-piece suit would make me look like a twelve-year-old. Too bad I didn't have a movie camera to capture the range of her expressions when I strolled out of the dressing room and modeled it for her. My friend's face had ended up a bright red. I wasn't a boy, you know, but the bikini bottom showed my little post all too well.

I had finally settled on a navy blue two-piece swimsuit with a halter-top and a miniskirt bottom with a white belt that rode low on my hips. The Mod style reminded me of a scooter dress Emma Peel had worn.

I glanced into the mirror one more time. "It's fine, Iseabail. No one's gonna see my little post." It wasn't like anybody went around checking under people's skirts, anyway. Every other girl I knew wore a swimsuit. Why not me?

Sean's reaction almost changed my mind. I pulled the door open with a nervous grin. I'd never let a boy see me wearing a swimsuit before. Well, not a girl one anyway. He stood outside the door in his swimming trunks and T-shirt and stared at me like he'd never seen a girl before. His eyes teased as he said. "Get dressed and we'll go."

I gave him a blank stare and mumbled, "Girls wear swimsuits to the beach."

Blue eyes pierced my soul with love. They held me in thrall while his arms slowly pulled me close. His kiss left me breathless and uncertain what I would have done had he not stopped. Had Lisa told him I could?

My body trembled in anticipation. For a heartbeat he hesitated, but then he smiled and tousled my hair. "You want all the boys chasing you then?"

Ooh! No. I didn't really want any other boys even looking at me. I threw on a white muslin blouse and rolled up its loose sleeves. Was that enough? It covered most of me. As I pulled the door closed, I watched our shadows intertwine on Sean's bed. "Soon," I whispered. *Lord, help me hold out until we're married. And please, please let that be soon!*

* * * *

Some summer days in Miami I took a shower in the morning and never did get dry again. Air conditioners seemed unable to keep up with the humidity. Putting my hair up helped a bit, so I asked Lisa to make a French braid for me. My friend had been all smiles since my engagement.

Rachael's fine hair refused to stay in barrettes, but I found some combs that seemed to work. I got her several with fake diamonds to go along with her little princess swimsuit. A feather boa and a wand for her to use as a scepter, a little rouge on her cheeks and some candy lipstick, and she was ready to go. "Go show Daddy. Okay?" The girl squealed and ran off toward the living room.

The children and their moms were supposed to come in their swim-suits. For me, Rachael's birthday party was an excuse to wear something comfortable and cool—hip-hugger jeans and a halter-top. Wasn't that what an elfin princess wore on a lazy August afternoon? After a year on hormones I had curves. Nice to show them off once in a while. Not that I'd wear something so skimpy in public. The only male at the party old enough to care was Sean, and I didn't mind teasing my fiancé a little. Not at all.

He set up a Slip 'n Slide in the back yard, along with some sprinklers. The adults sat under the awning and talked while the kids ran crazy. After everyone was soaking wet, I brought out scones and ice cream.

After the guests drifted away, Lisa and Aiko glanced at each other and walked inside, leaving Kaylah, and Sean, and me sitting alone. When I got up to put the ice cream away, Sean jumped up. "Here now. Let me get that. You rest for a minute."

"Where's Rachael?"

"She's asleep on the couch."

"Thanks." I'd been standing most of the afternoon, so I took the hint and parked next to Kaylah. "How's Mrs. Gillespie?"

My cousin patted my arm and smiled. "She still uses a walker sometimes, but the Gillespies are ready to have you and Rachael back at the manse. They'd like you to say your goodbyes and leave early next week."

I'd been in Miami for most of the summer and had gotten used to living with the Alexanders. The last month with Sean had been the best one ever, but my absence from the Gillespies and from my church weighed on me. Returning to Saint Andrew's, especially with Sean, would be wonderful, but my decisions had already been made for me. The path to marriage lay through some stupid gender clinic up north. "Mom says I have to go home, complete some gender program, and go back to school."

"Is that what you want?" Her eyes burned with a mix of tenderness and anger.

What I want? Kaylah was the only one who ever asked me that. Didn't I have to obey my parents? "Mom was supposed to arrange things with you so Rachael and I could go to North Carolina. She says Alicia can babysit while I'm in my classes."

"Would that be better for Rachael? Or you for that matter?"

Had Mom even spoken with her? I hated arguing for a position I didn't support. "They're my family, Kaylah."

"Are they now? If your heart is set on returning to your parents, I'll sign the necessary paperwork, but I can't allow you to take Rachael with you."

My heart froze. *Lord, please don't let her take my baby!* "But I—"

"Does an adopted girl have any obligation to obey her birth parents?"

"No, ma'am." Had they really given me away? *Lord, please*—Was I just being selfish?—*Lord, thank you. I'll put Rachael's needs before my own and trust that You'll straighten out the mess with my family later.* Wasn't that what a mother would do? "I'll take Rachael back to Saint Andrew's."

"There you are." Kaylah took my hand. Fond eyes studied my face. "A long time ago my little girl told me she was an elfin princess. What did she want to do when she grew up?"

The years fell away and we were back in Oswego, playing house and talking about our big plans for the future. I grinned at Kaylah and showed her my ring. "I'm going to be a wife and a mom."

Kaylah nodded, eyes intense. "You know what God requires of a husband and wife then?"

More than I could ever hope to live up to on my own. "Yes, ma'am."

"Are you sure God wants you to marry the boy?"

Even a little princess understood that marriage was more serious than playing house. A wife was supposed to be all sorts of wonderful things that I wasn't. "Yes, ma'am, but I'm not sure I'll ever be ready."

"Why not?"

Somewhere along the way I'd gotten lost in childhood, wandering the endless labyrinth of my imagination. "I'll never be a normal woman. Maybe not even a grownup."

"I love you exactly the way you are." I turned to see Sean standing in the doorway. He kissed me and sat on the other side of Kaylah.

My cousin winked at me and turned to Sean. "Jamie is returning to Saint Andrew's next week. Go with her and talk to Pastor Gillespie. He'll help you find work and a place to stay."

She smiled at me again. "You're already a fine mother, Jamie. God will show you the rest. The Gillespies will let the two of you adopt Rachael as soon as you've settled in to married life. Don't delay the wedding too long. All right?"

I glanced at Sean, but he seemed okay with going to Saint Andrew's. His eyes held a fire that would have burned through any objections I could raise. Wide-eyed, the elfin princess nodded at Kaylah.

"There you are," she said.

❧ 37 ❧

The best time for sleep was when I was supposed to be getting up. I bunched the pillow around my head and tried to ignore the soft whoosh of the ceiling fan.

"Potty time, Mommy," whispered my insistent cherub.

"Okay, pumpkin." I rolled over and stretched. The bed in the cook's quarters slept comfy, but was neither as firm nor as healthy as Sean's futon. Waking left me yearning for a few more minutes of sleep.

Rachael took a bath and got dressed with minimal help from me. The last few weeks she'd wanted to do everything herself, so I gave her some space. Since coming home, the girl had been all smiles and giggles, but she kept asking for Aiko, or Lisa, or one of her little friends. Well, Mrs. Gillespie would know the local children. We'd find my little girl some new friends and the Alexander girls would be at the wedding.

I read Rachael a Bible story, and we prayed together. My heart missed Sean the most in the morning. He lived on the second floor, but house rules prevented us from spending any time alone together. We'd agreed to that as a condition of Sean staying in the manse.

Breakfast had grown to be a production. The Gillespies were okay with oatmeal. Sean preferred bacon and eggs. Rachael's new love was hotcakes with maple syrup. When I discovered an old waffle iron in the back of the pantry, I went searching for pecans.

Sean grinned at me across the kitchen table when I handed him a plate piled up with waffles, scrambled eggs, and bacon. He'd been spending his days with Pastor Gillespie, working out the details of the manse remodeling effort. The pastor wondered out loud why a wealthy family from Chicago would donate a large sum of money to an unknown foster care charity on some little island in the Caribbean. I just grinned.

The doorbell rang as I sat down to eat, so I rushed to answer the door. I found Alicia standing on the porch, eyes dim, like she'd been up all night. Something had been spilled down one leg of her bell-bottoms and her blouse was all rumpled.

I set her small suitcase inside and hugged her as tight as I could. "I missed you."

We dropped her bag off in Heather's old room before I led her into the kitchen and introduced her around. Alicia ate in silence while I studied her, wondering what had happened. My parents had been reluctant to let their sixteen-year-old son take an airplane to Miami. Alicia would turn sixteen soon, but no way would Mom and Dad have let her travel alone. Had she run away?

Sean threw me a significant glance and offered to clean up the dishes, so I grabbed Alicia's hand and dragged her into the cook's quarters. "What's up, Ali?"

"Can I stay with you?" Her eyelids drooped, almost closed.

"Sure. How much trouble are you in?"

"Mom and Dad aren't coming to your wedding. We argued, and I got so mad I hitched to Miami. Lisa gave me a ride to the port and loaned me the money for a ticket."

We hugged again, but Alicia seemed ready to pass out, so I led her back to Heather's old room. Her suitcase was one of those little overnight ones, not much larger than a big purse. "Did you bring any clothes?"

"A couple of tops, a pair of jeans, and some underwear." Alicia swayed as she scanned the room. "I didn't bring any dresses."

"I don't think anyone will mind. Take a hot shower and get some sleep. There's towels here in the closet. Leave your clothes outside the door. I'll wash them." I kissed her on the cheek and pulled the door closed.

In the sitting room I picked up the phone and dialed my parents' number. My mom answered.

"Hi, Mom."

"How are you?" Not quite bitter cold, but she didn't sound happy to hear my voice.

I sighed, wishing I could make things better. "Alicia got here safely."

"What? She's still in bed. She got in late and went straight to her room."

"Okay, Mom." I let the handset fall back into its cradle and headed back to the kitchen. I managed to get Rachael cleaned up and out of her highchair before the phone rang again.

"Hi, Mom."

"I sent your decoy home. The fool was still asleep in your sister's bed. When did Alicia leave? Yesterday morning?"

"I'm sorry, Mom, but you'll have to ask her."

"Did you pay for her plane ticket?" She sounded downright hostile. I had to remind myself I was working toward reconciliation. Hanging up wouldn't help.

"All you need to hitchhike is a thumb and a pretty face. Be thankful she's still got both." Silence stretched out for several heartbeats while I prayed that Mom would be reasonable.

"Can you take her to the Miami airport? We'll arrange for a ticket to be waiting for her."

My sister was six inches taller than me and a lot stronger. She wasn't going anywhere unless she wanted to. "I'm kinda busy right now, getting married and all."

"Perhaps Kaylah can take her."

Like my cousin would force Alicia to go home. "Mom, if you and Dad don't come down for the wedding, I don't think Alicia will ever go home again."

"Are you threatening me?"

My first thought was to slap her face. For that I repented. Why did my conversations with Mom and Dad always go downhill? *Lord, please help me explain this to her.* "Alicia and I have been close all our lives. When we left Oswego, you and Dad tore Kaylah away from us and drove me into hiding. Now you're trying to split us apart again."

"Nonsense. We want you both home. Your father doesn't think you should even be thinking about marriage yet. We can't approve of your engagement, so it makes no sense to be at your wedding. You need to come home, get counseling, and finish school. God will provide you a husband someday, but not now, and not someone who loved Jameson."

Well, my parents had been frank with me about Sean. It bothered them that he'd befriended Jameson. But they didn't know Sean, and I didn't care that he had liked Jameson. He loved me. All of me. I couldn't change my past and wasn't sure I wanted to. "Dad should talk to Dr. Cameron. I don't need a gender program. And since when has Dad insisted his daughters go to college? If Alicia were living under the same roof as her boyfriend, you'd be demanding she get married. All I'm asking is that you treat me the same as her."

"All right." Mom sounded worn out, like she'd run out of steam. "I'll talk to him, but his mind seems made up on this."

What our family needed was better communication. Everything out in the open. At least Mom and Dad working together. "Tell him how I ended up on Saint Andrew's the first time."

"I don't think that would be helpful."

Yeah. I didn't think you'd want to share that.

But maybe if she knew Dad's secret, she'd open up more about hers. "Then ask him why he strapped Scott."

"Your father never used his belt on anyone. I don't even think Elizabeth disciplined Scott more than twice. He was always obedient."

I'd been hiding nearby when my dad and my brother quarreled. "The day before Scott joined up they had a big argument. Ask Dad what happened."

"He's swamped with work. I'm not sure he can get time off right now."

When we left Oswego, Dad had started working for Western Electric, doing secret government stuff. He got paid better, but he traveled more. There wouldn't be a family to come home to if he stayed away. "Never mind his job, Mom. Come down here and set this right or lose Alicia. We're a family, remember? We should start acting like one."

* * * *

A late summer storm rumbled in after dark, making a steady thrum on the metal roof of the cook's quarters. Flashes of yellow and blue projected eerie shadows on the walls. Rachael lay on the bed next to me, asleep with Sofie in her arms. With the lightning and thunder, she wanted to stay close by. In less than a week someone else would be sleeping with his arms around me.

The old manse creaked and groaned in the gusting wind. I wasn't afraid of the dark, but it was comforting to have Sean upstairs and the Gillespies down the hall. Some of the noises sounded downright creepy.

The cook's quarters door squealed as it swung open. While I tried to decide whether or not to scream, someone in a white nightgown floated across the room toward the bed. "Are you awake?" whispered Alicia.

My voice had hidden away somewhere, so I grabbed my sister's hand and pulled her on the bed.

"Can I sleep with you?" My sister's question flashed me back to Oswego. Thunderstorms rolled across the northern Illinois plains on a regular basis, and Alicia had always stayed with me so she wouldn't be afraid. I wasn't scared, you know, but it was easier to sleep with her next to me.

"Sure." Sleeping together was okay for little girls. We might have been too old for that sort of stuff, but Alicia needed someone to hold. I wasn't going to tell her to go away.

"You called Mom and Dad, didn't you?"

"Yes. If they show up here, stay with them. Everything will be okay now."

"You should talk to them before you get married."

"I'm not gonna argue, Ali. We'll all talk after the wedding. Sean and I are taking a week off for a honeymoon. After that, okay?"

"I'm not going home unless we're still a family."

"I know."

❦ 38 ❧

Early morning light squeezed through the gaps in the blinds, painting bright stripes across the wall. *Rachael!* I sprang out of bed before remembering that Kaylah was keeping the toddler for us.

Sean rolled over and gave me a sleepy grin. "She's fine."

It had been a long while since I'd been away from Rachael for more than a few hours. I sat on the bed next to my husband and worried about our daughter. "She's probably crying."

"Who? Rachael or your cousin?"

Ooh! The two-year-old could be a pill, but my cousin would have treated her like a princess. Sean sat up and pulled me back against him. His tender touch against my nakedness, familiar now, brought a rush of heat.

The elfin princess grinned at me from the armoire mirror. Her hair and skin glowed, but it was probably only a trick of the light. Well, the smile she wore was bigger than would fit in her cute little mouth, so some of her joy sparkled out through her emerald eyes. She glanced down and I nodded. "Yes, Iseabail," I whispered under my breath. "Such a fuss over nothing."

Sean wasn't a gynecologist or anything, and I was the only girl he'd ever been with in bed. He'd checked out everything, but couldn't find anything wrong with my little post. Actually, he thought it kinda cute. "Why would anyone want to cut it?" he'd said.

Arms around my waist, Sean ran his hands over my abdomen. "Maybe we'll have ourselves another little one." I whipped my head around, but all I caught was a twinkle in his eye.

I threw him back a teasing grin. "I'm willing to try as often as you are."

"Are you now? A little more than nine months ago you asked me for another baby. He should be a newborn by now. What would you think of Broden for a boy's name?"

He had to be joking. How did a mother with a bunch of little ones ever cope? "The foolish girl who asked you that has a better idea now how much work two kids would be."

"Children are a gift from the Lord, are they not?"

They were indeed. I studied his eyes and found mirth mixed with love. And yet he seemed serious. My heart rose to my throat as I pondered having two children so soon after getting married. I shook my head in dismay, but regretted it when I noticed the disappointment in his eyes.

A soft tapping on the door meant Mrs. Gillespie had our breakfast ready. Our weeklong honeymoon had zipped right by. The midnight hour had struck, changing my coach back to a pumpkin. The elfin princess had become a cook and a mother once again. Kaylah would drop Rachael off later in the morning.

After breakfast a long shower seemed to be in order. I stretched my sore legs and yawned. The girl in the mirror made wide eyes at my bruises, but I laughed at her. "Yes, Iseabail. I get hurt whenever I play with boys." He hadn't hit me, you know, but our bodies had bumped together, and I had whacked my arm against the bedpost once. "We'll figure everything out." A few little bruises in the beginning were okay.

The manse stood on high ground, overlooking the village of West End and, beyond that, the ocean. Even in summer a breeze cooled the mornings and evenings. I pulled on an old pair of jeans and a T-shirt. Over that I wore one of Sean's old flannel shirts.

With apologies to Mom and Mrs. Gillespie, anybody who pulled weeds in a dress wasn't right in the head. Either that or they had never knelt bare-legged near a fire ant colony. Well, Mrs. Gillespie didn't allow any ants in her herb garden, but still…blue jeans were made for playing in the dirt and Mrs. Gillespie's garden wanted weeding.

I had just showered again and changed into a dress when Kaylah arrived with Rachael in tow. The girl started wailing and wouldn't stop until I found her some ice cream and sat with her while she ate. After I washed her face and hands, I helped her find Sofie. Content, she curled up on my bed and closed her eyes.

Kaylah kissed Rachael on the forehead, and then hugged me. "Pray for me. I'm off to meet with your parents. It's time we all reconciled."

Mom and Dad had arrived the day before the wedding. Alicia had been a bridesmaid, so she'd been at the reception, but I hadn't seen my parents there. I hugged my cousin tight. "Thank you. God will make it all better. You'll see."

"There you are," Kaylah said, and left.

Sean, and Rachael, and I ate a light lunch. Mrs. Gillespie returned while I was drying the dishes. The newborn she carried brought me heart palpitations. I took a step back when she said his name was Broden. I nearly burst out laughing when I realized Sean must have known about the baby's arrival. Pastor Gillespie had probably told him.

Abigail smiled and held the baby out toward me. "Can you take him for the rest of the afternoon? I have some errands to run." She showed me his diaper bag and turned to go.

What did I know about newborns? I rushed after her, almost knocking Rachael down.

Mrs. Gillespie stopped at the front door and smiled. "You'll be fine."

Broden started crying and waving his arms as soon as she closed the door. Mrs. Gillespie had left a warm bottle of formula in the kitchen, so I grabbed it and sat in the rocker in my old bedroom.

Rachael stared in wonder, elbows on my knees, while Broden slurped from his bottle. After gurgling once, he stopped and closed his eyes. As I studied his face and his tiny hands, God softened my heart toward him. I smiled at Rachael. "Would you like a baby brother?"

The floor creaked, and I turned to discover my husband standing in the doorway. His smile said he'd overheard my question. Sean studied Broden for some time before speaking. "He's right handsome, there."

"As is his father." That earned the elfin princess a long kiss.

Sean brushed a lock of hair away from my eyes. "Kaylah called. They're on their way over." That my cousin was still alive seemed a hopeful sign.

Sean's steel-blue eyes found mine when the doorbell rang. I nodded and followed him to the front door. Rachael grabbed my skirt and held tight, her head poked around my waist to find out who was here. Broden squirmed until I stuck the bottle in his mouth again. I whispered words of encouragement to him, thinking that two little ones might not be so bad.

"Come in! Come in!" Sean just about pulled my Mom and Dad in the door.

When I looked up from feeding Broden, my parents were both staring at me. I did my best hands-full curtsey and grinned. "Dad, Mom, this is Sean. The shy one attached to my skirt is your granddaughter, Rachael. The little one is Broden." I shot a quick glance at Sean. His eyes were as cheery as the sky on a clear summer day.

He winked at me and nodded. "We're planning to adopt him as well."

Dad and Sean started drifting toward the sitting room, absorbed in quiet conversation.

Alicia pulled the door closed and gave me a quick hug. "We're moving to Saint Andrew's!"

"That's awesome!" Miracles still happened. Mom turned to follow the men. When she glanced back, I smiled and whispered, "Thank you."

I held Broden out to my sister. "Would you hold him while I fix dinner?"

"I don't know anything about newborns."

Neither did I. "You'll be fine." And anyway, Mom was here.

# # # #

For More Information

Disorders of sex development (DSD) is an umbrella term for a number of different medical conditions. Further details on individual conditions may be found at

The author's website: www.liannesimon.com

AIS-DSD Support Group   www.aisdsd.org

SUCCEED Clinic   www.succeedclinic.org

About the Author

Lianne Simon's father was a dairy farmer and an engineer, her mother a nurse. She grew up in a home filled with love and good books.

Tiny and frail, Lianne struggled physically, but excelled at her studies. In 1970, she was awarded a scholarship to the University of Miami, from which she graduated in 1973. Fond memories of her time there remain with her.

Some years later, after living in several states, and spending time abroad, Lianne settled in to the suburbs north of Atlanta, where she now lives with her husband and their cat.

While seeking answers to her own genetic anomalies, Lianne met a family whose daughter was born with one testis and one ovary. As a result of that encounter, she spent more than a decade answering inquiries on behalf of a support group for the parents of such children.

Lianne hopes that writing this book will, in some small way, contribute to the welfare of children born between the sexes.

CPSIA information can be obtained
at www.ICGtesting.com
Printed in the USA
LVHW04s2312180618
581200LV00001B/101/P